Sunset Downs

Christian Cerone

Do you have a story to tell? What's your animal spirit? Share it with us. #hellobeesties

Wildebeest Publishing Company, LLC
6456 Collamer Road
Syracuse, NY 13057

For more information about copyrights and usage, special discounts on bulk purchases, workshops, and engagements, please contact Wildebeest Publishing Company, LLC at (315) 220-0217, info@wildebeestpublishing.com, or online at www.wildebeestpublishing.com

Wildebeest Publishing Company, LLC Paperback First Edition July 2023, United States of America

Cover art by Ruby James Keeton

ISBN 978-1-958233-11-5

For Steve—
Thanks for letting me tag along.

The night wants to kiss you deep
And be on his way
Pretend he don't know you
The very next day
Isn't it hard sometimes?
Isn't it lonely?
How I still hang around here
And there's nothing to hold me
    - Patty Griffin

1984

Catherine

From above it looks like waves.

It looks like a sea of humanity undulating in waves against an immovable object. The rhythm drives every swell, surge, undertow. You can stand amid these forces and be swept off your feet, moved a measurable distance, and set back down. And just when you feel the confidence returning to your footing, you're swept up again.

Resistance to these forces takes its toll on the body. Abdominals strain to maintain balance. Leg muscles remain taut in an attempt to keep the body grounded. Arms constantly brace against others for support. The physical demand is not unlike that of treading water, and it leaves one exhausted.

Washing over everything is the music. It seems to both attract and repel these waves. The crowd surges against the stage, driven into a mania by the raw energy of the performance, while the brute force of sound streaming from the amplifiers seems to push back. Bodies recede briefly, gather into the new mass that has made its way forward, and crash again into the motionless platform upon which the artists enjoy safe refuge mere feet from the chaos.

Catherine was 18 when she went to her first concert—Day Two of the US Festival at Glen Helen Regional Park in San Bernardino. It was a fiasco—blazing hot, water scarce, drugs rampant, and people dropping like flies. The medical tents overflowed with dehydration cases, overdoses, and bad trips. Well over half a million attended, and at times it felt like all of them were trying to fit into the exclusive expanse of grass directly in front of the stage. She braved that throng for as long as she could until she felt her body would be bruised beyond repair.

Her friend Ashley had long since abandoned her, seeking refuge farther back where the crowd wasn't so frantic. Knowing it would be a longshot to find her before their agreed-upon meet-up time at the car, Catherine decided to reposition herself to the side of the stage. She remembered swimming lessons and summer camp beach days where they told her to swim sideways if she ever got stuck in a riptide. You could try to swim in or even farther out, fighting the tough current until exhaustion overcame you. But moving just a few feet to the side would put you in peaceful water.

Sure enough, she found her way out of the strongest surges of humanity fairly quickly, then bumped shoulders here and there until there were larger patches of daylight ahead. After freeing herself, she climbed a hill that was sparsely occupied because its sight lines originated behind the stage. A musician would have to be crowd-surfing to be seen from this vantage point. But the view of the crowd itself was breathtaking. Wave after pulsing wave crashed into the metal barrier at the foot of the stage where Ozzy Osbourne's band's driving drums, bass, and guitar whipped the masses into a frenzy. The retreating undulations seemed to reach those standing a hundred people deep from the stage, only to ripple back, turning again into swells growing in thickness until they appeared to crest, crashing, falling, futilely beating the wall of sound before retreating again.

In the clubs it was not much different, just on a smaller scale. Tonight, she took refuge on the balcony. The pit would be a gropefest, and the short skirt she wore would easily offer anyone with enough shrewdness a handful of her ass. She'd been there too many times before, wanting to spit in every innocent face because, chances are, all of them were guilty in some way or another. So instead, she watched from above, each surge of the crowd, each swell driven by the power of the music. Each wave picking up several before putting them down again, more or less right back where they started.

Glen

Tommy Aldridge had just thrown his drumstick nine rows deep into the Long Beach Arena crowd. Right at them. Paul didn't get off his chair fast enough to catch it on the fly and it hit him in the shins. As he leapt, he saw it spin and come to rest on the floor under the chair in front of him, its shaft chewed jagged from a night of pounding the edges of drum rims. Paul hit the floor, fell to his knees, and made a blind grab at it just as a wave of sweaty humanity pounded over his back. His head hit the chair in front of him, or perhaps the chair was pushed onto his head. He felt immersed in a sea of arms, but facing down, saw nothing except the tile floor and the feet of chairs now shifted from their once-tidy rows.

The mob that enveloped him dissipated faster than expected. Suddenly, he was rising to a knee with no one on his back, no lingering hands pushing through him to search the floor for the drumstick. He came up empty. He thought he had it. Thought his hand beat the others to it. But there was nothing, and no sign of it on anyone near him. The stick had evaporated.

Glen stood in the aisle waiting for him, looking more amused than concerned about him.

"Did you get it?"

"No. I don't know what happened."

"A dogpile is what happened. I'm glad you were able to walk out of it."

"I thought I had it. Came right to me."

"Too many people. Everyone jumped in."

Glen stopped suddenly, recognizing a man in bright spandex pants sporting a huge mane of teased and bleached hair.

"Hey Glenn! I didn't know you were here. Great show, huh?"

"Hi, man! Good to see you! Yeah, Ozzy rocked it! Totally awesome!"

"Glenn, this is my brother Paul. Did you see him going for the drumstick? He almost got it."

"Yeah, I saw the pileup. Pretty brave of you to mix it up in that."

"Paul, this is Glenn Holland. He plays drums for Pandemonium."

"You go to school with The Resches' sister Dadie, right?"

"Yeah, I had a class with her at CSUN. She recognized me from a show and invited me to check you guys out. Paul, their band is one of the first ones I saw in Hollywood."

"Well, here. Now you can both come see us."

Glenn the drummer handed Glen the fan a flyer featuring a studio shot of him and the three Resch brothers equally decked out in studded leather vests and long hair. Their next show was at the Country Club in two weeks.

"April 14th. Paul, you should come with me. You'll love these guys."

"Yeah, Paul, it would be great to see you there."

"He hasn't been to a club show before. I keep telling him he should come with me and be a part of the scene."

"Well, there you go. Come on out. We'll see you on the 14th."

They parted ways as Glenn lingered to pass out more flyers on the floor. Glen handed Paul the flyer as they made their way to the crowd packing the aisle to the exit. Paul felt some discomfort in his right hand. Looking closely, he discovered several splinters lodged in his palm.

Justin

THERE WAS A certain stigma attached to being from the San Fernando Valley. Parts of the Valley were okay. The Country Club was there in Reseda, and fans came over the hill by the hundreds each weekend to fill its floor. Other clubs lined Lankershim, and the entire east side had a gritty edge to it. It wasn't Hollywood, but it had its own sense of legitimacy. But parts of the Valley were far more privileged, especially south of Ventura Boulevard where he lived, and you didn't admit to having such an address among certain circles for fear of looking like a snob. Most of the scene was living paycheck to paycheck or handout to handout and had few financial plans aside from where they'd eat their next meal. To be born in more security meant to lose some credibility among those who either suffered or basked in penury.

He once showed his driver's license to a guy from the Crenshaw District with whom he worked. He had looked considerably younger at 16, and when his friend saw the photo he started laughing.

"Oh, Valley go home! Dude, if you ever came into my neighborhood when you were this age, we would have beaten the shit out of you. Little white Valley boy. People used to spray paint 'Valley go home!' all over the place. Dude, you might not have made it out alive."

People in the scene were from everywhere, though, and nobody ever made an issue of it. He knew plenty of people who piled into the cheap apartments that lined Reseda Boulevard and in more sketchy parts of the Valley like Van Nuys and North Hollywood. People came from the west side, Venice, Palms, Culver City, or areas east of Hollywood like Silverlake,

Eagle Rock, Boyle Heights. He once met a girl at the Country Club from Glendora. He got her phone number, but once he found Glendora in the *Thomas Guide*, he never called her. He liked to drive, but the last thing he needed to be doing was driving to the eastern San Gabriel Valley on a routine basis.

The Valley was alright. He'd heard enough people bad-mouth it to realize there was probably more to life somewhere else. But it was home. For now. And living in the foothills gave him easy access to places that didn't make him feel so tied down. When the heart of the Valley floor was a morass of heat and traffic, he went to quieter places and rose above it. Gateways to the LA basin on the other side. Mountains with passes to the greater city. And the ocean.

Paul

The night drenched me to the bone
Awash in the music
Soaked through
Until it dripped in excess from my ears
And from my virgin clothes

THE FIRST LOCAL show I ever went to was at the Country Club. The first band on stage that night was called Hostage. Their set had already begun when I arrived, and the guitarist was standing center stage in the middle of a raging solo. After going to a few large-scale concerts, I was surprised how empty the house was in comparison. I walked down the center aisle past tables where people drank and paid little attention to the band that was performing. I made it to the floor and continued unchallenged right up to the edge of the stage. Front row. Only a few other people nearby, and I stood cross-armed among them, looking up at this guy wailing on the guitar as if I'd just entered a gallery at an art museum and was inspecting the brushstrokes of the nearest oil painting.

I enjoyed the set immensely, most likely because of the novelty of the proximity in which I was able to witness it. I had never seen the making of music at such close range before, aside from the countless hours of music videos I had sat through. But this was different—unpolished, in the flesh, full of raw energy, raging volume, and distortion. The real deal. Wrapped up in muscle shirts and hairspray. Bandanas and spandex. Nail polish and calluses. Well, as real as it gets in the spectacle that is the LA music scene.

Pandemonium was the third and final act that night. The floor was packed by the time they came on. I left with a drumstick and plans to see them again two weeks later.

We stopped by the Resch family home for the after-party. I drank a beer faster than I should have, having worked up a thirst holding my position on the crowded floor. When I got up quickly to throw away the empty bottle, I felt a foreign form of dizziness. Glen called it a buzz and silently laughed at the fact it was my first so as not to embarrass me in front of those much older, much wiser.

I was 15 years old.

I went outside and got reacquainted with the night.

Catherine

PEOPLE TRICKLED OUT of the Resch family home and scattered along the sidewalk up and down the block. It had become too late in the night for the occupation of someone else's house, but never too late to take to the streets and prolong the party. Several small crowds stood around chatting with no concern for their effect on the slumbering neighbors.

Glen and Catherine talked briefly with a couple of friends of hers until they went their separate ways. Catherine immediately began grumbling.

"I swear, Janine annoys the hell out of me sometimes."

"Why?"

"Because she's a bass slut and gets all weird when people talk to Eric or any of the other bassists she knows. Michelle's not much better."

"Wait . . . she's a what?"

"A bass slut. You know, guitar sluts, drum sluts, bass sluts?"

"No, I don't know."

"A bass slut . . . a bass slut is someone who only has sex with bass players. Like a guitar slut only fucks guitarists. A drum slut . . .. you get the idea. Michelle's a drum slut."

"That exists?"

"Heck yeah, that exists. You've never heard of it before? Probably because you're not in a band. These girls are hardcore. They'll fuck anyone as long as they play the right instrument. No pun intended."

"So, as long as the guy plays bass, Janine will have sex with him?"

"Pretty much, yeah."

"Even if they're butt ugly?"

"Yep. You know the bassist for Odin? She fucked him. That dude's scary looking."

"This is crazy."

"No, man. It's just Hollywood. What did you expect?"

"Crazy."

"You can't be prude about stuff like this. It's Hollywood. Anything goes and everything goes."

"Yeah, but . . . what do they get out of it? I mean, they are groupies, I get that. But . . . what's in it for them? It's not like everyone is going to make it."

"Yeah, but a few do. And they can say they fucked them when. But it doesn't matter if they are going to make it. It's like a pure numbers game with these bitches. It's a competition. The more dicks they get, the better they are. Janine thinks everyone wants to fuck her. But she acts like she's all choosy, right? Even though she's not. I don't care. I don't want everyone to fuck me. That's totally skanky."

"Bruce and I call 'em hosebags."

"Yeah. Janine's one of the biggest hosebags of them all."

"You wanna get going?"

"We probably should. Where's your brother?"

"Oh, he's around. He had a little buzz on from a beer he drank. So, he went outside about a half an hour ago. Probably didn't want to make a fool of himself."

"There."

Catherine pointed to a palm tree on the mow strip next-door. Paul was standing next to it, staring back at the small crowds that now dotted the block on their side of the street. Glen jogged over, happy to see he hadn't wandered too far.

"Hey, you feeling alright?"

"Yeah, I'm feeling it."

"Still? After one beer?"

"No. I had another."

"Where'd you get another?"

"From this girl, Flor. She brought me one."

"Flor? Mike's sister Flor?"

"I don't know. She just said she was Flor."

"And just like that she brought you a beer?"

"Yeah."

"Did you talk to her at all?"

"Yeah, a little."

"What did you say?"

"We talked about the show. And I told her
I'd see her at the Troubadour on the 28th."

"Awww, Glen, your brother has himself a girlfriend."

"Nah, it's nothing like that. She's just a nice girl."

"Yeah, a nice girl bringing you beer and making plans to see you at the next Pandemonium show."

"Well, she did ask me if I was going to be there. And told me when and where it was. You're going, aren't you?"

"You mean, we're going. Yeah. I guess you want to, huh?"

"Sure."

"Well, I knew you'd like the club scene for one reason or another. Welcome in!"

"More than one. It's got music, and a lot of tight pants, and a lot of . . . tight pants."

"Ha! You would notice."

The three of them began walking up the sidewalk, Paul leading the way to nowhere in particular. He walked right on the edge of the curb, stepping with one foot in front of the other. He'd only make it a few feet before having to step off into the dry gutter to regain his balance. Glen and Catherine followed close behind, until Paul nearly stumbled into the street. They caught up to him and linked arms, walking side by side just off the curb.

"Ah, that's better. Thanks guys."

"Awww, Glen, your brother is drunk."

Bruce

He had talent. No one could deny that.

He had the prints that showed it and the negatives to substantiate them. He would let anyone who was interested in proof look through his suitcase.

Proof. He always thought it was funny that the word had two meanings. For him, both were essential for his career aspirations. "I was there!" his work could testify.

He'd show them piles of photos in that suitcase of every local band imaginable and several established artists he had the good fortune to get close enough to. Iron Maiden, Scorpions, Ozzy, WASP, Slayer. He shot Billy Squier while sitting on the stage, not pressed up against it, but no one could verify whether he had landed a special press pass to accomplish this or had simply taken advantage of a lax environment. It was Billy Squier, after all. His latest story was that Queensrÿche wanted to take him on tour with them opening for KISS in huge venues across the country. Maybe overseas.

He'd show them other artifacts in that suitcase besides his photos. Backstage passes, guitar picks, and autographs. Then there was the entire Randy Rhoads installation. Rarely seen photos, none of which he had taken (although he didn't offer that information freely); the business card Randy used while giving guitar lessons in Burbank (complete with the R/R logo stolen from Rolls Royce); a letter from Randy's mother Delores, thanking Bruce for his loyal fandom. The collection was the envy of any Randy follower who failed to realize that every one of those items could also be theirs with a little effort and resourcefulness. Bruce never claimed to have met Randy—he wouldn't go so far—but he did credit himself with having contact with each of Randy's surviving family members. Even his sister Kathy was supposedly a fan of Bruce's work.

He'd talk about befriending the guys from Mötley Crüe. He and Nikki Sixx bonded over a twelve-pack and it was "Nikki this," "Nikki that" ever since. He'd throw around the names of the other three members of the band as if they were acquaintanceships he didn't care much to develop, but Nikki was clearly a favorite. He didn't have any photos of him, however, aside from clippings from magazines he never worked for.

"Wait, get back to this Queensrÿche gig. What's up with that?"

"They want to take me on the road. I'll shoot every show."

"That's amazing, man. When do you start?"

"I don't know. I still have to work all that out."

"So, you don't have the job yet?"

"Not officially. I have to get some prints over to Karen, their manager."

"Wait . . . how can they hire you if they haven't seen your stuff yet?"

"They've seen my stuff. I go way back with Geoff. They want me. It's just a formality. Karen just has final approval."

"Well, when are you going to send the prints in?"

"I don't know. I should do it soon."

"Then, why don't you?"

"I will. I just have to get together some stuff I like."

"Just send her anything. It's all good."

"Yeah, I will."

"Do it, man. Don't fuckin' blow this. If she asked to see your stuff—"

"I will. I said I will."

The term *starving artist* definitely applied. Bruce officially lived with his father in Orange County, but his apartment was so far away from the scene that Bruce spent most of his nights on other people's couches and floors. He also subsidized his lack of steady income by grazing through their refrigerators until he'd worn out his welcome.

Still, people had patience. Why not, when the man who might shoot platinum-selling album covers and exposés in *Rolling Stone* and *CREEM* habitually slept on your floor and ate all your Corn Flakes?

The talent was there, like with so many of the artists who played the scene weekend after weekend. It was only a matter of time.

Mike

THERE IS A point on Santa Monica Boulevard where everything changes. As you drive east, northeast really, you are surrounded by lush green lawns, well-manicured hedgerows, and finely pruned eucalyptus and palm trees among other exotic species. Landscaped medians make the entire boulevard look like a pristine greenbelt, as if to disguise the fact that you are never more than walking distance from some of the most frequented intersections in the country and the most hair-pulling traffic that goes with them.

In the distance, you can see a large red "T" on a sign looming over the road. Once you reach it, everything is different. Concrete takes over for grass. A dense collection of storefronts replaces swaths of parkland and estate grounds. The boulevard narrows and appears more rutted and worn. Beverly Hills has given way to West Hollywood, and the contrast is uncomfortably stark.

Mike had been hanging out at the Troubadour and other clubs up the hill on Sunset for more than a few years. He'd started young. Too young, in retrospect. When she was only slightly older than he was then, his sister Flor began joining him most weekends. He had befriended many in the scene, and even worked for his friends in the band Poison, helping unload, set up, break down, and reload gear at every show.

Hanging out with the band was alright. Being one step away from the band members meant plenty of hot women were always paying him lots of attention. He met women who would do anything for a chance just to be introduced to a guy in the band and then do anything to that guy once given that opportunity.

Being connected to a band also meant coming to terms with living vicariously through them. Mike didn't play an instrument, he just loved the music. He had always known he'd never make it as a performing artist. But it was exciting to be friends with those who might. The scene was filled with people who wanted to see their friends make it big —more so they could take credit for having known them when they were nobodies than so they could be genuinely happy for their success. Knowing this, he questioned his own motives for working for the group, especially when he was reminded that other incentives—such as a steady income—were likely nonexistent in that line of work.

The band liked having him around because his large stature made him appear like a one-man security detail. He stood at least four inches taller than everyone else and weighed about seventy more pounds. Aside from his connections, Mike often thought his popularity was only attributable to his size. In an unpredictable city and an often chaotic scene, large friends were desirable, and there wasn't a night when Mike didn't have a group around him. But he also worried that people were too intimidated by him to get to know him—they were close in proximity but otherwise distant. It was a lot like being in a band. Everyone wants to meet you, but few know anything worth saying once they do. He felt simultaneously surrounded and alone.

"Hey Mike, you going for a walk?"

"Yeah, you want to come?"

"I don't know. Where are you going?"

"We can go anywhere. How about this way?"

"Into Beverly Hills? Nah."

"Why not?"

"Too . . . I don't know. It's different. It's all green and clean and the grass and trees."

"Nothing wrong with grass and trees."

"I know, but it's too . . ."

"Sterile?"

"Yeah, that's the word. *Sterile.*"

"How about the other way?"

"Nah, I don't want to go deeper into West Hollywood. The Rage scares me."

"You're afraid of gay people?"

"No, I'm not saying that. Just not that comfortable."

"I don't know what to tell you, man. We might pass the Rage, but it's not like we're going inside."

"Yeah, I know. But you know what they say. 'What do you do if you drop your wallet on Santa Monica?'"

"Yeah. 'Kick it to Sunset.' I know. So, you want to go to Sunset?"

"Nah."

"Why not?"

"Too steep."

"That hill? That hill's nothing. It's long and gradual. It's easy."

"No thanks, man. Not in these shoes."

"So that leaves only one last direction to go."

"Not really. There's Melrose. But that's just more freaky West Hollywood."

"You don't want to get a tattoo or something?"

"No thanks, man."

"I know. Joking."

"I guess we're stranded."

"I'm not stranded. You might be, but I'm fine."

"So, which way are you going?"

"This way, I guess."

"How far? I mean, where are you going to wind up?"

"Wherever the road takes me."

Justin

He often found himself with nothing to do. He had expected finally getting a car would open entire new realms of possibilities for him. But even with the freedom of driving around the city, he often felt out of places to go. The irony wasn't lost on him. Several times, he'd turned to a random page in the *Thomas Guide*, found the most interesting looking feature on it, and driven there, only to be disappointed by the lack of anything extraordinary. Too often, things look better on paper.

So, on those nights when the passage of time felt more like a burden than a luxury, he'd find himself returning to a select few haunts. If frequency of visitation was an indicator of his taste, Mulholland Drive was a clear favorite.

He spent plenty of time on foot where the road was unpaved, usually breaking off its course to scale a small hill nestled into an oxbow of the rutted dirt track. High points such as these offered a fuller view of the expanse of city lights below. But in the car, he always ventured east, where Mulholland continued to wind its way along the crest of the Santa Monicas, but paved, populated, and far more traveled.

Earlier that year, Annie had shown him the Hollywood Bowl Overlook. Past Laurel, on the descent toward Cahuenga and the 101, the city had recently adorned a turnout large enough to hold a handful of cars with painted parking spots, railings, and stairs to a couple of vantage points. Crowds had slowly begun to form on weekend nights as word of the lookout spread, but he always hiked up the stairs to the highest promontory and found space away from those encumbered by strollers or lack of stamina.

From this perch, the 101 looked like a great bejeweled red and white snake, emerging from the pass in a sweeping curve then straightening through Hollywood on its way downtown. The skyline could be clearly seen if the smog wasn't too thick, but beyond it was an oblivion of haze illuminated by the endless expanse of light beneath it. Closer, tucked snugly into the folds of hills pouring off the crest, sat the Bowl itself. A wide swath of bench seats, cut not too obtrusively into the mountainside, gave way to fancier box seats kneeling at the semilunar entrance of the famous white band shell, appearing from this distance much smaller than its actual impressive size. A few lights were scattered on the more pristine terrain, increasing in frequency as their distance grew until melting into the high-powered grids of brilliance that blanketed the greater basin floor.

He reminded himself countless times to get himself here on the night of a show to sample the acoustics and watch the crowd, like an omniscient looming over those blissfully unaware their engagement in the spectacle before them was capable of being observed from above.

Tonight was not unlike others. The parking lot was nearly full, but most who drove lingered close to their cars or strolled along the lower footpath to an area with benches and a metal display featuring pictures of the Bowl under construction and a written history of the region. One illustration warned about mountain lions. Someone had scratched a helpless stick figure in the lion's mouth.

He immediately ascended the stairs to see if he could find a private spot atop one of the higher vantage points. The first had several people on it, all looking out at the city. He climbed the next set of stairs to the highest man-made viewpoint and found only a young couple. They were struggling with a camera, each arguing for a turn to look at it. They both seemed intent on being the one to fix the problem. He nearly offered his assistance but decided if they were each so determined to take the challenge upon themselves, there was no way they'd let a stranger intervene and steal all the glory. Perhaps sensing that their bickering would be annoying to him, they quickly left, still wrestling for possession of the camera on the way down the stairs. He didn't like the idea of imposing his presence on others and usually would have gladly waited awhile for his turn to be alone after others were done with the view. But in this case, he didn't mind that his arrival might have hastened their departure. Their argument seemed to poison the atmosphere, and he was grateful to have cast it off the hillside—or at least back down to the crowds below.

He was always amazed how much the hill on which he stood buffered sounds from the lower vantage points. Anyone not within his view was silenced by the mass of the rock between them. The act of turning a corner had left him in solitude. An occasional laugh or burst of exuberance from someone in the crowd below broke through, but for the most part, he could stand and enjoy the view unaware of how many arrived or departed beneath him.

A few moments later, the conversation of a family that must have moved down the trail to the base of the stairs became faintly audible. He could hear a man, a woman, and at least two children. They spoke Spanish. He tested his memory of it from high school and wasn't too happy with the results. They said something about the ocean, but that's all he could make out. He doubted even this, as they'd have to be pretty disoriented to believe they could see the ocean from here. Eventually, their voices drifted away, evidence of them turning back instead of ascending to his viewpoint.

It quieted again until all he could hear was the distant hum of the city. He tried to dissect it into parts. Engines, mostly. The buzzing of electrical transformers or power lines, perhaps. An occasional horn. Tires gripping asphalt on the freeway. Wind, however slight, swirling in the basin and coursing up the hillside. Hundreds of thousands of microphonic conversations emanating from the entire landscape, made audible only by their simultaneity. He marveled at the phenomenon. How the city has a voice. How it spoke to the power that churned beneath him. How it testified to the potential that lay before him. Like many others, he came to look. But he secretly prided himself for being among the rare elite who also came to listen.

Glen

THE STRETCH OF asphalt separating the Rainbow Bar and Grill from the Roxy was prime real estate. Too narrow to be much of a parking lot, although everyone called it that, it was really just a driveway that led to an alleyway and parking areas behind the buildings. A few cars belonging to the Rainbow's VIPs were frequently parked along the wall on the Roxy side, however, so the parking lot moniker stuck.

When a show from the Roxy emptied, people gathered there to mingle with those stumbling out of the Rainbow. Here, the social scene raged onward until crowds began to thin, only to be refueled at two in the morning when the Rainbow booted everyone out. Those looking to continue the night's revelry formed circular clusters, filling the space between the buildings and overflowing onto the sidewalk. Talking within these clusters were established musicians, those aspiring to be established musicians, those aspiring to know them in several senses of the word, and those simply aspiring not to go home.

Whether the night's show was at the Roxy or at slightly farther venues, such as the Whisky-a-Go-Go or Troubadour, hanging out in the Rainbow parking lot afterward was a mainstay. For many, it was as interesting and amusing as the night's musical performances.

Standing outside amid the throng of regulars, Glen heard someone lay on the horn of a car driving slowly by. Many heads snapped around. He couldn't see the driver, but a disjointed chorus of "fuck you" burst from the crowd, accompanied by a host of raised middle fingers. Several immediately walked toward the car, willing to become better acquainted with the driver. The shifting of bodies provided an opening through which he could see more of what was happening, but by then the car had passed, speeding up enough so that chasing it on foot proved futile.

"What a dick."

"What happened, Mike?"

"Just some jerkoff flipping us off. Probably jealous of us hanging around with all these hot women. Asshole's got nothing better to do than honk at us as he drives by. Some people need to mind their own fucking business."

Glen liked to recall the time he saw Twisted Sister at the Palladium. At some point in the show, Dee Snyder pointed out the record executives and other suits who watched from the balcony. At first, Glen thought the desired response from the audience was applause, but then Dee began berating the executives for not having the balls to come down and watch the show from the floor. He made a few jokes about getting their suits wrinkled, and the audience began to boo those standing relatively comfortably above them.

A few songs later in the set, a cup of beer fell from the balcony railing, landing on those unfortunates below. Dee waited until the end of the song, then lashed out again.

"Which one of you motherfuckers up there threw the beer? Come down here right now! These are my people, and they are better than you'll ever be! They deserve better than to have beer poured on them by some stick-up-the-ass record-label clowns—rich snobs who don't know the first thing about how to rock! You think you know something because you've got your cush job in your cush office? You need to come down here and get yourselves a real education!"

The crowd went crazy. Glen wondered if a riot might break out. He imagined people in jackets and ties burning at the stake. He thought he saw a few in the balcony head for the exit and almost felt sorry for them. Evidently, Dee felt confident in whatever record deal the band had. He clearly wasn't scrounging and groveling for whatever help he could get like most of Glen's musician friends.

The crowd in the Rainbow parking lot carried on as if nothing had happened, the confrontation with the driver a distant memory.

His people. He felt comforted by the thought.

"Hey, Mike. Did I ever tell you about the time I saw Twisted Sister at the Palladium?"

Bruce

PAUL GOT UP in the middle of the night and tread lightly past a snoring Glen in the neighboring twin bed. On his way down the hall to the bathroom he found the light on in the kitchen. Thinking Glen must have absentmindedly forgotten to turn it off before retiring, he reached into the room and flipped the switch.

"Hey, I'm eating here."

"Wha . . . ? Who's there?"

He quickly flipped the switch back on.

"Who the heck are you? You scared the shit out of me."

"I'm Bruce, man. Your brother is letting me crash for the night. He said if I was hungry I could help myself."

On the counter by the sink, Paul noticed an open loaf of bread, an open package of bologna, an open package of American cheese slices, and an open jar of mayonnaise with a knife still sticking out of it.

"Uh . . . ok. Just make sure you put the food away. My mom will be pissed if she finds it in the morning."

"Yeah, no problem. You must be Paul, Glen's brother, right?"

"Yeah. Wait a minute, I thought I recognized you. You're the guy that's always taking pictures at the shows."

"Yeah, that's me."

"I see you all the time. You sort of stand out."

"Yeah, being tall helps me get the best shots. No one in my way. You should have gone tonight. Blackie was insane! Threw raw meat out to the crowd."

"Cool. Did you get any shots?"

"Of course. I'll get them developed this week. But I've got my port-folio with me. I'll show you some other shots in the morning if you like."

"Yeah, that sounds great."

Bruce took another bite of his sandwich.

"Well, I'm going to the bathroom. Are you crashing on the couch or what?"

"Yeah, Glen pulled out a sleeping bag for me."

"Alright. Have a good night."

"Thanks, Paul. Nice meeting you."

"You too."

"See you at breakfast!"

Charlie

"What's up, Charlie?"

"Mike! Hey, man. Have a seat."

Charlie sat on the curb on Sunset, just outside the AM/PM. The show across the street and up a block at the Whisky raged on.

"Naw, that's alright. I'll stand. What are you doing here?"

"Getting a couple cheeseburgers for a buck, man."

"You eat 'em already?"

"Not yet."

"Well, they keep the burgers inside under that light. What are you doing sitting out here?"

"Just trying to decide if I really want them."

"Tough decision?"

"Yeah."

"Whatever, dude. Well, I'm going in for a Coke. You going to the show? Keel's gonna tear it up."

"Uh, I don't know."

"Another tough decision?"

"I guess."

"Were you in there yet? The opener sucks. I'm trying to kill some time until they're off."

"No, I haven't gone in yet."

"Well, you gonna? C'mon, come check out Keel. They're great. You can't just spend your night sitting outside the AM/PM."

Charlie didn't move. Mike turned to head in the direction of the minimart but held himself in check. He sat down next to Charlie instead.

"Alright dude, what's wrong?"

"Wrong?"

"Yeah, what's wrong? It's like you're paralyzed or something."

"I'm just depressed, man."

"Depressed? You? Why?"

"I don't know."

"You been drink—wait a minute . . . dumb question?"

Charlie nodded.

"You drunk? Stoned? Wasted? What?"

"What have you got?"

"You know, I don't think I've ever seen you sober."

"Naw!"

"Yeah! Really, dude. I've been hanging out in the scene with you, what . . . three, four years? You're always high on something."

"Hey man, don't give me that shit. I'm high on life, man!"

"Yeah, I get it. But you say you're depressed."

"Oh, yeah, right."

"You forgot for a minute?"

"Not a minute, man."

"So, what about?

"I forgot."

Mike couldn't completely contain his laughter.

"You forgot?"

"Yeah."

"How the hell can you be depressed when you can't even remember why you're depressed in the first place?"

"Oh, yeah, huh?"

"Yeah, huh. If you don't even know what's making you sad, how can you be sad? I'd say you're pretty lucky."

"Well, I'm not just going to spring up and be all happy and shit. Just like that."

"Okay."

"I'm not just going to go into the club and start hanging all over everyone like they're my pals."

"I wouldn't expect you to."

"Wait . . . I remember."

"What is it?"

"It's not so much that I'm depressed. It's just that I was trying to figure something out. So, I took a seat here to think."

"Okay. Figure what out? Think about what?"

"Figure out who we are."

"What do you mean?"

"I mean what I said. I'm figuring out who we are."

"I know who you are. And I know who I am."

"Yeah, who am I?"

"You're Charlie. You're a fixture in there, dude. Everybody is like 'Hey Charlie! There's Charlie! How ya doin', Charlie?' all the time. Everybody knows you. Everybody loves you."

"They don't love me. I annoy them most of the time."

"Well, you aren't always a happy drunk, Charlie."

"No?"

"No. You get angry sometimes. But we all do. It doesn't mean people don't forgive you. For the most part, they think you're . . . I don't know . . . you're just Charlie. I bet they think you're cool most of the time."

"It's just this scene, man."

"What about it?"

"It's like . . . I got it. I figured it out."

"What's that, Charlie?"

"It's Halloween all the time. We're Halloween, man!"

"What do you mean?"

"It's like . . . dress up and wear your makeup and go out and . . ."

"Don't regular people dress up and wear makeup and go out?"

"Yeah, but this is different. This is like . . . be something you're not. These are not regular people."

"No, I never said they were. But who wants to be regular? That's boring, man."

"Yeah, but . . ."

"And, 'be something you're not'? What does that mean?"

"We're Halloween. Get all dressed up and pretend. These people are pretenders."

"Yeah, we talk about the posers all the time. But we're not all posers. There are the posers and there are the cool people. You're one of the cool people. We hang out with the cool people."

"But even the cool people are doing it. Everyone's doing it."

"Doing what?"

"Doing that thing. That act. That show. Show after show. It's always the same. I mean, the bands on stage are different. But it's always the same crowd. The same scene. And it's Halloween every fucking night, man."

"You tired of it?"

"No. I mean, I love it for the most part. Where else do I have to go?"

"You can go anywhere you want."

"But I fit in here. Yeah, I'm Halloween too."

"That doesn't sound like anything to be depressed about."

"Well, I guess I'm not depressed after all. Thanks, Mike."

"Wha—? Damn, I want some of what you're smoking. It was that easy?"

"I'm serious. I mean, look at us. We're all headbanging and shit. Everyone. There are the thrasher guys who like to slam in the pit. Just beat on each other. There are the pretty girls. They just like to be seen. The glam dudes. Shit, they wear more makeup and spend more time on their hair than their girlfriends. But we're all in there every weekend just tearing it up. Banging our heads. Pumping our fists. Rocking out, you know?"

"Yeah, I get it. Why don't we get in there and bang our heads, then?"

"Oh no . . . no, man."

"What?"

"I'm not falling for that pep-rally shit."

"That what?"

"That pep rally, rah, rah, let's get in there and fight, fight, win, go team crap."

"I never said any of that."

"But that's what you meant. Let's go team. Let's get in there and kick some ass."

"Whatever, Charlie. I mean, don't take this the wrong way. I love you, man. But you never cease to amaze me."

"Whatever. But just give me a second."

"For what?"

"To get up on my own terms."

"Okay, man. Take your time."

"Alright, I'm ready."

"Took you long enough."

Charlie stood and took a step toward the street.

"Hold on. I'll see you in there. I never got my Coke."

"No, it's okay. I'll come with you. I never got my food."

"Oh, yeah. C'mon I'll buy you a hot dog."

"Oh, no. That's alright."

"C'mon, it's just a hot dog."

"Nope. I don't eat that crap. That shit will kill ya. Cheeseburgers, man!"

"That's right. It was cheeseburgers, wasn't it?"

"Cheeseburgers!"

"I'll buy you a cheeseburger."

"Two for a buck, man. You can't go wrong."

"I'll buy you two, then."

Ashley

Ashley had the usual hard time finding a parking spot at Tower Records and had decided to just parallel park on Cedros and walk. She stuck to the sidewalk instead of cutting through the lot to the rear door. She'd seen a huge display for the new KISS album up front while driving and was not in the mood to browse. She sidestepped four guys playing guitar along the side of the building, a few yards down from the Ticketmaster window. They looked like they were still in high school.

The place was pretty jammed for a Wednesday night. She didn't have much trouble grabbing a copy of *Animalize*, though. She lingered at the display reading a review of the album that had been posted there when a young man interrupted her.

"Damn, $9.98. They just keep going up in price."

She wasn't entirely sure he was talking to her and not just complaining to himself. She decided it was safer to respond anyway.

"Yeah, I know."

She figured their conversation ended there, but after a pregnant pause, he spoke up again.

"I'm going to have to start hitting the used racks at Moby Disc far more often."

"Money a little tight these days?"

"Yeah. Very tight."

She decided not to wait for another pregnant pause.

"Do you work?"

"Sort of. I do odd jobs for family friends. Bookkeeping, stuff like that. It's hard to find anything these days."

"What are you looking for?"

"I'd love to work in the music industry."

She failed to stifle the laugh.

"Sorry. It's just, that's what everyone says. In LA, everyone wants to work for the music industry, or the film industry, or like, the entertainment industry, whatever the hell makes that different. Are you a musician?"

"Me? Oh, no. I was thinking more of the business end. I don't have any talent."

"Ah yes, behind the scenes is where everyone looks who doesn't have any talent."

"I know. It's a rat race. All about who you know. But you know what's funny?"

"What?"

"About everyone I know are people who are trying to make it in the music industry too. As musicians."

"Yep. Lots of starving artists out there."

"Do you work?"

"Yeah. Law office. But like, secretarial crap. They don't let me practice law."

"Ha, that's good. I mean, I guess that's good. I don't know."

"Don't worry about it. Hey, what kind of music do your friends make? I know a lot of bands too."

"Mostly hard rock, heavy metal."

"Really? That's what I'm into. I go to the clubs a lot. I don't remember seeing you there."

"Yeah? I only go once in a while. When I can get on the guest list, you know?"

"Yeah, I know. Like, who do you know?"

"I've known the guys in Lizzy Borden quite awhile. I know guys in Keel, Pandemonium, Sin, Hellion, LA Guns. Those types of bands."

"I've seen most all of them. Our paths have probably crossed a few times. I'm Ashley, by the way."

"Oh, uh, I'm Justin. Really? I don't remember seeing you either. Who do you go to shows with? Maybe we know the same people."

"Probably. But I'm not going to, like, just start naming everyone I know. My best friend is Catherine. She has really black, black hair. Wears leopard and tiger print spandex a lot. I hang out with her mostly, so if you knew her, you'd probably know me. There are a bunch of other regulars I see all the time. Too many to name."

"Yeah, don't worry about it. Many of the ones I see regularly, I don't even know their names. So, whatever."

"And what do you do the other days of the week when you aren't going to shows or hanging out in record stores?"

"Umm, not a lot. Just hanging out mostly."

"Yeah? Doing what?"

"You'd think it's stupid."

"No. Try me."

"I look at the city lights a lot."

Paul

AND YOU, TOO?

Were you in love with the night?

Were you one of those lonely hearts on the streets after dark, pulsing with its rhythm?

Did you embrace every adventure, rising from the ashes of extinguished days,

Ready to take flight?

We'd hold each other's hands as we negotiated flat stones across dark rivers, never fully comprehending the power of the current that ran underneath every step, never knowing we were plugged into it; it gave us life.

We were surrounded by those who dove from great heights to test its depths, emerging with a glow, an effervescence of newfound vitality.

I'd sit on the bank and dip in a toe, never daring to ask for more from a rebirth.

Glen

The freeway was flowing smoothly this time of night. The ringing in his ears coupled with the steady drone of the Firebird's engine, creating harmonic overtones that carried him over the pass and back into the Valley. But he knew this was the calm before the storm.

They had been forbidden to go, but they went anyway. Pissed off at something so trivial that they both had since forgotten what it was, their mother demanded they sell the tickets. Not on a school night. Not when Paul was only 15. It was too late to be out. Especially on a school night.

Glen was old enough to come and go as he pleased. He still lived at home but was no longer held accountable for his whereabouts. But Paul was another story. And since they both planned on going to this show together, the restriction applied equally.

He had a twinge of guilt about taking advantage of their mother's work schedule. She couldn't help it that she had to work so late that she couldn't always keep track of where Paul went after school. She couldn't help it that she had to be in bed so early as to allow her to be up and out of the house in the morning before he awoke. It was easy for him to pick Paul up from school and head off to the show with plenty of time to kill and no one standing in their way.

He had many ways to cope with the guilt. Too many ways, actually. He wasn't hurting anyone. Paul stayed up late all the time, and doing so on a school night wouldn't make a difference. He was old enough to make that judgment call himself. The music was more important than the lateness of the night. The music. That's the only thing that really mattered. How dare she deny them the chance to witness the raw, passionate performance of such incredible music?

They both figured by the time the concert date arrived, their mother would have forgotten what night it was scheduled. They made certain not to remind her. They were going, that was final. It was just a matter of how to come home late with the least amount of backlash possible. This was their first chance to see the Scorpions live. Bon Jovi was opening, and he showed promise as a new artist. No way were they going to miss this because of some stupid, impulsive grounding.

"Mom will be in bed by the time we get home. Don't worry, we're in the clear."

"No way. I bet she's still awake. I bet she's staying up until I show up. I never called her, never told her where I was going."

"Yeah, you should have called from somewhere when we got there . . . made something up. Oh well, she'll be mad and yell like she always does, but it was worth it."

"Totally worth it."

Still, Paul would rather not face that kind of music unless he had to. He had managed to avoid it most of his life. Having an older brother had deflected most of the wrath. He didn't want anything to spoil the brilliance of the concert he'd just witnessed. He wanted the only ringing in his ears putting him to sleep to be from Marshall stacks, not screaming in his face.

Glen negotiated the car off the freeway and through the stop signs and curves on the final mile to their house.

"Do me a favor. Just slow down and drive by first. Don't pull in the driveway."

"Why?"

"Just do it. I want to see if she's still up."

She stood in the dim glow of a single kitchen light bulb, arms crossed, staring out the window at the mouth of the driveway, waiting for a set of headlights to make an appearance.

"Holy shit! She's up!"

"You called it, man."

"Do you think she saw us?"

"Naw. Too dark in the car. So many cars drive down this street, she probably didn't think it was us."

"Drive back to the boulevard."

"Why? You've got to go home sometime. You think she's going to give up now and go to bed?"

"Just drive back. There's got to be a plan."

They had it by the time they pulled into the Chevron station on the corner. Glen turned the car around, stopped long enough to let Paul out, then headed back up the street toward the house. Paul counted a minute and a half off his watch, then hopped into the pay phone and fished a quarter out of his pocket. He hoped the heat he faced on the phone would be the only heat he faced that night.

"Mom?"

"Where the hell are you? I've been worried sick!"

"I'm sorry. I'm at my friend Jason's house. I came over after school because we have a big test in Jackson's class tomorrow. He's helping me, and I lost track of the time."

"You don't call? Why can't you call to tell me where you are?"

"I forgot. I lost track of time. I'm stressed out because I'm not doing too well in that class, and I have to do well on this test."

How could she argue against such dedication to his schoolwork?

"Well, next time, let me know where you are! I was about to start calling the police, the highway patrol, then the morgues. I have to be up early in the morning. I don't have time to be messing around with this! How are you getting home?"

"Isn't Glen around? Can he come pick me up?"

"He's not here. I'm not about to go out now to get you. Why don't you think!? You do things without thinking them through! Oh wait, Glen just pulled up. Hang on, I'll have him go back out before he gets settled."

Paul sat in silent amazement at how smoothly the plan was working.

He could hear the stress in his mother's voice as she assaulted Glen with instructions to get on the phone and figure out where to pick up his irresponsible little brother. Glen got on the phone.

"Hello? Where the hell are you?"

"Hey man, is she buying it?" He was amazed at what a good actor Glen was, pretending to be pissed off at the inconsiderate way he'd made his mother stay up with worry for him.

"Yeah . . . Jason's house? Who the hell is Jason? Just tell me the address, I'll find it."

"Heh, heh. I can't believe it's working!"

"Yeah . . . okay, got it. Dumbass! Why didn't you call?"

"Sorry, man, it was the fucking Scorpions!!!"

"Alright, I'll be there to get you in about ten minutes. Stay put, dipshit!"

"Don't worry, I will!"

He hung up, pumped his fist in the air, and slowly exited the phone booth, knowing it would be roughly a minute and a half before he saw his brother's car taking the turn a little too quickly into the gas station.

He opened the door and hurried into the passenger seat like a bank robber grateful for an accomplice.

"Did she buy it!!!? Totally buy it!!!?"

"Totally bought it, man! Great plan."

"Oh man, I can't believe we pulled that off. You were awesome . . . getting pissed off at me! Very convincing."

"I used to be in drama, you know. I can act when I have to."

"Oh man, that was fucking awesome!!! I can't believe we pulled that off."

"You want to know the best part?"

"What?"

"We get to drive around for like 20 minutes because I'm supposed to be picking you up in Woodland Hills! We're not due back for a while!"

"She'll be in bed by the time we get home. I know her. As soon as she heard I was okay, she went upstairs. I won't have to face her until tomorrow, and by then, she'll have cooled off."

When they returned home, the lights were off save for the one on the stairway. His mother summoned him from the darkness above.

"Paul?"

"Yes?"

"Come to the foot of the stairs."

"Yes."

"Don't ever do that again. If you're not coming home for dinner or going to be out late, call and let me know where you are."

"I will. Sorry, I lost track of the time. It was a good night, though. We got a lot done. It will help me a lot for tomorrow."

"Alright. Turn off the light please."

"Good night."

Best concert ever.

Justin

HE COULDN'T HEAR it until his head hit the pillow. Not until all other sound disappeared. No longer the clamor of voices in parking lots and on sidewalks. No longer the drone of engines making their way down the Strip. No longer the steady hum of his own car as it negotiated the freeway, accompanied by whatever was playing on the tape deck. It wasn't until the lights were out and demand on all other senses was reduced to a minimum. And then it was clearly apparent. So prominent he was amazed he couldn't hear it before.

His ears felt muffled, as if stuffed with cotton. Or filled with glue. Numb. And the sound he heard wasn't originating anywhere on the outside. It was coming from inside, bouncing around his brain and eustachian tubes, as if trying to find a way out. An unending, steady tone. Lingering vibration in a constant frequency, left behind after all other vibrations were extinguished. A high, unmistakable ringing.

Weeeeeeeeeeeeeeeeeeeeeeeeeeeeeeee.

Not loud. But persistent.

A screaming that mimicked the screaming he'd heard blasted into microphones and out of amplifiers all night long.

Bruce

"Dude, let me drive."

"Bruce . . ."

"What? I won't crash it. When have you ever known me to crash a car?"

"I haven't known you that long."

"Very funny. The answer is I haven't. I've never crashed a car. C'mon, Mike lets me drive his car all the time."

"Mike has a piece-of-shit Dodge Dart. Used to be his mom's or something. Mike doesn't care about that car."

"And even so, I take good care of it. I'll take extra good care of yours, knowing how much you care about it. C'mon man. Trust me."

Glen looked at Paul who shrugged.

"Alright, man. But if you crash it, it's going to be your ass. You'll owe me until you die."

"Ha! Just get in. You won't regret it."

Bruce grabbed the keys from Glen's outstretched hand before he could change his mind. He dashed around the front of the car, tapping on the hood in random places as he went as if to make sure it was secure before getting in the driver's door.

"What the hell was that?"

"Victory dance. And a blessing. Praying to the Firebird gods."

"You're not making me feel any more confident in your abilities, you know that?"

"Don't worry about it, man. Firebird . . . Sky Bird . . . Insane!"

He fired up the ignition and backed out of the parking spot in the Geffen lot slower and with more caution than his excitement would have predicted. He put it in gear, rolled down his window, and hung a right on Sunset.

"Hey, where are you going?"

"Going to cruise the Strip first!"

"Bruce . . ."

"What? Don't be so uptight. I'll take Laurel home."

He floored it to catch the light at Doheny and laid on the horn as they passed the Rainbow, sticking his arm out of the window in a perpetual wave.

"Hey, Grant! Mike! Dave! See ya!!!"

A collection of heads turned to see Bruce's toothy grin flashing from the driver's window of the Firebird. He floored it again and didn't let up the gas until they had flown past the Whisky.

Traffic slowed their progress all the way to Crescent Heights. Just as well, thought Glen. Bruce waited for the light to turn red before hanging a left from the intersection.

"Guys run that light all the time. I always let it go red before turning. See? I'm careful with your little car."

"Yeah, right."

"Hey, whatcha got in the tape deck?"

"Iron Maiden. *Number of the Beast.*"

"Steve Harris, man! He's insane! Let's crank it. Running to the hills, man!"

Bruce rolled up the window as Crescent Heights turned into Laurel Canyon Boulevard. He hit play on the deck, grabbed the volume knob, and quickly looked over his shoulder at Paul in the back seat.

"You ready, man?"

Paul braced himself and nodded.

Bruce turned the knob to an earsplitting level. Then turned it a little more.

"Hallowed Be Thy Name" had just kicked into high gear when Bruce hit the first tight turn on Laurel. He put the right tires in the gutter and hugged the curb all the way through it. The car didn't lose speed as it drifted across the lane to hug the centerline on the next turn. Paul had to grab the headrest in front of him to stop himself from being dragged off the seat. The next turn pulled him too far the other way and he hugged the side of the car's interior with his face. The speakers sent immense sound waves crashing over his head, numbing his ears. Each turn pulled him against a current, only to release and toss him in the direction in which he strained to maintain his center of gravity.

Bruce screamed above the raging guitar, asking Glen if he trusted his driving ability yet. Glen just smiled and hung on tighter. They caught a green light at Lookout Mountain and Bruce opened it up on the straightaway.

"If you get a ticket, it's also your ass!"

"Don't worry, man. They won't catch us!"

Bruce laid the wheels in the gutter on every right turn as the car rose through the steep canyon.

"You think I'm going to hit the curb, don't you!?"

"Probably!"

"Well, don't worry about it, man!"

In the next straightaway, he grabbed the volume knob and turned it again, but Paul didn't hear a difference in sound. Either his ears or the speakers were already maxed out.

The higher they climbed, the more in control of the inertia Paul became. He leaned into each turn, riding the current each afforded, shifting sides as the car straightened. One more sweeping right turn and he could see the light at Mulholland was green. Bruce wouldn't have to slow down. The rise of the car reached a crescendo. They would crest at Mulholland, sail through the intersection, and then hurtle down Laurel on the valley side.

Paul grabbed the headrest again, anticipating losing his stomach as the car broke that threshold.

But Bruce slammed on the brakes.

An old Chevy Monte Carlo approached the intersection on Mulholland from the east, not slowing for the red light. In a microsecond, all three of them thought it was just another case of delayed LA reflexes, that the driver would surely stop short before entering the intersection. But he saw the Firebird before he saw the signal. He didn't hit the brakes until he was in the crosswalk.

Both cars came to a screeching halt in the middle of the intersection. The front bumper of the Monte Carlo came to rest inches from Glen's door.

Their bodies recoiled from the sudden stop and their heads came to rest facing the occupants of the Monte Carlo. Both were young men, short dark hair, tank tops. And both were laughing their asses off.

"Jesus."

"Motherfucker . . . Are those guys laughing? They're actually laughing?"

"God damn that was close."

"Are they fucking drunk, or what? YOU COULD HAVE KILLED US, ASSHOLE!!! WHY THE FUCK ARE YOU LAUGHING!!?"

"Just go, Bruce. Just go."

Bruce hit stop on the tape deck, silencing the entire scene.

"Motherfuckers! Run the red, nearly plow into us. You would have been dead, dude. No doubt. No fucking doubt!"

Bruce gave it enough gas to slowly cross Mulholland but continued to stare out the back window at the driver of the other car. The Monte Carlo sat patiently for the red light to change, nearly blocking the intersection.

"Just go Bruce. What are you going to do, fight them or something?"

"No, I just can't believe that guy. He almost killed us and he's laughing."

"He's probably fucked up. Just hope the cops pull him over before he does kill someone."

"My god. You alright, Paul?"

"Yeah, I'm fine. That was crazy, though. Fucking crazy."

"Insane."

Bruce accelerated down Laurel but kept a slower pace than before. The three of them continued to catch their breath. One turn later, Bruce reached for the tape deck again.

"You ready, man?"

"Yeah."

He hit play, grabbed the volume knob, and turned it up.

Daisy

"Is Debbie around?"

"No, thank god."

"Still off working in the entertainment industry?"

"Still off period, more like it. I think she's still paging . . . paging? Is that a word? Being a page at ABC. You know, grabbing coffee for some producer and thinking she's better than the rest of us. Something her daddy got for her."

"What does he do again?"

"Heck if I know. Some big shit at ABC. Big enough shit to buy this place for his baby girl."

"Must be nice."

"I still don't know why she wants a roommate. It's not like she needs money to afford the place."

"She said something about safety."

"Yeah, like I'm going to protect her ass if a rapist breaks in."

"She could escape when the rapist decided he wanted you first."

"Very funny. Yeah, her dad doesn't want her living alone. Probably thinks I keep her from bringing home strange men, too."

"Ha! That's ironic."

"What's ironic?"

"The part about her bringing men home when you're the one bringing men home."

"Huh?"

"I'm just assuming, mind you."

"Assuming what?"

"That you're the one . . . never mind."

"I swear I don't understand irony."

The front lock clicked and the door swung in. Debbie emerged slowly, neck craning, looking for Glen after recognizing his car out front.

"Oh, hey, speak of the devil."

"Hey Glen!"

"Hi, Debbie. We were just talking about you. Are you still being a page?"

"Yeah, why?"

"Just wondering what that entails. What do you do all day being a page?"

"Not much . . . hey, Daisy. Do you mind doing that in the bathroom?"

Daisy had laid out what looked like her entire makeup case on the living-room coffee table. More than one mascara tube, several eyeliner pencils, blush and other powders, and two eye-shadow kits lay in disarray in front of her as she sat cross-legged on the floor, her face parallel to a vanity mirror lying on its back at the table's edge.

"What's the big deal?"

She said it with half her face pulled down in an attempt to better expose her lower eyelid to the dull point of a coal-black pencil. Not every consonant sound was heard.

"You can't even take that thing out of your eye to talk to me?"

Glen thought he might head out early, in case there was a line at the Troubadour.

Daisy put down the pencil and turned her face to Debbie, a freshly slathered streak of black underscoring one eye.

"Geez, I think that eye is done."

"Hey, I don't tell you how to do your makeup."

"Sorry, I'm just not used to so much eye makeup. It's crazy how much you use."

"That's the style. You should come out to the clubs sometime. You might like it."

Daisy gave Glen a smile as if to ask, "Can you imagine?"

"No thanks."

Debbie turned to head to her room, but lingered.

"What do you guys see in going every weekend?"

Daisy froze with the pencil inches from her eye.

"What do you mean, 'what do we see?'"

"You know, like what's the attraction?"

"There's no place I'd rather be."

"Sure, but every weekend? Doesn't it get a little old?"

"No. I get to spend time with my people. I'd miss them if I didn't go."

"Yeah, but you don't get tired of it?"

"Different bands, you know? It's not like we're seeing the same show every night. So, no, I don't get tired of it. It's cool to hang out with friends."

"How about you, Glen?"

Glen knew it was coming about a second before Debbie turned her attention to him. But too late to make a break for it.

"It's sort of a place to fit in. I mean, we're not a bunch of posers or followers just trying to fit in somewhere. But it's a place to feel you belong, I guess, that doesn't ask anything in return. So, we just, I don't know . . . fit in. It's hard to explain."

"Sure, fitting in is fine. But why the same thing over and over, every weekend? The clothes, the makeup. It's like you're going out to a costume party every night."

"It *is* a costume party, in a way. Definitely a party. Great music and talented people working really hard to play it and to make it. It's exciting watching people make it."

"Hardly anyone makes it."

"A few do, here and there."

"Whatever guys. I'm getting changed."

"Hey, you're working in the entertainment industry. You're in the same business. It's the same deal."

"But I'm not decked out in Spandex, wearing a ton of makeup and a can of Aqua Net every time I go to work."

Daisy grabbed a handful of her makeup kit, dropping a pencil or two as she rose from the floor.

"I'll go in the bathroom. Sorry to soil your precious living room."

Debbie waited until she heard the bathroom door close.

"Was it something I said, Glen?"

"Of course it was something you said."

"But why? What's so offensive about asking what the appeal is?"

"I don't know. It sounds condescending, that's all."

"How?"

"Well, just because you don't understand the attraction of the Hollywood scene doesn't give you the right to talk about it like it's some sort of freak show."

"I never called it a freak show. I try not to judge your music or your friends. It might not be my thing, but I don't judge."

"Yeah, but just asking makes it sound like you're passing judgment."

"How can I be passing judgment? Daisy doesn't give a crap what I think. She puts herself above all that. She doesn't think her scene is a waste of time."

"Well, it still sounds like you're passing judgment to her."

"Why?"

"Maybe she doesn't fully believe it isn't a waste of time."

Charlie

THEY HUNG OUT on the bench at the bus stop even though none of them was going anywhere. Charlie couldn't sit still. He stood on the bench, planted a foot on the backrest to gain a height advantage, and wildly jumped in an attempt to touch a dead palm frond that jutted askew from the trunk of a nearby tree. His apparent goal was to grab it and tear it from its home, but he could barely get his fingertips on it.

Nobody said anything. With each jump, he landed right at the curb, often stumbling into the street. If a bus were to come by and the timing were right, it would surely plow into him. But nobody warned him. Everyone expected Mike to fire off a short joke or two. He'd be the first to tell Charlie to give it up, he's dreaming if he thinks he can jump that high, to go get someone like Ron, who stood a foot taller, to try it. Mike would be the first to remind Charlie that he was acting like a fool, but he stayed quiet. Some nights, you just let Charlie do his thing.

Distracted by the spectacle Charlie provided, no one noticed from which direction he appeared. An older man, much too conservatively dressed for any Los Angeles street at night, much less Santa Monica or Melrose, stood patiently at the bus bench waiting to be acknowledged.

Mike wasn't the first to notice him, but he was the first to speak.

"Hey, what's up?"

To this, the older man responded with questions about the bus lines, making the naïve mistake that people sitting on a bus bench in LA knew the first thing about how the buses ran. His thick accent and broken English explained his appearance. There was nothing local about him.

He explained that he was in town for the Olympics and was out taking in the sights. Mike wondered if the tourist had intended on seeing Hollywood but had gotten sidetracked. He couldn't picture The Troubadour making an appearance in a foreign guide book. West Hollywood seemed a little too gritty a recommendation for any self-respecting travel-guide publisher concerned for their readers' safety. He found a pause in the conversation to chime in.

"Where are you from?"

He hoped his question hadn't come off as a threat but rather as the sincere curiosity of someone interested in other parts of the world and others' places in them.

"West Germany."

Charlie had just completed his sixth leap for the palm frond when he noticed the newcomer.

He immediately went on the offensive.

"Hey, man. What the fuck are you looking at!?"

"Aw shit, Charlie."

Someone muttered under his breath in a tone that mixed the here-we-go-again resignation of what it's like to hang out with a guy like Charlie with the dread that this time it might be different. This time he might snap and do something nobody wanted to see.

When he received only a blank stare of confusion in return, Charlie continued, walking slowly toward the tourist.

"I said, 'What the fuck are you looking at!?' Are we interesting to you? Did you come down here to watch the freaks? Why don't you take a fucking picture, man!? Hang it on your refrigerator!"

The tourist allowed an uncomfortable chuckle to escape his throat, although he didn't retreat as those witnessing the exchange predicted he would. Mike made a mental note that the man probably considered himself cornered and didn't want to make any abrupt moves. He needed only turn around to realize he had all of Beverly Hills to run to.

Charlie was inches from his face.

"What the fuck, man!? Why don't you go back where you came from!? I mean, why are you here, anyways? You don't belong here!"

The tourist replied with more composure than seemed possible, given the bitter look on Charlie's face and its proximity to his own.

"I'm just here visiting. For the Olympics. I saw the club here, and the people, and—"

"Well these aren't your people! All these people like you, coming down here gawking at us! You know?"

Charlie took his eyes off the tourist for a split second as if to appeal to his comrades, but nobody made a sound or motion as if to support him.

Perhaps sensing he was alone in this, Charlie became more agitated. The tourist attempted to defend himself, but Charlie cut him off again, nearly leaping in his face to meet his gaze straight on. Face red, eyes bulging. He was going off the deep end now.

"It's always the same with you people! Coming down here. Coming here—thinking—looking...but . . . but, you know what? You remind me of my dad!"

At least one of the onlookers might have laughed if it were not for the distraction brought on by the sudden realization that Charlie had just seemingly confessed a legitimate reason for his unpredictable bursts of irrational behavior. Mike pictured a young Charlie at home, reluctantly playing Scrabble with a man dressed in a fedora and lederhosen, getting the crap beaten out of him every time he misspelled something.

Perhaps most insulted by this comparison, the tourist's discomfort appeared to get the better of him, and he tried to liberate himself from the interaction.

Mike finally broke the silence of the spectators.

"Whoa, whoa, cool it, Charlie. He's on our side."

Charlie's face kept its angry scowl as he turned to face Mike.

"Seriously, Charlie. Calm your shit down. The man's not causing any harm. He has a right to be here. You don't own the fucking street."

Charlie at first appeared ready to engage in this debate about rights and who belonged where, but then his countenance softened into something more like sadness.

As all eyes turned to Charlie to see if he had gotten so irrational as to challenge Mike or perhaps might burst into tears, the tourist made a hurried departure down Santa Monica away from the group without so much as a goodbye. Those embarrassed by Charlie's behavior hoped he found others in the city more hospitable.

"Charlie, what the hell is the matter with you? Why you so damn angry?"

"I don't know, Mike. He doesn't belong here. It pisses me off."

"Why? What does it matter to you if he belongs here or not? He's visiting. He's just checking out the scene. Why can't you be welcoming?"

"Because I'm not a freak on display, man. Like a friggin' animal in the zoo."

"I know that. He knows that. He didn't treat you like an animal."

"Yes he did, man."

"How?"

Charlie silently stared at the sidewalk.

"How? He didn't do anything. Why don't you give people a chance? Maybe learn something about somebody else's culture for a change?"

"I don't know, Mike."

"You don't know? It's not a difficult question."

"Should I go apologize?"

"That would be nice. The dude's long gone, though."

"Which way did he go?"

"I don't know. Down Santa Monica. Probably broke into a sprint when no one was looking. He got out of here fast. I bet the old man could haul ass."

"Heh, heh."

"What's so funny?"

"Maybe he's here for the Olympics because he's running in a race."

There was a collective groan from the onlookers.

"Go home, Charlie. Go home and go to bed, man."

Justin

HE GOT BACK from the show early enough to drop by Victor's place down the street and see that he was still up.

"Hey man, I was just going to bed. I wasn't expecting to see you tonight."

"Yeah, Jared didn't want to stay to see the headliner. I only knew the guys in Lizzy Borden, so we cut out early."

"Jared, man. That dude never wants to stay out late."

"Probably in a hurry to get home and jerk off."

"Heh, heh, yeah. . . . You staying up for a while?"

"Yeah, I was thinking about taking a drive."

"You just got back, man."

"I mean a drive without the car."

"Oh . . . shotgun!"

"Yeah? You were on your way to bed."

"I can be convinced."

"Alright, dude. Your stash, though."

"No problem, man. You'll pay me back. . . . Not!"

A few hits off a water pipe later, the two were walking up the street in the right-hand lane. Cars were so infrequent there that time of night, neither of them could remember a time they had to use a sidewalk. It was a game they played, especially when they were stoned. Justin was the driver and Victor his loyal passenger, as they walked side by side down the middle of the lane. Each imagined a windshield in front of them and a mellow tune on the radio. And thus, walking briskly and concentrating their perspective on a distant point well ahead of them, they could make parked cars and houses seemingly whiz past their peripheral vision. The road seemed to retract beneath their steps at a comfortable 25 miles per hour, as gentle turns and inclines were negotiated effortlessly. The walk was long and nearly entirely uphill. But the numbing effect of the marijuana pushed any thought of physical exertion out of their minds. They drew from an apparent endless well of energy and shared the remainder of a joint along the way to refill the tank, just in case.

They slowly made their way up into the foothills until they hit Clarinda Drive, perhaps the newest and steepest street in the neighborhood. Fresh pavement rose, curved, and ended abruptly in a cul-de-sac, yet Justin guided their imaginary car up a dirt path that would someday serve as the driveway of a newly built hilltop home. Well off the asphalt, among vacant lots overgrown with weeds, the two dragged out the game as long as it would go, then turned a tight 180 and stood facing the valley lights below. The entire route was a mile and a half with about a 500-foot elevation gain. Neither breathed heavily.

They simply stood and stared. Conversation was minimal, although Victor was known to bring up a bizarre topic for discussion now and again. Justin was known to begrudgingly humor him with his input. Sometimes, in warmer months, they brought a couple beers and savored them while admiring the view. Sometimes, they brought friends. Jared lived nearby. Paul and Glen also lived at the base of the foothills and enjoyed the walk as well. Friends were alright. But Justin didn't mind fewer numbers. He was embarrassed to admit he had forgone extending polite invitations to make the journey alone several times. He enjoyed the solitude that made it possible to hear only the distant city.

A dog's bark funneled up the hillside. A siren slowly grew louder, cutting a path from east to west along the nearest edge of the valley floor until abruptly ceasing, leaving a faint echo desperate to catch up.

He picked out Reseda Boulevard, the street that extended farthest up the hillside on the opposite end of the valley. A faint white "S" revealed where it broke from the straight illuminated gridlines and wound its way to higher elevations beyond. He wondered if he stood on top of those hills on the other side, what shapes of light would be visible here at his feet, or if the nearby streetlights and porch lights would be strong enough to carry their glow all the way across the valley at all. He made a mental note to drive Reseda to its greatest heights someday to find out.

He had a harder time distinguishing streets that flowed east to west across the valley floor. Their parallel lines were stacked more closely from this vantage point, and no headlights or taillights helped define them.

Every so often, a dark smudge on the landscape interrupted the glowing lines on the grid. Parks, most likely, vacant for the night. Even so, many featured tennis courts whose especially brilliant lights canceled any notion of darkness nearby. There were very few empty spaces large enough to have a negative impact on the shimmering array.

He briefly averted his gaze to look at Victor, who smiled in return.

"You know what this place could use?"

"What?"

"A telescope."

"You want to look at the stars?"

"No, the lights. And what they illuminate."

Paul

Foothold on a gray hill
A shadow overseeing
The million and one lights
Beneath him
The faint, steady drone
Of machinery
Traffic, sirens, horns, and screams
Peace above a rotting world
Of sweatshops, sex parlors
And tourist traps

Captured in the glint of her eyes
Subtle shades of gold
Bring out green hues
Soothing tones that say to him
He is warm
He is safe

They'll separate into the madness beneath them
Secured in the knowledge that the other
Will always long to be in the colorless hum
Sharing together this peace

Out of the light

I HAVE JUSTIN and Annie to thank for showing me the Hollywood Bowl overlook. I had no idea you could even see the bench seats from Mulholland, much less the band shell and stage. And there's a nice distant view of the downtown skyline from there too, complete with a graceful "S" of the 101 in the foreground, leading the way to it. But if you were to leap from this perch—if you had superhuman strength and could actually soar for miles from a single jump—you'd find yourself hitting only freeway or sagebrush. Or the luxury boxes below. It's a beautiful view, but it keeps you far removed from what you're seeing. There's a huge safety net there. Even the sounds emanating from the city blend together and soften, like pastels on an auditory canvas.

The views from where Mulholland turns to dirt and other high points in the surrounding foothills are no different. Many residential streets lay in calm darkness at your feet, creating a buffer between you and the busy streets that glow the hottest.

But the bluff under the Hollywood Sign is another story, and I found this one all by myself. Just the *Thomas Guide* and me, if I must share any credit. A leap from that little hilltop—that little altar on which to kneel in the shadow of the landmark—and you'll find yourself right in the thick of it. Dodging traffic. Dodging junkies and muggers. You'd probably hit the traffic signal at Sunset and Vermont, or plow into a façade on Vine, depending on which way you angled yourself before takeoff. There's no safety net here. You are suspended above it, shit and all, like a tightrope walker with a death wish. The palette of distinct sounds at your feet reveals every felony and misdemeanor, every lost cause, every wayward soul who thought he'd land only among angels if he took the plunge.

And it's fucking beautiful.

Catherine

"You've got to watch what you say."

"How's that?"

"I'm serious, Glen. You have to be careful. Like, I can't just say whatever I want about guys in bands."

"Why not?"

"Because bitches get possessive."

"Ooh, cat fight."

"Shut up, Bruce, I'm serious."

"Why even care?"

"I try not to care. I don't care. But other people care a lot. I can't control that."

"But why care so much about what other people say about some guy that isn't even your boyfriend? That you barely even know?"

"Glen, that's too logical. Nobody uses logic around here. This is the way it goes—"

"Hang on a second, I want to take notes."

"Shut up, Bruce! God, can't you take anything seriously without teasing people and shit?"

"Alright, alright. I'll shut up."

Denny's was at capacity, as usual, and especially full of chatter. Bruce leaned forward to better hear what Catherine had to say.

"This is the way it goes. You've got these girls whose only goal in life is to have sex with guys in bands. Come on, we've talked about this. It's like a competition. One's not enough. Like a steady boyfriend? No. You've got to jump from guy to guy. Bed to bed—"

"And the most lays wins?"

"Pretty much. You've got these girls who will say pretty much whatever they can say to get in. They manipulate people. They use the most calculated moves to get in good with the right people. To talk to the right people."

"Why?"

"So they can get close to the bands. So they can do the musicians."

"Why not just talk directly to the musicians?"

"You can, but that's just small talk."

"Huh?"

"You can have small talk with the musicians. But to get in, you have to manipulate. These guys have layers and layers of people around them. Like protecting them. Most of them haven't even made it yet—but it's like they have bodyguards."

"I don't get what you're saying. I've got friends in bands. I know a lot of guys in bands. I talk to them. I don't have to 'get in' with them. I just know them and talk to them. I don't have to break through layers of 'bodyguards.'"

"That's because you're a guy and you don't want to do them."

"But why can't a girl?"

"You just can't. And it's more than that. More than just doing them. It's getting backstage passes. Getting to go to the after parties. Getting . . . it's almost like getting to be a girlfriend for a while. Getting in."

"So, they play that role for a while and then move on to the next guy?"

"Yeah. And that role can be really rewarding if the band has made it, or is on its way. You're exposed to a lot of stuff. Drugs. Money. Fancy restaurants and parties."

"Well, yeah, if you happen to get to know the famous ones."

"Exactly. That's 'getting in.' So, here's the thing. These girls get in and then they are totally paranoid about what all the other girls also trying to get in are saying about them and the guys. It's like that game King of the Mountain. You fuck your way to the top and then worry about everyone else trying to knock you off."

Daisy walked in.

"Hey guys!"

"Hey, Daisy." Glen got up and moved to the other side of the booth. "Here, sit next to Catherine. I won't make you sit by Bruce."

"Har, har."

"Thanks. What are you guys up to?"

"Catherine is telling us your secrets."

"My what? I don't have any secrets."

"She's talking about how girls manipulate people to get close to bands."

"To get really close, if you know what I mean. And I bet you do."

"Shut up, Bruce!"

"See, Glen. It's not just me. Do you annoy every girl you know, Bruce?"

"Pretty much."

"I was telling them about how you have to be careful talking about bands. Because girls get jealous and think you're moving in on their territory."

"Ah, yeah. Hey, I gotta pee before I order."

"Why don't you order and then pee?"

"Because I don't know what I want yet, and it's kind of an emergency."

After Daisy excused herself, Bruce leaned in close again.

"She's one of them, isn't she?"

"What?"

"That's why she left to go to the bathroom. Because she's uncomfortable talking about this. Because she's one of them."

"One of who?"

"One of the manipulative girls."

"Daisy? No. Daisy says whatever the hell she wants. She doesn't care."

"Yeah, but doesn't she get to know guys in bands? You know what I mean? Doesn't she have to manipulate to get in?"

"Daisy? No. She's already in."

"How?"

"Not everyone has to manipulate. Some just get in naturally."

"You're not making any sense at all."

"You get it Glen, don't you?"

"Not really. But I do agree Daisy says whatever she wants. And she's in something, alright."

"More like something is in her."

"Geez, get off it, Bruce."

"That's what she said."

"Look, Daisy doesn't have to manipulate because . . . because she doesn't care about other people manipulating."

"Huh?"

"She's not threatened by anyone else. So, if someone is all manipulative to get next to some drummer she just fucked the night before, she doesn't care. That other girl can have him, for all Daisy cares."

"So, the other girls aren't a threat because there's nothing there to threaten?"

"Yeah, exactly."

"What the fuck did you just say? That didn't make any sense."

"It does make sense, Bruce. You just don't listen."

"I'm listening. I've been listening."

"So, Bruce. It's kind of like all these girls don't trust any other girls because they know they can't be trusted themselves."

"That's it, Glen."

"Except Daisy."

"Well, Daisy's not the only one, but yeah."

"So, how do the other girls feel about Daisy?"

"Oh, they hate her."

"But, if she's not a threat . . ."

"Oh, she's a threat. There's nothing more threatening than someone who isn't threatened by you."

"Wha—?"

"Bruce, you should be aware of this. I mean, you're a photographer. You've got to have experienced girls trying to get close to you because they think you're close to the bands."

"Girls tend to avoid me."

"I wonder why."

"Har, har."

"But you talk to them, don't you? Don't they approach you sometimes?"

"Yeah, I guess."

"That's the manipulation. They don't have to make a pass or anything to get in. They'll just talk."

"I don't think I've ever been manipulated. I mean, by them."

"Don't they ever talk to you about the bands? About the musicians?"

"Sure, but doesn't everybody?"

"You've been manipulated. I promise."

Daisy made her way back to the table. She was not surprised to hear the waitress hadn't come.

"I don't feel manipulated."

"That's good, I guess. I mean, ignorance is bliss, right?"

"Bruce is full of bliss."

"See? And you tell me to shut up? She just got back and already she insults me. She insults me just as much as I insult you guys."

"Because you deserve it."

"Har, har."

Daisy quickly flipped through the menu, then pushed it aside.

"You ready?"

"Yeah, I'm just going to have a chocolate milk."

"So, how do you do it, Daisy?"

"Do what?"

"Catherine was telling us about the girls in the scene and how they manipulate to get close to the bands."

"Yeah?"

"But she says you don't. You don't have to."

"No, I guess not."

"And you don't get involved in all the drama either. All the talking about each other and about the musicians?"

"No way."

"Why not? I mean, why is it easy for you to ignore it?"

The waitress approached the booth from Daisy's blind side, with order pad and pen in hand.

"Because fuck those cunts."

The waitress turned on her heel and began to walk the opposite direction.

"That's what he said."

"Dani! No, Dani! We weren't talking about you! Goddamn it. Go get her back."

"I'll go."

Catherine climbed over Daisy and bolted from the booth to retrieve the waitress.

Bruce tossed a napkin in front of Daisy.

"Daisy, you have a dirty mouth."

"Fuck you, Bruce."

Mike

MIKE DROVE TO the rehearsal space to help drop off gear so he was later than most to the after-party at the apartment on Sweetzer. The living room was packed and a small contingent hung out in the kitchen. Flor had disappeared after the show, and he had assumed she got a ride home but was relieved to see her sitting on the floor in the corner, talking to Rikki, as usual.

He paused and listened to a conversation near the front door before making the rounds.

"Dude, you still working at the Wherehouse?"

"Yeah, of course. I'm not quitting that job. Hey, Mike, how you doing?"

"I'm good."

"Hey, Mike. Why not?"

"Employee discounts, man. You think I want to pay full price for albums again?"

"That's why I asked. Do you think you can get me a discount on *Powerslave*?"

"Ah, man. You know how often I'm asked? I can't just get discounts for everyone who walks through the door."

"Yeah, I know. But I was hoping you could buy it with your discount and I'll pay you back. I promise. I'll give you the money before you give me the record."

"Dude, I'm not going to buy you an album. You want someone to buy you an album, get a girlfriend."

"But I said I'll pay you back."

Mike stepped away from the group and headed deeper into the living room, passing Danny who was on his way into the kitchen where the crowd had considerably thinned out.

"Is there anything to eat?"

"Not really. Just look in the fridge."

"I don't want to look in their fridge. I'm not comfortable doing that. Like I'm raiding their food."

"No, it's alright. Help yourself. There's probably not much in there anyway. Don't get your hopes up. Go ahead, man. Nobody cares."

"Alright."

Danny opened the refrigerator door to reveal shelves sparsely stocked and nothing in the way of snack food. Then he spied a small bag of peanut M&Ms on the top shelf. He grabbed it and strolled toward the living room.

He had just popped the last M&M in his mouth and scrunched the empty bag in his hand when he heard a disappointed cry from the kitchen.

"Who ate Bret's M&Ms? "

"Huh?"

"There was a bag of M&Ms I put in here for Bret. And now it's gone. Somebody ate them. And Bret didn't get even one!"

"That sucks."

"Damn right it sucks. Who goes around eating other people's M&Ms?"

Danny stuffed the empty wrapper in his pocket and headed for the side of the apartment farthest away from the kitchen. Bret coincidentally walked by on his way to a small group on the couch but hadn't heard about the disappearance of his candy yet. Or didn't care. He nodded hello to Glen.

"Great show tonight."

"Hey, thanks Glen."

Bret got called to join another group on the other end of the living room and abruptly changed direction.

"Great roadie-ing tonight, Mike."

"Fuck you, Glen."

"Not tonight, sweetheart."

"You would."

"I'm still loving you-u-u!"

"Yeah, I bet you are. I'm still loving your mom."

"I'm serious. You guys hauling gear and setting everything up do good work. That's a thankless job."

"Tell me about it."

"You know how those guys walk out on stage at big concerts and everyone gets excited for a minute? And then when they realize it's just the roadie checking something out, or tuning a guitar they get all disappointed. That must suck for them. 'Ah, it's only you. Hurry the fuck up so the band can get out here!'"

"Funny, but true. Hey, you should try it sometime. I think I heard the guys say Bobby's bass tech is leaving. I can get them to hire you."

"I don't know anything about the bass."

"You don't have to. They just give us these titles so we feel special. All you do is haul crap on and off stage. So, as Bobby's bass tech, maybe you'd be responsible for his amps and his bass. But that's about it. It's not like you have to know anything."

"Do they even pay you?"

"Not really."

"Not really?"

"Yeah, if the show pays really well, they'll give us a little. But that's rare. We do it more for the fun and the free admission. Sometimes a free beer from the bartender."

"What time do you have to be there?"

"It varies. Usually late afternoon. For sound checks."

"I don't know, Mike. I'm taking classes Friday afternoons. I probably couldn't make it over the hill early enough to help. I could probably only do Saturdays."

"Oh. They'd want somebody to be available every show."

"I understand. I'll pass on that. Maybe some other time if I'm not tied down."

"What are you taking classes for, anyway?"

"I don't know."

"Roadies don't need an education. Think about it."

"Heh. I will."

The group near the front door blocked the way of a couple who were trying to leave.

"C'mon, man. It's *Powerslave.*"

"Yeah, I've already got it. Awesome album."

"So, why can't you? Help share in the awesomeness."

"Relax, man. It's just Iron Maiden."

"Did he just say, 'It's just Iron Maiden?' Get the fuck out."

"What? It's not like it's holy scripture or something."

"Damn right it's not holy scripture. It's better."

"Well, I . . ."

"The Bible doesn't have power chords, man."

"I bet Jesus could play the bass, man."

"What the hell?"

"Think about it. He already had the long hair."

"Hey, get the fuck out of the way."

"Out of the way of what?"

"Of people. Look, they're trying to leave, dipshit."

Daisy

The guy stumbled out of the Rainbow and staggered right into Daisy's arms. He smiled at her and laughed as if he recognized her and then planted a kiss right on her lips. She reciprocated. They remained that way for what seemed several minutes, as the crowd slowly trickled past them, jostling shoulders occasionally, but never hard enough to disengage their embrace.

Paul didn't recognize him as a musician. His hair was on the shorter side. He looked more punk than glam. Eventually, sensing the crowd swelling around them, they moved off to the side of the parking lot and immediately resumed their make-out session. Paul thought Daisy had intended to begin the walk back to the car, so he headed up the sidewalk past several doors before turning around and realizing she was not following him. He slowly retraced his steps until he found Glen at the edge of the parking lot waiting on her as well.

"Are they coming?"

"No, not yet. I'll try to get her."

Glen headed for them, and they disengaged themselves long enough to walk toward him. Both Daisy and the stranger followed Glen like sheepish children being escorted home by an impatient father.

The group crossed at the light and quickly made it to the Geffen lot. Daisy and the guy resumed where they left off when they got to Glen's car—on top of Glen's car. He had laid her down on the hood and climbed completely on top of her.

"Oh, Christ. He's not going to bone her right here, is he?"

"I hope not. No, I doubt it. Just saying goodbye, probably."

"Who is that guy?"

"I don't know. Never seen him before."

"How does he know Daisy?"

"I don't think he does."

"You mean, they just met?"

"Yeah."

"Tonight, you mean. Earlier tonight?"

"No, just now when he walked out of the Rainbow."

"They'd never seen each other before then?"

"I don't think so."

"How is that possible? I mean, c'mon . . . oh, c'mon! If I were to just approach a pretty girl and start making out with her in a parking lot, you know what would happen? I'd get my face slapped and maybe my ass kicked."

"Maybe not."

"Maybe not? Right. I mean . . . how the hell did he know she didn't have a boyfriend or a date standing right there?"

"I don't know. I guess he could tell."

"Jesus. Is it really that easy? You can just go up to a girl you like and start making out with her? And she'll reciprocate?"

"If it's Daisy, yes . . . I guess so."

"Jesus. All this time I've been doing it wrong, then. You know, talking, being polite, asking questions like "What's your fucking name?""

"Some guys just got it, I guess."

"More like some girls just give it."

"That too."

Glen decided he'd seen enough.

"Alright you two, break it up. I think I might need new shocks and I don't want you to find out the hard way, you know what I mean?"

"That's what she said."

"Not even funny."

Justin

Justin let Annie walk into the Roxy first while he asked Jamie, who often took tickets at the door, for their stubs back. Walking a few feet behind, Justin could see all eyes follow Annie's long legs from high heels to mid-thigh hemline as she strolled by. When they passed Mike and Bruce, he made sure they noticed who was bringing in this fiery redhead with thick waves of hair flowing down her back and a dress to compete with the best head-turners on Sunset. They often teased him about his inability to get laid. Heck, Bruce was one to talk. Justin doubted he'd had sex in years.

He walked her right down the aisle, through a gaping hole in the crowd on the floor, and right up to the edge of the stage. He hoped it filled her with the same sense of excitement that had filled him those years ago when he came to his first show here. The opener was a bit tiring, even for Justin, and he soon relented when Annie suggested they move to a table farther back. Two opening acts did make him feel guilty that she would have to stand that whole time in order to save a great place on the floor for Stainless Steel. Mike and Bruce had set up camp at a table near the soundboard, talking to a drummer and guitarist of another band Justin hadn't heard of. After the musicians moved on, they made room for Annie, but Justin chose to stand. He made the introductions, and Annie was great at being social. He stayed out of the conversation as usual, admiring the fact they'd get to know what a cool girl she was.

Eventually he sat, but didn't talk much over the noise of the bands. He didn't like having to shout directly in her ear to be heard. Two big plates of stuffed potato skins arrived—Mike had ordered them for the table—and the waitress put in front of Annie what looked like her favorite drink—Diet Coke. Justin felt like an idiot.

"You should have told me you wanted something to drink. I would have gotten it for you. Let me know if you want another."

"I will, thanks."

As the second band made its way off stage, Justin was feeling relieved that they could finally move down to the floor to get a closer look at the headliner. Just before he raised the possibility to Annie, Grant from Stainless Steel appeared, clapping Mike on the back and shaking Bruce's hand.

"Hey Grant. You remember my friend, Justin? And this is his girlfriend Annie."

Grant smiled, shook hands, and said hellos all around. He chatted briefly with Mike, but Justin had a hard time hearing what was being discussed. He eventually said something about having to go help set things up and excused himself. Bruce followed him down the aisle, scoping out a good vantage point from which to shoot the show. With his height, he didn't have to look too far.

Glen suddenly materialized from the growing crowd, quickly side-stepped off the aisle and jumped into Bruce's seat.

"Hey guys, sorry I'm late. Was that Grant I just saw?"

"Glen, what's up buddy? Yeah, you just missed him. I told him we'd catch him after the show."

The floor was filling up and Justin knew it was now or never to grab a good place to stand. He asked Annie if she wanted to stand with him, but she declined. She said she was worried about getting her feet stepped on, but she'd join him in a little while.

He turned to go as another Diet Coke was placed in front of her. He cursed his forgetting to watch her glass.

The set was good, but after a while, it became clear Annie had no intention of hurrying down to the floor to be with him. He made his way back to the table about four songs in and asked Annie how she was enjoying it. She smiled, and Justin felt there was nothing weird about his leaving her to watch the show from a table with his friends. It's not like he abandoned her among strangers or anything. Mike appeared to look at him uneasily, though. Justin didn't understand why. Everything seemed fine.

He declined to sit again, choosing to stand behind Annie's chair. He noticed her drink was full. She either hadn't touched it or it was a new one. The way she eagerly sipped it, he assumed it was the latter.

When the house lights came up after the third encore, Justin finally grabbed a seat. They let the house empty around them, always the case when it was friends of theirs who were playing as headliners. Mike and Glen always wanted to hang back to talk to them, and they knew no one would make an appearance until the house was almost completely empty.

They saw Peter first, but he was being mobbed by a group of girls and their dates. He made his way up the aisle on the side of the house to avoid the crowd down the middle. Seth soon followed and took the same route.

"Hey, looks like if we're going to talk to Grant and the guys again, we should probably make our way over to the side. Or maybe outside. They don't look like they want to hang around inside very long."

Mike got up but stood close to Annie, gesturing with a nod to Glen. Justin didn't understand what it meant.

Annie tried to stand and immediately stumbled into Glen's waiting arms.

"Yep. Just what I was afraid of."

"What's wrong with her, Mike?"

"She's drunk. What do you think is wrong with her?"

"I thought she was drinking Diet Coke this whole time. What was that in her glass?"

"Long Island ice teas."

"How the hell did she buy those? She doesn't even have a fake ID."

"I bought the first two. After that, I cut her off. So, she started asking

Glen for more, and he figured she could handle it. I figured otherwise . . .
I guess I was right."

They made their way out to the street through what was still a good-
sized crowd, Glen holding Annie up on one side, Justin struggling to pull
his weight on the other. They jostled through the bodies and stares. Justin
suddenly cursed his desire to see a packed house. This is what he got for
wanting to show off his date to a big crowd. Guys couldn't take their eyes
off her when she arrived, and now everyone couldn't take their eyes off the
spectacle of her being carried to the car.

It made sense why she didn't care if he went down to the stage himself.
She'd rather get drunk than watch the bands up close. She probably didn't
pay for a thing, and she knew a good deal when she saw one.

They managed to get her in the passenger seat of Justin's car and buckled her in. Her condition had worsened greatly since she stood to leave.
She no longer spoke, and her face had lost the happy countenance of one
who is a little tipsy. She was flat-out wasted, and Justin wondered if she'd
be unconscious by the time they made it home.

Glen opened the rear door and jumped in.

"Hey, let me come with you. I can help you carry her in. It's the least I
can do after helping get her drunk."

"What about your car?"

"I don't have it. I got a ride in tonight with Danny. Mike, you'll find
him and tell him what happened?"

"No problem. The dude was over there laughing at you carrying out a
hot redhead. He probably knows not to expect you."

"Very funny. Alright, let's get the fuck out of here, Justin. Shit,
hang on."

Glen hopped out, opened the front passenger side door, and rolled the
window all the way down. He closed the door, then pulled Annie by the
shoulders until her head was leaning on the door frame.

"You trying to force some fresh air into her?"

"Nope. I just don't want her puking in the car."

They sped on the freeway, both getting blasted by the cold night air pouring in the open window. Justin thought Glen was being a little excessive in his fear for the car, but sure enough, Annie's stomach began to convulse on the freeway and didn't stop until they had crossed under Mulholland and descended into the Valley.

Justin couldn't hear much on the ride and didn't realize how bad it was until he got out of the car. A streak of vomit stretched from the passenger door to the bumper. Had a woman joined them for the ride, or if Annie had been sober enough, she would have reminded them to tie her hair back. It was now wet with puke—soaked, actually. They negotiated their way up the steps into the house, careful not to let Annie fall while trying to avoid the vomit dripping from her.

"You're going to have to get her in the shower or something. She's going to make a mess of wherever she sleeps tonight if you don't. Are you going to take her home later?"

"No, she told her parents she wouldn't be home tonight. And my mom will understand."

Glen helped Justin walk her down the hall and into the bathroom.

"Can you take it from here? You got her?"

"Yeah, I'll be alright. She'd probably prefer you weren't around for this."

"Yeah, I figured. I'm going to take off. I'll just walk it, you don't need to drive me home. You sure you're alright? Don't let her fall in the shower. She'll crack her head open on the tile."

"I won't. I've got her. I'm just going to sit her down in it and wash her off."

Justin unzipped that red dress. He laughed to himself about the irony of the moment. Everyone had been undressing her with their eyes all night, and he had gloated inside at the fact that only he would have the privilege of doing it for real. But this was about the least sexy context he could have created for that moment. He may as well have been a mortician. It was like undressing a cadaver.

Washing her hair proved to be far more difficult than expected. It was already considerably matted, and her thick tresses seemed impenetrable by water in places. He could tell from the brown color of the water going down the drain that he was accomplishing something in the way of cleaning, but soon realized that the hair was holding onto anything solid, like a great auburn filter. Figuring the shower was the safest place to get his hands dirty, he resorted to picking out chunks of vomit with his fingers. It all had a peculiar consistency—very durable and fibrous, with thin pieces half the size of postage stamps proving to be extra sticky and stubborn to remove from the long strands of hair they'd latched onto. Justin was dumbfounded until the realization nearly made him vomit himself.

Potato skins.

Until that moment, he didn't believe you could be too intimate with a girl like Annie. He tried to excuse it as a labor of love but didn't really know how he felt. He imagined the guys who were gawking at her would have just left her on a front lawn somewhere. He performed what he thought of as one of those good deeds made better because no one was watching, not even the girl too drunk to realize what a mess she'd made of her beautiful self. He'd never tell her. She'd only think he was going to hold it against her forever.

For days, he would scrape thin remnants of speckled brown that had plastered themselves to the tile. He'd finally feel rid of them, only to find a stray scrap on the soap tray, then another on a faucet handle, a large one behind a shampoo bottle. As time passed, they'd become harder to remove, until his fingernails tired of attempting to efface every reminder of that night.

Paul

How many times have I mistaken
The carbon monoxide–laced
Sulfur-infused
Grit-infested
Blast of combustion
Basting sunbaked macadam
Tarred, greased
Slicked indifferent

For the ever-long respiration
Of a city
Accused of being heartless
Yet whose circulation is evident
Along every corpuscular road
Every venous boulevard
Arterial highway

Whose thousand arrhythmical hearts
Feed the pulse in every intersection
And beat under layers of concrete
Haloed by smoggy exhalations
Of its own stunted breath?

1985

Mike

HE CARRIED A comic strip in his wallet. It featured two young kids drawn in an exaggerated, grotesque style. They ran freely in the night, seeking adventures. It was the stuff of innocent picaresque, but the romantic expectations of such an image were washed away by the darkness surrounding it all. They more resembled animals in some sort of nocturnal ritual. They stepped over sleeping—or dead—bodies, amid the refuse of an urban wasteland—rotten food, stray animals, used needles, discarded cigarette lighters, and bent spoons. They fled the comfort of their homes to revel in these urban wilds. Followed only by the moon, they explored haunts new and familiar. They engaged in unspeakable mischiefs with those wedded to the landscape. And when the sun showed the first inkling of starting its ascent on the eastern horizon, they fled the night and returned home.

The comic was yellowed and tearing along its creases. He would preserve it with Scotch tape when the time came. Because it was a necessary keepsake—the only portrayal he'd ever seen of what he considered to be that secret feeling he had whenever he left the house after dark. It captured the demon side of him that roamed these streets, seeking adventures of his own among fellow creatures of the night.

Tim

"HEY MIKE, WHO'S the little guy?"

Mike looked past a few bodies filling the Rainbow parking lot until he found to whom Charlie was referring.

"That's Tim."

"Tim? Is he like a midget in a band or something or just a young kid hanging out with us?

"Young kid. C'mon, Charlie. Don't talk stupid about him, man."

"Why not?"

"Because he's cool. He's been around the scene his whole life. His dad is huge in the business."

"Yeah? Who's his dad?"

"He works for Capitol. Lives up in the hills above the Strip."

"What does he do?"

"He's in A & R."

"A & R?"

"Yeah, A & R. Artists and Repertoire or something like that. He scouts bands. He finds new talent. He's the guy that decides who gets signed and who doesn't."

"Damn, really!? More like anal and rectal. That guy has us bent over and is fucking us up the ass."

"What do you mean?"

"The power he has. Everyone kissing his ass all the time. Everyone wants to make it, you know?"

"Of course, I know. But how is that getting fucked up the ass?"

"He can just do that to anyone he wants."

"I'm not following you, Charlie. As usual."

"He can just bend you over and you have to take it. Because you'll do anything to make it."

"I doubt he's actually bending people over, Charlie. He probably knows the power he has and stays out of it. Won't let anyone socialize with him, schmooze him, you know? He probably gets sick of being kissed up to."

"Who gets tired of getting their dick sucked, though?"

"By a bunch of guys in lipstick and spandex? Probably a lot of men."

Charlie walked over to where Tim stood chatting with Flor, Glen, and Paul. He didn't wait for an opening in the conversation.

"Hey Paul, how does it feel to know you're not the smallest shrimp in the scene?"

"Leave him alone, Charlie. He's cool. Glen, Paul, and my sister are cool too."

"I'm not hurting anybody, Mike. I bet nobody messes with this kid because his dad is a hotshot in the music industry. Everyone wants to get signed. So, nobody messes with him. This kid probably has more friends here than any of us. Hell, he probably gets more pussy than any of us, too."

"Charlie, I'm telling you. Leave him alone."

"No, man. I'm telling you, I'm not bothering anyone. I'm not bothering you, am I? Is it, Tim?"

"Yeah, and not really."

"Not really bothering you or not really Tim?"

Charlie laughed at himself. Mike rolled his eyes and tried to grab Charlie by the arm to walk him to the sidewalk.

"Hey, leggo, man. I'm not doing anything!"

"Tim, you alright?"

"Yeah, Mike. It's cool."

"See? It's cool, Mike. Go beat up somebody else, man."

Tim smiled. Charlie put his arm around him.

"See? I'm not messing with him. We're buds, right?"

"Not really."

Everyone within earshot laughed.

"Not really? No, you see, I'm different."

"How?"

"I'm not in a band. So, I'm not kissing your ass, man. Or your dad's ass."

"Nobody kisses my ass."

"I bet they do. You just don't know it. I bet if you dropped your pants right now, there'd be little smoochy marks all over your butt."

Mike grabbed for Charlie again.

"Alright, that's it. You're sounding like a child molester, man. Let's go."

"Alright, alright. Geez. Can you believe this guy, Tim?"

"Yeah."

Everyone laughed again.

"Yeah? Yeah? Mike, you been kissing this kid's ass?"

"Oh god, Charlie. That's it. We're going."

Mike half dragged Charlie out of the parking lot and down the sidewalk several paces before Charlie interjected again.

"Hey, wait up. Hey, Tim?"

"What?"

"Do you think your old man can get me some front-row tickets to Iron Maiden?"

"No."

More laughter. Charlie threw up his hands in resignation.

"That's cool. That's cool. That's his choice."

Glen leaned in close to Tim's ear.

"You should have told him to kiss your ass."

Bruce

WHEN HE GOT to Denny's, they already had a table. A plate of french fries between them, Daisy sipped from a straw floating near the surface of a gigantic glass of chocolate milk, while Glen, as usual, nursed the plastic cup of complimentary tap water.

He slid into the booth next to Glen and reached for the ketchup bottle in one fluid motion, unscrewed the cap, and pounded a small puddle on the corner of the plate closest to him.

"Hey guys. Ya mind?"

Glen, as usual, shook his head as the first french fry was already crossing the threshold of Bruce's lips. Daisy rolled her eyes at both of them.

"What's up?"

"Not much, Bruce. You get any good shots tonight?"

"Maybe. You never know until you get 'em back from the lab. But I always do. Man, Jackie was on fire tonight. Insane!" He pantomimed a riff on an air guitar before reaching for another fry.

"Yeah, good show. Very good show."

"How about you Daisy? You didn't stick around long enough to get backstage? You'd rather hang around with this guy?" He gave Glen a nudge in the ribs.

"Whatever, Bruce."

"No, seriously . . . have you already banged everyone who was on stage tonight? No reason for you to stay?"

"Fuck you, Bruce."

"Evidently not. I think I have to be in a band for that. But what if I'm touring with the band? A bunch of people want me out on the road with them as their photographer. How about that? Would that count?"

Daisy ignored him.

"Leave her alone, Bruce."

"Hey, I think if she's going to act that way and not care what other people think, she shouldn't care what I think now that I'm talking about it."

"Who said I didn't care what other people think? Everybody cares what other people think. That's normal."

"You always act like you don't care, so all I'm saying is act like it now and don't be so offended."

"You're just jealous because nobody wants to fuck you."

"Yeah, right."

"Alright, both of you. Just let it go. C'mon, Bruce. We're having a nice time, and then you come along and—"

"Hey, it's not my fault she's a hosebag."

"Don't you fucking call me that!"

"Daisy, you'll be a lot happier in life if you just come to terms with what you are."

"Shut the fuck up! What about you? What the fuck are you? Besides a loser?"

"Hosebag."

"You call me that one more time, I swear—"

"Hosebag."

She grabbed the ketchup bottle and cocked her arm as if to throw it at his face.

"Whoa, whoa, wh—!"

Bruce lunged forward to grab her wrist as her arm came forward, deflecting the throw before it even had a chance to leave her hand. The bottle fell to the table with a loud bang but didn't shatter. A sudden hush took over half the restaurant seated close enough to hear it, but was quickly consumed by chatter again as it was assumed to be a harmless accident.

Bruce let go of Daisy's wrist.

"That would have hurt, you bitch."

He reached for the edge of the plate and gave it a quick flip, sending every french fry flying straight at her. She reflexively ducked to the side but too late. She was pelted in the face and chest. Many stuck in her teased hair.

Before Glen could intervene, Daisy grabbed her glass of chocolate milk and sent a contiguous brown wave airborne across the table. While it seemed the next logical choice of arms in this quickly escalating war, neither of them could believe she'd actually do it. Before his next thought, Bruce was wearing the entire contents of the glass.

The lady sitting behind him gave out a short yelp as the residual milk not deflected by Bruce's large frame came crashing down over her neck and shoulders. She immediately stomped off to the restroom, stopping along the way to have a word with the manager, all the while glaring at them.

It was surprisingly calm after that. Daisy stared wide-eyed, mouth agape, still holding the empty glass sideways as Bruce slowly dripped. Bruce casually removed his glasses, grabbed the unused napkin in front of Glen and began to dry the lenses. Glen sat frozen, dreadfully anticipating an even more violent response, ready to grab Bruce and restrain him as best he could should he decide to attack her. He surreptitiously gripped his cup of water, hoping it wasn't being considered the next weapon of retaliation.

Bruce put his glasses back on, and Glen chuckled to himself. Their cleanliness only magnified the mess covering the rest of him.

"You! You, out of here! I want you out of here!"

The manager stormed over, brandishing an admonishing finger.

"Oh, shit . . ."

Glen quickly pulled his wallet from his back pocket, found a five-dollar bill, and slapped it on the table.

"C'mon, let's get out of here. I'm not in the mood to deal with this asshole tonight."

They quietly exited the booth, as if quiet wasn't such a futile aspiration at this point. They hit the door in a few strides, the cold night air surprising them. Bruce noticed the smile Glen had been suppressing as they made their way down Sunset.

"What the fuck are you laughing at?"

"You."

"Thanks a lot. I'm going to fucking freeze in this shit."

"You remind me of the Nestle Quik bunny."

"Har, har."

"You're like a fucking giant Nestle Quik bunny!"

"Well, now I'm crashing at your place. I need a shower."

Catherine

"Glen?"

"Hey, Catherine. Come on in."

She stepped over the shoes strewn across the floor in the entryway, then swept most of them aside with a single stroke of her foot to make the passage easier for her companion.

"Don't mind the mess. I'm just making a sandwich before we hit the road."

"Didn't you eat dinner yet?"

"Yeah. Your point?"

"You're pregnant, man. Eating for two."

By now they'd entered the kitchen. Glen immediately dropped his knife and wiped his hands on a nearby dish towel when he noticed Catherine wasn't alone.

"Hey, I brought a friend. This is our exchange student I was telling you about, Ynez. Ynez, this is my friend, Glen. *Mi amigo Glen.*"

Glen extended his hand.

"Nice to meet you."

The tall, slender young woman with caramel skin and a mane of long, layered black hair smiled shyly, revealing a mouthful of perfectly straight teeth, and shook his hand.

"*Hola, mucho gusto.* Er, hello."

"Hello. So, how long have you been in America?"

"*Tres semanas.* Ah, three weeks."

"Yes, I understood. Three weeks. Your English is pretty good. Did you study in Mexico?"

"Yes, I study. But not very good."

She smiled again shyly, and Glen was taken aback by her attractiveness.

"Close your mouth, Glen."

"Hey, leave me alone."

"Ynez is going to get her first taste of the Hollywood club scene tonight. I've told her all about it."

"Yeah? Cool. Does she like heavy metal?"

He looked at Ynez but directed the question awkwardly at Catherine.

"Yeah, I think so. I've played her some records. She seems to like it. It's the crowd I'm worried about. I don't know if they have a scene like this in Mexico."

"She'll be alright. Everyone's fairly harmless."

"Yeah, but I'm still putting you on bodyguard duty."

He turned again to his sandwich.

"No problem. I'm sure I'll look very intimidating. I can bring this with us if you're ready to go."

"No rush. Let's hang out awhile."

"Let's hang out in the bedroom, then. My mom is weird about having people over."

He made his way down the hall and motioned for them to follow.

"Hey, Paul. What are you doing? We've got company. Coming in."

Paul sat up on his bed.

"Nothing, just lying here."

He got up and shut off the tape deck as the three of them entered.

"Hey, Paul. Was that Journey? You can leave it on."

"No, that's alright. Hey, Catherine."

Paul stood stunned when he made eye contact with Ynez.

"Ah, Ynez. This is my brother, Paul. Um . . . *él es mi hermano, Paul.*"

"*Sí, mucho gusto.* Nice meet you, Paul."

"Look at Glen, busting out the Spanish! Way to remember high school, dude."

"Leave me alone, Catherine."

Catherine took the *LA Weekly* off Glen's bed and chucked it on the floor.

"Go ahead, you take the bed, Ynez. We'll just sit here on the floor a bit. Do you want the music on?"

"Music? *Sí.* Music is good."

"Paul, go ahead and put the tape back on. Not too loud."

Paul pushed play and retreated to his bed on the other side of the room.

Catherine got up and turned off the light leaving only the one in the hallway to silhouette their figures.

"You coming with us tonight, Paul?"

"Me? No. I'm just going to hang out here."

"Really? You should come out with us. Get to know Ynez."

She winked at Glen, in clear view of Paul, knowing it wouldn't be perceived from across the room in the newfound dimness.

"No, that's alright. I'm not really into the bands tonight. Going to save my money."

"Alright, big spender. Suit yourself."

"He's alright, Catherine. Leave him alone. Don't get his hopes up for anything."

"I'm not getting his hopes up, am I? Just trying to persuade him."

She winked again, more in Paul's direction this time.

"Believe me, my hopes are not up."

"Good. You're too young for her anyway."

Glen gave Catherine a silent admonishment for talking so openly in front of Ynez, but, stretched out on the bed with her back against the wall, eyes closed, Ynez gave no sign of having heard their latest exchange.

Paul flipped the tape back to side one and the three of them chatted in hushed tones. Every once in a while, Ynez spoke up to confirm a fact when

Catherine spoke about her. Catherine explained how her mother, a teacher in the nursing program at Pierce College, had heard about the exchange program there. About twenty students from Mexico came to study computer science on scholarships and temporary visas. Each needed a sponsor to offer a bedroom, use of a bathroom, a shelf in the refrigerator, and use of the kitchen, all for very little rent. Catherine agreed to host Ynez. Her mother had asked Glen and Paul's mother to do the same for another student, but she had declined.

"You falling asleep, Ynez?"

"No, but I'm a little tired. Thank you for letting me here. To relax."

"That's okay. *Mi casa es su casa. ¿Verdad?*"

"*Sí, muy bueno. Mi casa es su casa . . .*"

"*Y, mi cama es su cama.* Oh, that sounded wrong."

Ynez chuckled.

"Geez, Glen. Hitting on her in her native language. Smooth."

Again, the silent admonishment seemed to have no effect on Catherine.

"Es alright. *Mi cama es su cama.* Yes, that is true. I am on your bed, thank you. You make joke in Spanish. That's good. *Un juego de palabras.* How you say? Play of words?"

"Play on words? Word play? Yeah, something like that."

"To make play with words in other language is difficult. No es easy. That's good."

"Thanks. See, that's good."

He practically stuck his tongue out at Catherine. She rolled her eyes in response. She and Glen had only ever been platonic friends, but his obvious attraction to Ynez was annoying.

"Glen, before we go, I was actually wondering if you could take a look at my car. It's making a weird noise. I think it's just a belt, but I don't want to take any chances."

"Sure, no problem."

"Ynez, we're going to go look at the car. *¿Mi coche? ¿El ruido?* We're going to go look for it. Stay here and relax. We'll get going soon."

"Okay."

"Paul, keep your eye on her. That's all you keep on her, got it?"

"No problem. I'm over here minding my own business."

"I don't know what we're going to see this time of night, but I'll try. Let me get a flashlight."

Glen and Catherine exited, leaving Paul suddenly feeling very self-conscious.

It seemed darker in the room and he wondered if Catherine had shut the door on her way out. He bolted upright to see if he could see the hallway and felt very conspicuous after he discovered he could.

"You okay?"

"Ah, yeah. Just . . ."

He didn't want to mention the concept of a closed bedroom door.

"Just thought I heard Glen call me."

"I hear nothing."

"Yeah, I guess not."

"How old are you?"

The timing of her question threw him. He suddenly felt younger than he was.

"Me? Sixteen. I'll be 17 in August. Uh . . . *yo tengo diez y seis años.*"

"*Ah, habla usted español también cómo tú hermano. Muy bien.*"

He didn't know if this was a compliment or sarcasm.

"*Si, un poquito. Como mucho gente en Los Angeles.*"

"*Ay, sí. Aquí hay mucha gente de México, Guatemala, El Salvador . . .*"

Her voice trailed off before running out of countries.

They lay in silence. Each on a twin bed against opposite walls of the room. Paul thought to ask her about music, about what she liked, and if she was looking forward to the show tonight. But it seemed too complex a topic to discuss in her broken English, and his Spanish wasn't good enough to carry on a conversation about it in her language.

"So, sixteen. *Diez y seis.* You still in high school?"

He was surprised she spoke first.

"Um, yeah. One more year after this one."

"Only one more? Es good. You like school?"

"Uh, not really."

"Then es good. You almost done."

He nodded while staring at the ceiling, unaware that she was doing the same.

Minutes passed again in silence until Glen shouted from the hall.

"We're back. You ready to go, Ynez?"

The tape stopped and the deck snapped the play button back into the upright position.

Paul

We lay on separate twin beds
Situated across the room from each other
Lined up against opposite walls
Listening to "Still They Ride" on the tape deck

And I ask myself
What was I thinking?
Would a girl lie on a bed
In the dark
Anywhere near a guy
Without offering an invitation?

Maybe it was cultural differences
Maybe just the communication breakdown
Those differences are sometimes responsible for

But maybe boldness doesn't need a language
Some things are never lost in translation
Maybe what makes us human
And the power of truth and love
Transcends all that

There are something like 200 countries on this planet
And I'm a wuss in all of them

It played "Still They Ride"
It had a profound meaning, although now I don't know what
It's just the way the soulfulness of the voice carried over us
That made us feel inspired
He sang to our plight
In a voice of our people
Wild and restless
It was our anthem for one night

It played "Still They Ride"
That song is too damn short
I'm certain another minute or two of it
Would have carried me over the infinite distance
That can separate twin beds in the dark

Another minute
And I would have had the courage to combat cruel geometry
Placing lives so painfully askew
Into the sweetest parallel

Charlie

MIKE HAD ONLY stepped a few feet into the bar at the Troubadour before Charlie practically leapt into his arms.

"Hey, Mike! How ya doin?"

"Hey, Charlie."

"Fancy running into you here!"

"Why is that, Charlie?"

"I don't know. Isn't that what you're supposed to say, though?"

"You can, I guess."

"Yeah, man. That's what they all say in those movies. 'Fancy running into you here' like they are all fancy."

"Whatever, Charlie."

"You mad at me, Mike?"

"Me? No. Why'd you get an idea like that?"

"You don't seem very happy to see me."

"I'm happy to see you, Charlie. You just sort of jumped on me. Took me by surprise."

"Oh yeah, huh?"

"Yeah. You don't have to do that, you know?"

"Do what?"

"Jump on me. Just say hi. I'll see you. You don't have to leap onto me like that."

"Yeah, like a panther."

"Yeah, whatever, Charlie."

"You going in to see London, Mike?"

"Yeah, of course. That's why we're here isn't it? Aren't you into London?"

"I guess so. I'm into the bar, though."

"You could say that again, Charlie."

"No, seriously. I'm into the bar. See, I'm here. In the bar. Get it?"

"Huh?"

"Into the bar. In the bar?"

"Oh my god, man. You must be freakin' wasted. You wasted, Charlie?"

"Why do you say that?"

"Because only someone wasted would find humor in that."

"Hey, be nice, Mike. You know I can't help it."

"Sure you can, Charlie."

"Well, maybe I don't want to help it."

"I guess not."

As usual, the bar was packed between sets. The energy inside the showroom seemed to spill out and infect the room. The tension created by the anticipation of the headliner's arrival on stage seemed to translate into the bar as well. People were quick to order so as to grab a drink and get back inside before missing anything.

Mike recognized several familiar faces in the crowd, a few of whom most people would recognize due to their fame. Mike rarely approached established musicians. He preferred to say hello to them as if they were old friends, nothing more. He had chatted with some here and there, but it was never due to his initiation of conversation. Despite his intimidating size, people found him approachable. And the ones who stopped to talk appreciated not being fawned over.

"Hey, you going in, Mike?"

"In a little bit. I'm cool hanging out in the back. I'll wait until they cut the lights. You coming with me?"

"Naw. I'll just listen from here."

"I bet. Sounds good, Charlie."

Suddenly, a commotion erupted from the end of the bar closest to the door. The men on the last two barstools began shouting and gesticulating wildly at a third man who sat next to them. Mike recognized the third man as Chris Holmes, the guitarist of W.A.S.P. He didn't know the other two guys.

"Sounds like a fight."

"Maybe."

"You going to jump in, Mike?"

"Why the hell would I do something like that?"

"Because you're a big dude. You could break it up."

"I'm not getting involved, Charlie."

"Ah. Yeah, that's probably smart."

Holmes seemed to restrain himself from the altercation, however. He kept his head down, and wagged it from side to side frequently, as if in a stupor. The two other men continued to speak loudly at him. Mike couldn't hear a word, but surmised from their tone they were berating him. They conspicuously avoided any physical contact. Mike was fairly confident there would be no fight, unless someone else decided to get involved.

As Mike was entertaining the idea that someone might find it heroic to come to the rescue of a prominent musician, Holmes suddenly stood, unbuttoned and unzipped his pants, pulled them down far enough to allow his penis to dangle freely, and then grabbed one of the men's freshly served drinks and submerged it as deeply into the glass as he could. He proceeded to swirl it around, being sure to rub it sufficiently on the sides and edge of the glass.

The section of the bar that had by now gotten caught up in the curiosity of what the argument was about and what it might turn into laughed uproariously.

"Damn! Giving him a refill?"

"Ooh, cock on the rocks, man."

Holmes continued to swirl himself around among the ice cubes.

Charlie was appalled.

"Oh my god. And you thought I was wasted."

"You're both wasted."

"Hey! Put that thing away, man!"

"Charlie, shut up. He'll hear you."

"I want him to hear me. That's why I'm shouting."

"Well, I don't want him coming over here deciding what he's going to stick his dick into next."

Deciding that Charlie was the last guy he wanted getting involved, Mike grabbed him by the shoulders and walked him to the other side of the bar.

"C'mon Charlie, let's take a walk."

"Where are we going, Mike?"

"Just over here."

"I'll be quiet. Honest. I'm done yelling at him."

"I know. I'd just rather be safe than sorry."

They settled into an open space between the bar and the first tier of tables in the middle of the room.

"I know you think I'm drunk all the time, but I'm never doing that to someone's drink."

"I know, Charlie."

"I mean. You have to be seriously out of your head to just whip it out in public like that. If you ever see me do that, just take me home, man."

"Deal."

"Dude was like the human swizzle stick."

"Pretty foul, man."

"What do you say to a guy to make him stick his dick in your drink?

"I don't know, man."

"I mean. I've had guys want to punch me out before. A few of them probably did, I don't remember. But I've never had a guy do that before. Guys don't whip it out for other guys. He must have been seriously pissed or seriously wasted."

"I'm betting on both."

"Yeah, me too."

The commotion seemed to have died down.

"I'm going in, Charlie. Last chance, you comin'?"

"Naw, I'm just going to stay here. Although I'm afraid if I stay I'm going to have to see his dick again."

"Then come inside, man. C'mon."

"Alright, alright."

Charlie followed Mike out of the bar, passing Chris Holmes who had reseated himself and was hanging his head again and wagging it from side to side.

Glen

THE SHOWS AT the Whisky and Roxy had let out over an hour before, but a good-sized crowd still mingled outside the Rainbow. Glen and Paul mostly people watched until Mike liberated himself from a group debating the vocal abilities of various singers and made his way over to say hello.

"Hey, guys. What's going on Glen?"

"Hey, Mike. Not much. You?"

"Same old shit. You know."

"Yeah. Hey, can I ask you something?"

"Sure."

"Do you ever wear eyeliner?"

"Me? Oh, fuck no. Not me."

"You never tried it?"

"No. That's cool with the guys in the band. A lot of bands these days, actually. But it's not my thing. C'mon, look at this face. There's nothing pretty here."

"It might not look bad."

"No way, man. Nothing pretty about this face."

"You don't have to be pretty. It'll just bring out your eyes a bit."

"My eyes don't need bringing out. These boys need to stay right where they are. Nothing needs bringing out, actually. You guys with the spandex, I don't know how you do it, speaking of bringing things out."

"You've never worn spandex?"

"Have you ever seen me wear spandex? C'mon."

"I guess I haven't."

"I'm a blue jeans and T-shirt kind of guy, Glen. You know that."

"I guess so."

"Glam is going to be dead in a few years, anyway. Don't invest all your money in Aqua Net and lipstick."

"Why do you say that?"

"Why? Because it's the way it is. Nothing lasts that long. A trend comes along, people follow it, then it dies out. Then it's uncool to follow. It happens all the time. It'll happen with glam, trust me."

"But rock and roll will never die."

"Oh, no shit. That I believe. But the look of the bands will change."

"If you say so."

"I know so. C'mon, glam especially. Think about how much time people put into their looks. It's hardcore. Too much work. People are going to get sick of it. It'll die. I guarantee. How long does it take you to get ready when you go out?"

Glen tried to duck the question.

"I don't know, I don't time myself."

"Yeah, but it takes you some time, right? It's not like you just throw on a shirt and boom, you're out the door like me, right?"

"Yeah, I guess so."

Paul had been listening silently, not wanting to get involved in the conversation, but he saw an opening and took it.

"Glen, it takes you like five minutes just to pack the kid. And then there's all that time you spend on your hair."

"Wait a second . . . the hair I believe, by the way. But back up. What did you say? Pack the what?"

Paul smiled.

"You want to tell him, or should I?"

Glen reluctantly tried to explain.

"I'll tell him. It's like what you said before, about bringing stuff out. In spandex?"

"Yeah, but I'm not following you."

"Well, you don't wear any underwear in spandex, because it'll show."

"Yeah, I know. You guys and your panty lines to worry about."

"Right. Well, packing the kid is adjusting yourself. You know, so you look your best?"

"Oh, my god, Glen. You call it "the kid?""

"Just a nickname."

"What is it with you guys and your dicks? I swear."

"Well, you want to look your best. So, you adjust everything to make it stand out. You have to sort of arrange—"

"Look, I don't want to know. I get it. You don't want to look like you're hung like a baby."

"Exactly."

"Why don't you just use a sock like most guys."

"I'm not faking it. Too obvious."

"Paul, can you believe this guy? You don't wear that crap, do you?"

"No. I'm like you. Jeans and T-shirts."

"Right on, little man. So, how much time do you spend on your dick, Glen?"

"I don't know, not too long. You want to time me sometime?"

"No thanks. And no offense. I'm not leaving because I know you've been touching yourself recently. But I've got to go flag down Bobby before he leaves. I've got questions about tomorrow night's show."

"No problem, Mike. I'll just wave."

"Yeah, please. Take care guys."

After Mike stepped aside, Glen realized a drummer he knew was standing in a small group nearby.

"Hey, Steve! It's been a long time."

"Hey . . . Glen, right?"

"Yeah, how have you been?"

"Been alright. Can't complain."

Glen suddenly remembered his manners.

"Oh, Steve, this is my brother Paul. Paul, this is Steve."

The two exchanged pleasantries as Glen resumed his train of thought.

"So, what have you been up to? I haven't seen you around at all these days."

"Yeah, I guess it's been awhile. I've been busy."

"What are you working on?"

"Well, I just joined a new band. My last band broke up a while ago and it's taken me a while to find another group."

"Yeah? Anyone we know?"

Steve looked sheepish. He may as well have been tracing a circular pattern on the sidewalk with his big toe.

"Guns N' Roses."

Both Glen and Paul scoffed simultaneously.

"Aw, man! What do you want to get hooked up with those guys for?"

Steve acted as if he'd already had to explain his choice numerous times.

"I know, I know. It's just a job. It probably won't last. But for now, you know, I'm just going to see what happens."

"You realize the reputation they have, don't you? Those guys don't seem to be going anywhere. Everyone calls them Scums N' Posers."

"Yeah, man. I know. I've heard. It's just a job. Just something to keep me busy for now until a better deal comes along."

"Alright, but be careful, man."

"I will. Don't worry."

Ashley

SHE DIDN'T TURN on the porch light as she left the duplex because she anticipated being out so late that the sun would be up by the time she got home. She'd rather sacrifice a little home security to avoid the terrible sense of waste that came upon her when she saw something like an outdoor light burning in broad daylight.

She almost didn't go out. It had been a long, tedious work week, and she had momentarily thought it might be better to stay home and catch up on her sleep. There was always Saturday night. But that sense of waste crept up on her. You only get two nights a week, she thought. Why blow half of them staying home doing nothing?

But it was just another Friday night. Nobody that exciting was playing. Most were going to see Sin at the Whisky, and that's where she'd head. She'd mingle at the bar, flirting with the bartender as always. She'd see the usual suspects, talking to everyone while secretly resenting the couples. Singles make far better drinking partners. She'd look for new faces but find few worth approaching, all the while dreaming of that moment when her eyes would lock on the gaze of a handsome face from across the room. An innocent face. And her heart would race for a change. But she'd soon write this off as childish fantasy. She'd soon see just another room of faces with nothing to offer her.

They say love provides or love feeds the heart, but she always felt empty. Whereas lovemaking is said to have the power to fill, she'd argue that it only drained. Men didn't provide anything. Men took.

She didn't remember who it was, but someone had told her the after-party would be at the Holiday Inn near Hollywood and Highland instead of John and Jessie's apartment. John had a cousin in town who got adjoining rooms for himself and a few of his friends who had come with him on the trip. There were some cute guys in the group, and most everyone else said they'd be there. So she went.

She'd had a lot to drink so she got a ride from someone. The car was full, but she didn't remember who drove. Both rooms were already packed when they arrived, but it seemed there were enough bottles for everyone to have their own. She didn't remember a single conversation or with how many people she spoke. The only memory she had of the hotel was that more and more people kept coming through the door. She wondered vaguely how the rooms would accommodate everyone but didn't worry about it too much. She didn't worry about anything when she was with her friends. She couldn't recall anything more about that night.

She wouldn't know what songs serenaded her on the drive home. Wouldn't know who thought enough to put her in her sweats before putting her to bed. Wouldn't know who tucked her in before letting themselves out, locking the door after turning on the porch light, summoning a guardian to watch over her through at least one more hour of darkness.

Paul

THIS IS ALL I remember.

A room at the Holiday Inn. Two rooms, actually, with a doorway joining them.

A crowd. Not unlike the crowd you'd see crashing against the stage at any club show. But all guys. No girls this time.

A bed. A russet-colored quilt crumpled against the headboard. White sheets and a thin green blanket pulled down and hanging off the foot of the bed. Just the fitted sheet remaining on the mattress. The bed is visible because the crowd has parted. They have formed a semicircle around the bed but are keeping their distance. They don't want to be too close.

A small patch of the burgundy wallpaper above the bed is torn leaving a gray hole. The top part is a straight line, along the seam of two pieces. The sides tatter at downward angles meeting at a point. It is almost a triangle, but not quite. The tear lines are slightly curved. It is the size of a fist, but I don't know what caused it.

There is a commotion in the room. A lot of shouting. Men's voices. Laughing, howling, yelling. All eyes are on the bed.

There is a woman on the bed. She is completely naked. Her hair is bleached blonde but her pubic hair is dark brown. Her hair is long and blown straight but her pubic hair is curly and tightly cropped, appearing matted on the mound between her legs. Her breasts are small, flattened more so because she is lying on her back. Her nipples are pink but do not protrude much.

A man is standing at the edge of the bed, pants dropped to his knees.

His hair is patchy on the backs of his legs and ass. Each arm has a hold of a leg, each leg rests in the crook of an elbow. Each arm keeps the legs spread wide. Each arm keeps the woman's body still at the edge of the bed where it receives him. He thrusts his hips quickly in violent bursts, arms holding her close and still to allow him the deepest penetration. He rhythmically drives himself into her, speeding up only to abruptly freeze, body tense, buried within as completely as possible. He withdraws, grabbing his pants to quickly cover his nakedness before turning to face the cheering and jeering crowd.

Another man immediately rushes forth and falls to his knees at the edge of the bed. He buries his face in the woman's crotch and begins to violently lick her. The crowd groans and laughs, joking about the wetness and taste of what's just been left behind there. The man comes to the realization that he is being laughed at, quickly stands, and clumsily drops his pants. It is clear he has been drinking too much. Instead of lifting the woman's legs to enter her while standing, he lowers himself, lying on top of her. The woman has been completely inert throughout the experience.

Bruce comes up from behind Tim, grabs him by the shoulders and shouts, "I'm going to get this guy laid!!!" to which the crowd bursts into laughter and applause. Tim wriggles himself free easier than he could have if Bruce had really meant it.

That is all I remember. Nothing happened to disperse the crowd. No cops arrived. No one came to the woman's rescue. They just scattered after they ran out of volunteers, I guess. The fact I don't remember how it ended makes me wonder if it was all a dream. Maybe I just woke up. Who said you don't dream in color?

Russet, white, green, burgundy. Pink. A torn piece of wallpaper the size of a fist.

Torn.

Justin

His eye was trained on a single point of light. He slowly brought it into focus.

"It's the bowling alley! Oh my god, that little red dot is the sign for the bowling alley!"

"Let me see!"

"Hold on, hold on. This is cool. Just let me make sure."

He kept his eye pressed to the aperture and continued to peer through. The words "Canoga Park Bowl" gleamed in red neon in perfect focus in the circular frame. He pulled his face away and directed his gaze down the top of the barrel of the telescope. The sign was just a red point of light in a sea of thousands. He looked again through the viewfinder and again away, finding the point among the others with his naked eye, making sure it was indeed the same point being magnified through the series of lenses and mirrors at his fingertips.

"Yeah, that's it all right. That little dot. An entire neon sign. Big one, too."

Justin carefully pulled away from the eyepiece of the telescope so as not to bump it out of position and let Victor slide in for a look.

"Holy shit! That's so cool."

After everyone had a look and shared in the fascination, a game was created. A point of light was chosen, singled out, and the telescope trained upon it. Guesses were made. Billboard? Street light? Store signage? Then the truth revealed itself through the lens. The rest of the night was spent finding landmarks for each other. Little surprises to discover inside the viewfinder. Or unusual lights were located and the secrets of their purposes exposed.

He couldn't quite put his finger on why this fascinated him so much. He didn't understand why it captivated his interest so utterly. Something about how such an intricate arrangement could be reduced to a blur, to a smudge, to a nondescript pinpoint of color, if given the distance and the vantage point. Without the telescope, distinct images were merely tiny glowing masses, disembodied. The entire scene was a mass of thousands of these unidentifiable points. Yet each maintained a unique identity when given the chance to look closer. This game at the top of Mulholland reminded him of a poem he had read by Ezra Pound about faces in a subway station. Each dissolved into a smear of color like a watercolor left out in the rain. They were like pastel cherry-blossom petals soaked to transparency against the wet black branch of a tree.

The telescope somehow gave a context to it all, made them feel like giants towering above an entire world where every light held a distinct purpose too tiny to discern with the naked eye. Each store sign beckoned shoppers. Each street light guided motorists and pedestrians along their way. Each porch light stood sentinel over one of thousands of homes darkened in silent meditation. Each carved a circular nimbus out of the negative space.

He was fascinated as much with this darkness as with the lights. He wondered what filled all the spaces between. But training the telescope on a dark area didn't clarify what he was looking at. It only served to magnify the darkness, providing no positive spin on negative space.

The lights were dazzling, captivating. Yet he often wondered if what he couldn't see comprised all of what he really should be looking for.

The game continued, with creative variations, deeper into the night. The mood was festive, almost celebratory. Everyone toasted this new way to see. Everyone left less blind. More enlightened.

He'd find moments to distance himself. He'd stand apart, staring out at the vast expanse of brilliance, tuning out all of his companions' noise until there was only the quiet of the winding streets at his feet. And the distant hum. Victor grabbed him at one of these times, drunk on the revelry.

"It's like you can float, man. Just spread your wings and soar. Dude, I wish we had a hang glider. Now that would be a party, man!"

He was reminded of dancing with a family friend's daughter last year at a wedding reception in a penthouse ballroom twenty-one stories above the street. They looked out on this same sea of lights from another angle, bathed in light themselves, a mere pinpoint among thousands laid out against the darkness below. From this perspective on Mulholland, they'd be floating. An illuminated dot against a black backdrop. And within the ballroom, they'd be floating above the random array that disguised itself as orderly beneath them.

And now again he longed for release from the chaotic. Longed to be held and to dance over an endless sea of light.

Summer

The crowd in the Roxy poured out onto Sunset, many of them lingering as usual in front of the Rainbow next-door and on the stretch of asphalt that separated the two buildings. Glen stayed behind to find out where the after-party would be. He told Paul he'd catch up to him outside, so Paul made his way out alone and lingered on the outskirts of groups of people who all seemed to be discussing the highlights of the show and reveling in the night. He sidestepped occasionally, avoiding small throngs of people moving up the sidewalk or toward the entrance of the Rainbow, all the while keeping his eyes on the Roxy's doors, waiting for Glen to appear.

Suddenly, a gorgeous woman with a head full of thick brown ringlets cascading over her shoulders caught his eye. She stood just outside the Roxy, talking to a young couple. Her smile was infectious. She seemed to embody the pure joy everyone sought out there on the sidewalk, trying to be a part of the scene. It looked effortless for her to enjoy herself, and he imagined this was true in any setting, as long as there were people around. It was the sort of smile that seemed to draw its power from others. She radiated but also reflected the positive energy of those around her.

He was about to chalk all this up to yet another frustrating experience of seeing someone with a special sort of attractiveness and charm only to let her slip away without having spoken a word, when she suddenly bid farewell to her friends and walked directly toward him. His instinct tried to force him to break eye contact and look away, lest he allow his attraction and fascination to show, but something affixed his gaze to her, so much that he feared he would be accused of staring in lecherous pleasure.

She towered above him, breaking six feet in heels. She was apparently unbothered by his gaze.

"Hey, are you Glen's brother?"

His heart sank . She probably only wanted to know where Glen was.

"Yeah."

"Nice to meet you, I'm Summer."

She extended her hand and he shook it, trying to be firm but delicate.

"Hi."

He forgot to tell her his name.

"I thought I saw you in there standing with Glen. I know him through Dadie. Dadie Resch? She and I are friends and he had a class with her last year. Do you know Dadie and the Resch brothers?"

"Yeah. I mean, not Dadie so well. I met her once, I think. My brother introduces me to people."

He almost visibly winced at how pathetic that sounded.

"I just wanted to say hi. It's cool to see someone so young at the shows. Um, I'm assuming you're pretty young? You look it."

"Well, I'm older than I look, but I am young. I'm younger than most everyone here, I think."

Again, he struggled to contain his frustration at how stupid he was sounding.

"Seems like it. Have you been coming to shows for a while?"

"For a year or so. Glen goes more often, but I join him once in a while."

"That's nice. It's good to broaden your horizons. There's a lot out there in this city. Hopefully, you're finding your way through it, figuring out what interests you. There are a lot of good times to be had. A lot of great music to be heard, huh?"

He was struck by how confident and intelligent she sounded. She hadn't said much, but there was a depth to her that fascinated him. He could tell they'd have a lot to talk about, if he could only bring himself to say something more profound.

"Yeah."

That was about as profound as he was going to get, it seemed. He simply could not believe this woman had gone out of her way to talk to him.

"There are a lot of stories out under these lights. Plenty to learn. And plenty for you to tell someday."

He stared at her in amazement. He wanted to take her to one of the many overlooks he'd discovered so they could look at those lights together. He wondered if there were any places he could show her that she didn't already know for herself.

"Um . . . yeah. Sorry, that's just . . ."

"Just what?"

"Just what I was thinking."

"It was? Then that's kismet, isn't it?"

"Huh?"

"*Kismet.* One of my favorite words. Hey, I gotta run, but tell your brother I said hi."

"Okay."

For a split second, it seemed like she wanted to kiss him goodbye. Ever so slightly, she leaned closer to him. His face warmed under the radiance of her smile. He quickly pulled his eyes away as if he'd go blind if he lingered any longer. But it was an illusion after all. She seemed to only slightly nod, as if they'd just shared an important secret that she wanted to make sure he understood and wouldn't go around repeating to others. Or it could have been her way of getting a better look at him to determine just how young he was.

Glen appeared out of nowhere but had obviously seen them talking as he approached.

"Hey, I see you met Summer."

"Yeah."

"Nice girl, huh?"

"I like her."

"Good. Yeah, she's nice."

"She's different."

Mike

Mike had been holding court in the parking lot of the Rainbow for half an hour by the time Glen and Paul arrived from the Whisky. His sister Flor stood close by, chatting with some friends as best she could despite Mike's voice drowning out everything in its vicinity. He interrupted himself briefly to acknowledge Glen and Paul's arrival.

"Dude! What's up?"

"Good to see you, Mike."

"Hey, what's up, little man. Stop fucking my little sister."

"I'm not fff— . . . I'm not doing anything. We're just friends."

"I know man. I'm just messing with you. You can fuck her if you want."

Paul's face reddened.

"Mike!"

Flor had clearly overheard. She slapped Mike on the shoulder and returned to her friends, too embarrassed to say hi to Paul at the moment.

"Really, Glen. Tell your little brother it's ok if he wants to fuck my sister."

"Leave him alone, Mike."

"Alright, alright. Just looking out for you, little man. Hey, Glen, I'm glad you're here. I was just about to tell these guys about James and James. Remember those guys you met last week?"

"Sure."

"My cousin introduced me to them. Or rather, told them to call me when they were desperate. They barely got here and they're already living the dream. Check it out . . ."

Everyone huddled close in rapt attention.

"They're both from New Jersey. Been best friends since kindergarten. That's where they met my cousin. They all go way back. They're both musicians. One sings, one plays guitar. Both are named James and neither of 'em goes by a nickname. They don't like Jim or Jimmy. Both want to be called James. So, the singer, we just call him Dude. James the guitarist said some other friends of theirs in Jersey started calling him Dude and it just stuck. So, it's James and Dude now. Even though Dude hates it. But tough shit, you know? Get another nickname if you don't like it. What's wrong with Jim or Jimmy?

"They've been playing together for a while now. Supposedly hung out with Bon Jovi before they got signed. James shreds on guitar. The guy can play like Eddie Van Halen, I swear to god. And Dude's a pretty badass singer. Took lessons from the guy who taught David Lee Roth or something. So, these guys don't have much going for them in Jersey, right? I don't know the whole story. Can't keep anyone in the band. Drummers coming and going, bass players. I don't know if they're hard to get along with or just choosy as hell. They seem pretty full of themselves. Like you better be damn good if you want to play with them."

"So, have they signed?"

"No, they haven't signed. They don't even have a band yet. I'm getting there, let me finish.

"So, a couple months ago, they decide to move to LA. Just pack up and go. Strike out to make it in the scene here, right? Sound familiar? Like most everyone else who's already here. So, here they come, driving cross-country from Jersey in this piece of shit van, everything they own inside it, which isn't much. Except for some really expensive gear. James is like a total audiophile. Has to have this high-end gear to get the best sound. The dude shreds—I've heard him play through just a little amp—but he has to have this expensive gear to protect his sound, you know? Like nothing less will do.

"And they're driving cross-country, right? And they run out of money. I mean, who the hell sets out on a cross-country road trip without enough money? They run out of gas in, like, Kansas or Colorado. They panhandle some change here and there. Everything they get goes in the gas tank. They make it to like Utah and then have to sell some old tools they've got and the jack to the van. James won't sell his gear, of course, but everything else in the van is fair game. They make enough money to fill the tank a couple times. Then they run out of gas in Fontana."

"Damn."

"I know. Can you imagine? You drive 3,000 miles from New Jersey to LA to come to Hollywood to make it in the music scene, and you get as far as Fontana. Jesus, that sucks. Fontana. So, that's where I come in.

"They call back home. I don't know what the fuck anyone at home can do for them. Maybe it was for emotional support or some shit like that. And my cousin talks to them and gives them my number. He tells them to call me and tell me that he sent them to me. Tells them I'm a great guy who'll help them out."

"You are a great guy, Mike."

"Yeah, fuck you."

"Seriously."

"Whatever. So, these two guys I don't even know call me up and beg me to help them. I swear, if I didn't love my cousin so much, I would have told them to fuck off all the way back to Jersey. Or hitchhike or something. But I drive all the way out to fucking Fontana and bring them a full can of gas and enough money to get their asses to Hollywood. What they're going to do when they get here, who the hell knows? But I get their asses into town."

"Dude, can you imagine? If they make it, you're the hero, dude."

"That's a big 'if,' Charlie."

"I can dream, can't I? I can dream for others, too."

"Where they go first, I have no clue. I'm driving separately. I lose sight of them somewhere on the 10. I offered them my place if they needed to crash for a couple days until they figured things out, but they said no, they couldn't take advantage of me any more than they already have, blah, blah, blah. So, I'm like, whatever, good luck to you, and I'm off, right? I guess the guys are going to sleep in the van and figure something out.

"So, they call me a week or two later to thank me again and tell me they both got a job at a Box Brothers in Studio City. Pretty cool for them. I guess they drove around like maniacs looking for work and this store hires both of them pretty much on the spot. And they both request to work the late shift every day, to close the place down. You know why?"

"Why?"

"I drive out to see them. You know, since they called, I figure I should keep in touch. They are my cousin's friends, after all. And what do I find when I get there?"

"What?"

"They're living in the fucking store!"

"Really?"

"Yep. There's this little back room and they sleep in it every night. I guess the manager trusts them right away for some reason. Lazy bastard is probably just happy he found somebody to close the store every night so he doesn't have to. And they're living in the store. They've got these two little mattresses and their sheets and blankies. They have a little travel alarm clock that they set every morning so they can get up, pack up, and get the fuck out before whoever opens the store shows up. They put boxes up all around them so if anyone is snooping around, peeking in, or if the manager comes by for some reason, they're all hidden in there. And they're living in the store."

"Why don't they just sleep in the van?"

"That's exactly what I asked them. They said they were sleeping in the van at first, but a cop came by one night. Started shining his flashlight in the windows and knocking on the doors. I guess someone called it in. Strange van with Jersey plates parked on the street or left in the lot or wherever the hell they were. They stayed still and quiet until the cop left.

So, no big deal there. But now they're too scared to sleep in the van. Dude refuses. Can't sleep for fear that cops are going to bust their asses at any moment. So, they've set up a little home away from home in the back of a Box Brothers."

"Can you imagine that? Making millions of dollars as musicians and getting to tell everyone they got their start living in a Box Brothers in the Valley. What a story."

"Pretty pathetic story unless they make it, dude."

"Yeah, but a great story if they do."

"I don't know, man. These guys have talent. But they just aren't doing anything yet. I tell them to come hang out with us, start meeting some people. I tell them to put an ad in the *Pennysaver.* Get a band together. Start playing. Get tapes out to the clubs and play some gigs. But they aren't doing shit."

"Why not?"

"I don't know. James was saying something about saving up money for some more gear. Like he wants this special-effects device on the vocals or something before they record. He won't send tapes out without this perfect sound he wants to create."

"Dude, whoever is listening to those tapes and signing bands doesn't give a shit about special effects. They look right through that shit . . . or listen right through it. They can tell who has talent and who doesn't without all the effects. They should just record something and send it out if they're as good as you say they are."

"I told them that. I tell them to just send something out. No big deal. If they don't get any calls, they can always send something out again after they record with their fancy equipment."

"Or they can pay someone at a studio and get all the fancy equipment they want. Fancy mix jobs. Fancy production. They just have to pay for it. Borrow some money. It's not that hard."

"I know."

"Damn, plenty of talented guys busting their asses every week. Playing every week and going nowhere. And these guys are too stuck up to even start playing? Like what they have is beneath them? I'd give my left nut for talent like that. Maybe for the gear, too."

"I know. I don't get it either, man."

"Maybe they really suck. Maybe it's just a cop out, man."

"No, I've heard them. I heard James play and I heard an old tape of theirs. Dude sounds really good on vocals too."

"They've already got a tape then? If it sounds good, why don't they start shopping it around?"

"I don't know."

"I don't either."

"Shit . . . . Jersey, man. All the way from Jersey. They may as well be back in fucking Fontana at the rate they're going."

Glen

Nobody knew the kid. He appeared among those milling about the crowd outside of the Rainbow. Nobody saw him walk up, nobody knew from which direction he had come. He just materialized. He had spoken to a few people, but Mike was the first to give him the time of day.

"Hey Glen, this kid needs a ride. Can you help him out?"

"Yeah, maybe. Where do you live?"

The kid stayed quiet until Mike gave him a nudge in the shoulder.

"Where do you live, kid?"

"I'm not going home. I just want a ride down the street a little."

"Yeah? Where to?"

"Just over to Oki Dog."

"You know where that is, man?"

"Yeah, I've passed it before. It's not too far, I don't think. What do you think, Paul? You okay if we give him a ride?"

"Sure, no problem."

Paul took a good look at the kid. He felt certain that he was older, which said a lot, considering Paul was used to being the youngest one around just about everywhere they went.

"We'll take him, Mike. Thanks."

"Thanks for helping out, man."

Paul tried to get Glen's attention as they walked to the car, not wanting to let the kid know they were talking about him.

"He's pretty young, ya think?"

"Yeah, he looks it."

"Don't you think we should take him home? What if something happens to him out on the street?"

"I doubt much will happen to him. Even if it did, it's not our fault. We're just giving him a ride. What's your name, man?"

Glen's question was met with silence.

"Pretty weird. I wonder what his story is. Where he lives."

"Don't worry about it. He's probably used to getting hassled about being on the street."

They got to Glen's Firebird, but the kid continued to show little interest in being social. Now that they had stopped walking and he was sure he was being understood, Glen asked again.

"Hey, what's your name?"

Fearing that refusing to answer might make Glen renege on the ride offer, he relented.

"Call me JC."

"Is that what everyone calls you? JC?"

"Yeah, most people."

"Where do you live?"

"Around. Just take me to Oki Dog. I'll be fine there."

"Are you from around here? I mean, did you grow up in LA?"

"Yeah."

"Alright. Oki Dog it is."

They climbed into the Firebird, Paul stepping aside to let JC in the back after his offer of the front seat was denied. He slid the seat forward a bit before shutting the door but this gesture was met with silence.

Nobody spoke as they drove, even though Glen turned down the stereo. He made his way to Santa Monica Boulevard quickly because he didn't know how far east Oki Dog was. He was still paranoid that he'd passed it and would be driving a street urchin around most of the night.

"It's this way, right?"

"I don't know."

"Have you been there before?"

"No. They just told me to get to Oki Dog and I'd be okay."

"Who's 'they'?"

"People. People I've met. I'll be fine if you can just get me to Oki Dog."

"Are you sure that's where you want to go? I mean, it's just a hot-dog stand, right? I can take you somewhere else if you'd like. Do you have a place to sleep tonight?"

"You don't have to do me any more favors. Just get me to Oki Dog."

Glen debated whether he should more specifically offer up their place as a point of refuge but decided not to push it.

They made no small talk on the ride. Nobody tried. They didn't even ask JC if he knew any of the bands on the scene or if he'd been to any shows. They were pretty certain they hadn't seen him before. He dressed the part—torn jeans, Vans—but his hair was shorter than most. If he cleaned himself up, he could be the kid in math class nobody pays much attention to.

Paul was surprised. Glen was usually pretty social with just about anyone. Typically, Glen would have been asking someone like JC for his life story by now. But maybe he got the point. The kid seemed to have something to hide. Or rather, he just seemed ashamed of his situation.

"I think this is it . . ."

They crept up to a small building with palm fronds on the roof and other tropical décor.

"Yep. Oki Dog."

They all saw the sign at the same time.

The tables outside were packed. Music played over speakers and also spilled out of the kitchen. Many people were in line outside a window, but patrons could go inside as well. Paul saw a small crowd at a pinball machine through an open door.

JC offered a brief thank you as he stepped out from the back seat.

"Do you know anyone here?"

"No . . . I don't think so, I mean. Don't worry, I'll be alright."

"I hope so . . ."

Paul climbed back in and closed the door. Glen didn't take much time to survey the crowd before putting the car back in gear. He noticed a few skateboards, a few Misfits T-shirts, a Ramones, an Adicts, a couple Black Flags.

They accelerated down Santa Monica looking for a good place to hang a U-turn.

"Think he'll be alright?"

"I don't know. He seems to think so. I guess there's that."

"I mean, where's he going to sleep? Probably just meet someone there who can offer him a place to stay?"

"Probably. Or stay up all night on the streets. That place doesn't look like it closes."

"We didn't ask him if he had any money for food."

"I doubt he was going there for the hot dogs. He'll be alright."

The Firebird made its way back through West Hollywood, past the Troubadour, whose crowd had dispersed a long time before, and through the cleaner streets of Beverly Hills and Century City before finding the freeway.

Justin

The end of Clarinda Drive stood perched on a hilltop high above the Valley, illuminated after sundown by three streetlights—three points of light among countless others that seemingly splashed out of the vibrant bowl of colorful jewels below that was the Valley floor at night. These three lights were higher than any others that dotted the nearby hills, making the cul-de-sac a prime vantage point and a favorite spot for Justin to go when he wanted to experience that paradoxical sensation of feeling simultaneously isolated from and connected to the city. It was always quiet and peaceful, far enough removed that the terrible din of freeways and busy streets was a mere faint hum. But it offered a perspective of the entire Valley at night, as tangible as if it lay in the palm of one's hand. It was as if one could merely lean forward out of the darkness and bathe in the many colors that filled this space surrounded by mountains, like dipping one's face in a Technicolor basin and emerging dry again but nevertheless cleansed.

Justin knew his nights on Clarinda were numbered. The cul-de-sac featured three large lots that had already been cleared and graded, with naked frames of large houses already rising from the dirt of two of them. The remaining construction would place a future living room of some lucky family in the spot where he most liked to stand. He marveled at the view these privileged souls would have as their own someday soon, and he wondered if they'd appreciate it as much as he had.

As building materials started appearing on top of the hill, he made it a point to walk to the top more frequently. Tonight, a joint had already made several rotations around the room when he suggested a trip to the viewpoint to Jared and Victor.

"Too burnt. I'm going home. Gotta be up tomorrow."

"For what?"

"Dunno. Something important, probably"

Victor was up for anything, as usual, so the two of them headed south and left Jared slowly making his way down the block and a half to his own bedroom.

They immediately got into formation for the game they always played. Justin had the "driver's seat," walking close to the painted lane dividers. Victor was riding shotgun, walking on Justin's right. The two stared straight ahead as if looking out a large windshield into the night that surrounded them. They imagined moving faster than they could walk. Houses zipped by in their periphery. Hills were climbed with ease.

When they got to the top of the short, steep, dead-end street with the best view around, they put on the brakes. The notion that something was wrong hit them both before their impaired minds had the chance to process what it was.

"Holy shit."

It still took several moments before they realized how it was done. Someone had taken scraps of gypsum board—drywall that would soon adorn the frames of these future houses, enclosing spaces with boundaries that would keep such trespassers at bay—and scraped words into the street, as if writing with sidewalk chalk. Another moment prolonged by the ethereal haze in their brains revealed the intent of those words.

Eight or nine testaments of hatred lay at their feet. Each message was a clear and direct statement of anti-Semitism.

"'Jews go home . . . ' What the fuck?"

Scattered across the entire cul-de-sac were chalky white swastikas. And among them, in varying degrees of vulgarity but uniform themes of ignorance, were messages threatening the imagined future residents of Clarinda Drive.

Justin was crushed. This spot he held so sacred was tarnished. What pissed him off the most was the fact that someone, or several people, had so callously entered his sanctuary. It felt like a rape—a gross violation. They didn't deserve the peace the cul-de-sac offered. They didn't deserve the amazing view afforded by such a vantage point.

"Did they even open their eyes?"

"Say what?"

"How could some asshole enjoy a view such as this and still feel the need to do that?"

"Life goes over some people's heads, man."

Justin looked around.

"We've got to do something. We have to fix it."

"How?"

Justin ran to the curb and grabbed a scrap of gypsum board that had been tossed in the gutter. He tore it in half, sending a cloud of powdery mist over the street, illuminated by those three streetlights.

"C'mon, man. Help me out."

They both began scratching out the words and symbols, digging the gypsum into the hard asphalt. The coarse texture of the street made the going difficult. It was hard to sustain a good line while rubbing the board back and forth like a crayon. It skipped and scudded recklessly off the pavement, leaving only perforated lines that did little to obscure the messages underneath. Victor soon discovered the best method was to drag the board over long distances with slow and steady pressure to keep the writing edge firmly in place. It took longer than they thought, but they soon had significantly undone a lot of the damage. Many of the messages and symbols were now illegible.

They sat on the curb to catch their breath. The vision that had greeted them at the top of the street seemed to sober them up. Suddenly, it was physically taxing to undertake such a project.

"Still looks like crap."

"Well, we don't have an eraser, man. We did alright."

"Not good enough."

"We scratched them out as much as we could."

Victor suddenly felt the urge to just get home and go to bed.

"Come on man, it's like two in the morning."

"Just wait."

Justin didn't want to leave. He'd come for perhaps one last look at the view, and he hadn't even taken the time to enjoy it. He'd hardly even noticed the thousands of twinkling lights beneath him. He hadn't had the time to get quiet—really quiet—and take in every sound of the nearby neighborhood, framed by the distant cacophony emerging from those lights. He hadn't had a moment's peace.

"That's it!"

He sprang to his feet, revitalized.

"What's it?"

"Get up and help me."

He started walking around the perimeter of the cul-de-sac. He'd never noticed how the street swelled into a perfectly round bubble at the end. Most cul-de-sacs ended in variations on the theme of oval. It suddenly seemed impossible to find one that formed a terminus in as perfect a circle as that of Clarinda Drive. Starting at the point where the circle was broken to allow the street to flow down the hill, he dug his gypsum board into the pavement and ran a perfect arc from the inner edge of one gutter to the other, enclosing the open end of the asphalt circle in chalky dust. He continued drawing, following the sweeping curve of the sidewalk all the way around the dead end, about half a foot away from the gutter, until he met up with the point where he began the first arc. He knew if he got that first curve right, the rest would be easy.

And it was. Victor still wasn't sure what he was up to, but he followed his lead. The two of them ran around and around, dragging their boards behind them, tracing around the entire cul-de-sac and all the graffiti. They continued for several revolutions, each time making the chalk lines thicker and darker, until everything at the top of Clarinda Drive was surrounded by a perfect circle.

Victor was spent.

"What are we doing, man? I'm getting dizzy."

"Hold on . . ."

Justin ran up the incline to the top of one of the graded lots to get a higher vantage point of their work.

"It looks great, man!"

"It looks like a circle, dude."

Justin noted his next point of attack from his position above. Never losing sight of it, he ran down, grabbed a new piece of drywall, and dug its edge into the asphalt. He ran a straight line from one end of the circle to the other, cutting a perfect diameter straight down the middle. He ran back retracing the line. Victor got his breath and followed along faithfully. Several tracings later, a line as thick as the edge of the circle cut the entire shape in half.

Once he was satisfied with the clarity of the line, Justin walked to the very center of the circle. He calculated a 45-degree angle as best he could, and ran a light line from the midpoint to the edge of the circle, creating a diagonal that branched off from the diameter they'd just completed. He returned to the midpoint and ran a symmetrical line to the opposite side of the circle.

Victor finally saw the light.

"Holy shit! You're a genius, man! A freakin' genius! It's a peace sign! How fucking awesome is that!? It's a peace sign!"

His glee echoed down the hillside beneath them.

After returning to his vantage point above to check the angles and the symmetry, Justin was satisfied. He handed Victor a new piece of board.

"Come on. Let's get it done."

They both traced and retraced the new lines, making their thickness and clarity equal to those of the others. Then, with a newfound energy, they retraced the entire symbol many times as if to leave no doubt of its intentions. Each layer of chalk added a level of clarity more satisfying than the last, and the final image was so deeply etched into the pavement that they were certain airplanes overhead would be able to see it.

They both climbed to the vacant lot above and admired their work. It was amazingly accurate. And the message behind it was clear. Every scratched-out bit of vulgarity was now encompassed by a symbol that trumped hatred. They reveled in seeing the result of their labor. They felt vindication for anyone who might have happened to witness the ugliness that was there before they arrived.

Victor clapped Justin on the back.

"It's perfect, man. Take that, fucking skinhead cowards!"

The image of the street winding its way up the steep hill to end in a perfectly circular peace symbol inspired Justin's weary mind.

"We should do this every weekend."

"I think the new neighbors would catch us eventually, dude."

"No, man. In a new cul-de-sac each time."

Victor laughed.

Justin continued, growing more certain that his idealism wasn't in vain.

"Think about it. Almost all these hillside streets are dead ends. How cool would it be if every Sunday morning a new group of people woke up, got their newspapers, and saw that the circle at the end of their street had been transformed? They'd have helicopters taking pictures of the latest peace-sign vandalism. It would be on the news. People would wonder where we'd strike next. If their street would be the chosen one. We'd be, like, unknown heroes."

Victor smiled, taking it all in.

"It would be hard for people to get pissed at us. I hope a lot of people see this, man. It's totally clear, the story behind what happened here. It's like . . . symbolism, you know? You said more in response to that anti-Jewish shit than anyone could have said . . . and with just a little chalk."

Justin continued to implore.

"Think about it . . . We might start a trend. Others would do the same thing in neighborhoods all over LA. It would sure look nicer than all the bullshit assholes like that leave behind. Way better than plain asphalt, too."

Victor continued to smile.

"You get me stoned enough, I might join you."

The two stayed awhile admiring their work and the view of the city below. Justin was eager to see the look on the faces of those who showed up—the construction crew on Monday or just those who might walk up the hill to enjoy the view as he did. For now, it was only the two of them. He felt like they had a tremendous secret, and he wanted to share it now with everyone he could.

He found his quiet. They remained for quite some time, silently staring down on the thousands of twinkling lights. Every point a brilliant eye bearing witness to their small miracle.

Paul

From Clarinda, the top of Vanalden looks like a runway
Straightened from the contours of an ancient river
Girded by parallel blasts of white
Exaggeratedly lit up in contrast to the darkness of the hillside on
    which it lies
Angled upward at an almost impossible angle
As if in a haphazard attempt to assist airplanes in their ascent
Looking as if it would otherwise launch something clear over the
    mountains
Into the ocean
If given the speed
And lack of wings

There's a cave up there somewhere
Filled with the graffiti of another era
Carved into solid rock
Beyond where the lights fade
Off a dirt road much narrower than Mulholland
But I've yet to find it
Seems I'm always there in the dark
Turning my back to the possibility
Of a new escape
Bearing witness instead
To the multitude of lights
Lying seemingly unchanged for generations
While the city constantly changes beneath them

Daisy

THE PALACE EMPTIED onto Vine Street. Throngs of people continued chanting "Black and Blue, Black and Blue" as they dispersed along the sidewalk.

"You think we'll be on TV?"

"Probably. We were right up front. I felt like I had one camera on me most of the show."

"That was awesome. When is it going to be on? We should all get together to watch."

"They said like two or three weeks. We'll find out."

"Hey, thanks again for the tickets, Daisy. Thank Debbie for us."

"You're welcome, I will. She said it was no big deal. Not a lot of people in her department know or care about Black and Blue. Pretty easy for her to get."

"We're going to head out, Glen."

"Hey, no problem, Grant. We'll see you guys next weekend."

"Take care."

Glen, Daisy, and Paul made their way up the hill and around the corner on Yucca where the car was parked.

"What do you think, guys? Denny's?"

"You know, I'm getting a little tired of Denny's."

"Then where to, Glen?"

"How about Pink's?"

"There'll probably be a line."

"No big deal. I can wait. Can you wait, Paul?"

"Sure."

"Okay, cool. Pink's, then."

Paul piled into the back seat.

"Your brother's such a gentleman. Always lets me sit up front."

"He lets everyone sit up front. "

"Still, that's nice. When are you getting a car, Paul?"

"Probably never. I don't know."

"That's alright. I drive a piece of shit. That's why I always make your brother drive."

"I'd take a piece of shit at this point."

"Yeah, sorry."

"He borrows our mom's car once in a while. You can't complain about that."

"Yeah, she never wants me to go more than like a mile away, though."

Daisy took his exaggeration seriously.

"C'mon Paul, I'm sure she lets you go farther than that."

"Not much."

"Do you, though?"

"Do I what?"

"Go farther?"

"Sometimes."

"She won't find out?"

"Not unless she checks the odometer and does the math. She doesn't pay that close attention."

"Shit, if I had a son and loaned him my car and told him not to go too far, I'd be damn sure checking my odometer."

"Yeah, I guess I'm lucky."

"What's the farthest you've gone?"

"When I wasn't allowed? Probably Santa Barbara."

"What the fuck? You drove all the way to Santa Barbara in your mom's car and she never found out?"

Glen was genuinely shocked.

"You never told me about that, Paul."

"I didn't want you saying anything. Besides, how's she going to find out? I put gas back in it. She doesn't check anything else."

"What did you do in Santa Barbara?"

"Had an ice-cream sundae and came back home."

"Wha—? You're crazy. Your brother's crazy, Glen."

"Never trust the quiet ones."

"Where else?"

"Huh?"

"Where else have you driven?"

"Nowhere that crazy. I went exploring one night and wound up at the Forum."

"How did that happen?"

"No reason, really. Just started driving. We probably wound up on Sepulveda or La Cienega and just kept going. I don't know how I made it to the Forum. I wasn't trying. Just happened to drive by it and thought, 'Oh, now I know where we are.'"

"Really? That's pretty crazy. Inglewood? Not exactly a place to be exploring."

"I know. I've never had any problems, though. Well, not really."

"Who were you with?"

"This guy Brian from school. He doesn't go to the clubs. But I'll do other stuff with him from time to time."

"You said 'not really?' Have you run into problems?"

"Wow, Daisy. Give him the third degree. You sound like you're going to report back to our mom."

"I'd never do that. I don't even know your mom. I'm just curious. I never just drive around. Kind of scary out there."

"I should tell you the Korean Mafia story."

"The what?"

"Korean Mafia. I don't think I told you this one either, Glen."

"Doesn't sound familiar. How many stories do you have?"

"Not many. But you'd remember this one. Freaked me out so much I probably tried to wipe it from my mind. Never told anyone."

"Ooh, how special for us."

"I was with Brian and this guy who was closer friends with him, Andy. We went out one night in mom's car. Just driving around, and we get this idea to go to McCabe's."

"What's McCabe's?"

"It's like a guitar store, but they have shows there. You see them listed in the *LA Weekly*."

"Oh yeah, sounds familiar."

"We'd never been, so we figured, let's go check out the guitars and see what the place looks like. Maybe we'd go to a show there sometime. I don't know."

"Right."

"So, we grab a *Weekly* and find the address. It's on Pico. And the address had me going really far east on Pico. I thought it would be in or near Hollywood, but it's farther out. Or so we thought."

"Okay."

"We keep driving and driving down Pico, looking at the address numbers. And we get all the way into Koreatown before they are even close to what we're looking for. We were practically downtown. On Pico the whole way. From the 405."

"Yeah?"

"And I don't know if it was before or after, and who found out first, but we realize that the place is on Pico Boulevard in Santa Monica. Not LA. The street numbers are all different there. It's like you're driving down Pico out of Santa Monica and all of a sudden, the address numbers totally change. As soon as you cross the city limits, the block numbers are all different. So, there can be an address on Pico in Santa Monica and a place with the same address on Pico in LA. But this place would be way the hell east in, like, Koreatown or downtown."

"That's confusing."

"Yeah, no kidding. Turns out, we were on the entirely wrong part of Pico."

"So, what happened? 'Before or after' what?"

"Before or after we got attacked by the Korean Mafia."

"Oh my god."

"That's just the nickname we gave them. This group of thugs. Not like the real mafia. But who knows? Maybe gang members."

"What happened?"

"I changed lanes in front of this guy in a pickup truck. I guess I didn't signal. I rarely do, especially when there isn't any traffic. I mean, why bother letting everyone know you're changing lanes when they are nowhere near you?"

"Okay."

"He was way behind me. It was an easy lane change. No cars close. No big deal. But he pulls up alongside me at the next red light and rolls down his window. He motions for me to roll down mine."

"You mean, your mom's."

"Yeah, right. So, I roll the window down and look at him like 'What?' And he says, 'Hey, signal next time.' I didn't even realize I hadn't. No need to, I thought. So, I just kind of nod and say 'Okay' and roll the window back up."

"Yeah?"

"And I guess he thinks I said something like 'Fuck off' because all of a sudden, he's all pissed off."

"Oh my god!"

"I know. And there are all these guys riding in the back of the pickup truck. Just out in the open. I don't know how he told them what happened, but all of a sudden, they are all pissed off as well. At the next red light, they all pour out of the back of the truck and pose in their like, karate, Tang Soo Do, or whatever, moves."

"No shit? Oh my god!"

"Yeah. And one of them is going 'Come on!' outside like he wants to kick my ass, and I just keep the window rolled up and the doors locked."

"Yeah, no kidding."

"And the guy kicks my window."

"What?"

"Yep. He does this martial arts side kick, right into the window. Jumped off the ground, extended his leg, and wham!"

"Did he break it?"

"No, thank god. He kind of bounced off it without even making a crack. Pretty hard to believe."

"Damn, that's lucky. What did you do?"

"This guy Andy wanted to fight. He's like, 'Let's all rush out of the car at the same time. We'll surprise them.' There's like six or seven of them and three of us, the dumbass. We would have gotten our asses kicked. Good thing he was in the back seat and Brian refused to let him out. He would've died."

"No doubt. What did you do?"

"I floored it. I got the hell out of there. I think the light turned green or was about to. I didn't wait for it. I hung a right turn and drove like a madman down the street. I figured, if a cop sees me and pulls me over, I can point out the truck and tell him what happened. I wanted to get pulled over. It's like, where's a cop when you need one?"

"Oh my god."

"I can't believe you never told me this, Paul. Mom would kill you if she found out."

"Yeah, no shit."

"So, what happened?"

"They chased us."

"No!"

"Yes. They must have gotten back in the truck in a hurry, because the next thing I know, he's on my ass, chasing us down."

"Oh my god."

"We get to the next intersection and I hang another right at the last minute. I don't know if he took the turn or missed it. Maybe he got cut off by another car. But I looked in the rearview mirror and he was gone. I made another quick right on the next block in case he was just coming around the turn and saw me. I wanted to be out of sight before he saw which way I went."

"Oh my god. It's like a chase scene in a movie. You were driving like a maniac, I bet."

"Pretty much. I didn't care who saw me. Like I said, I wanted a cop to see me being chased and bust them."

"Unbelievable."

"So, we pretty much lost them. And what do we see the next turn we make? A cop car."

"No!"

"Yes. They were on the side of the street. They had someone pulled over."

"Did you stop and tell them?"

"Yep. It was weird because they were writing this guy a ticket and were all nervous about all three of us coming up on them in a hurry, all out of breath and excited."

"Ha, no kidding."

"So, they made us wait at a distance while they dealt with the guy they had pulled over. And then one of them got the chance to talk to us. So, we told him what happened."

"What did he say?"

"Not a lot. Like, "We'll keep an eye out for the truck and pull them over, talk to them if we see them.""

"Did they?"

"I doubt it, but I don't know. He didn't sound too convincing. Like if he didn't see it with his own eyes, there wasn't much he could do. We made our way back to Pico and back toward Santa Monica. We never did find McCabe's. Too freaked out by what had happened. How I was inches away from having to explain to my mother why her driver's-side window was shattered.

"Or why you wound up in the hospital. Oh my god, can you imagine?"

"I don't want to imagine. So, we called them the Korean Mafia. Bunch of Korean guys, defending their turf against us white Valley invaders. They were totally looking for a fight. I wasn't rude to the guy. I didn't say anything that could be confused as cursing him out. I just nodded and said 'Okay.' I guess that was too casual or something . . . like I didn't care for his feedback too much and blew him off. Or maybe my long hair pissed him off. Threatened his sense of conformity."

"That's crazy, Paul. What other secrets do you have?"

"Yeah, my own brother. What else are you keeping from me so that I don't tell mom?"

"Nothing."

"Yeah, right."

"No, I'm serious. That's pretty much it. Just some stupid adventures driving around when or where I shouldn't be."

There was no parking anywhere near Pink's, so Glen circled around.

"How about you, Glen. What kind of trouble have you gotten into?"

"Not much. Anything crazy, you've probably already seen. Stuff at the clubs."

"Nothing else?"

"Once we were going to Perkin's Palace and wound up in Azuza."

"Ha!"

"It's in Pasadena, Perkins Palace, and Danny was supposed to be looking at the map telling me where to get off the freeway. I'm driving and driving. We get all the way out to Azuza and right when I'm about to ask him if he knows what he's doing, because it seemed like we'd gone way too far, he's like 'I think we missed the exit.' I wanted to kill him."

"Did you miss the show?"

"No, we turned around and made it back. Missed some of the opener, probably. I don't remember."

"How about you, Daisy? I bet you have some stories that have ours beat."

"Oh, I've got a lot of stories. Mostly the scene, though. Not really driving around."

"Tell one."

"Well, one that involves driving was this time I went downtown in the middle of the night."

"What for?"

"It was this job someone told me about. I don't even remember how I got into it. I was still in high school. Or high-school age, at least. Someone told me about this job making copies of video tapes."

"What kind of video tapes?"

"Ooh, I know what you're thinking. It's not that. Although I could tell you about the number of times I've been asked to be in a porno. Funny how many people are suddenly amateur filmmakers when I come around. Everyone wants to put me in their movies, can you believe it?"

"I can believe it. Must be hard."

"That's what she said."

"Ha!"

"Anyway, this was nothing like that. And it's funny you mentioned the Korean Mafia, because I think this guy was Korean. He was some kind of Asian. And he had a business selling videos. I don't know if they were pirated movies. I mean, it was real movies, but he was making copies and selling them."

"Uh, yeah. That's called pirating."

"And he had this weird office with all these VCRs. The job was, basically, put in a tape, push record, let the movie play in another machine and make a copy. Several copies at once. He had several machines hooked up to the main one."

"Just regular movies?"

"Yeah, I think. That's all I saw. I only did it once. It creeped me out to be down there by myself. Someone let me in and then left. I was there in the middle of the night alone. I had to hang around so I could switch tapes when the movie ended. Rewind and start again. It was weird."

"Sounds weird. And illegal. And dangerous. You went down there alone?"

"Yeah. I had a friend who was going to come, but she flaked out, so I went alone. But I didn't give a shit. It was like ten bucks an hour, which was great money for me then."

"Not too bad today, either."

"Yeah. But it was weird, so I didn't do it again. You know what the weirdest thing was, though?"

"What?"

"I never go downtown. Especially at night. And now I know why. There is literally nothing going on."

"I never go at night either."

"It's like a ghost town. I got out of there around three in the morning. Everything was totally quiet. I was on a pretty big street, like 8th Street. It was totally deserted."

"I went with some friends to Gorky's once. The one downtown. Same thing. It's really quiet after dark."

"Yeah. And this weird thought I had—I was surrounded by all these totally dark tall buildings. The only lights were the traffic lights and maybe a streetlight or two. No lights on, hardly at all in the buildings. And you know what it reminded me of?"

"What?"

"Tombstones."

"Tombstones?"

"Yeah. It's like there's all this activity in those buildings and on the streets during the day. All the fancy business people in suits going in and out of them. All the activity, right? And at night, it's like everything shuts down and it's all quiet and weird. And I pictured it like a cemetery. And these tall things sticking out of the ground were like tombstones. That's the only thing sticking out of the ground in a cemetery. And it got all creepy to me. Like all the activity was dead. All the people that were there, all the energy, it had all died. And it was just graves now. Like the buildings are really just tombstones in disguise."

"That's crazy."

"I know."

"You have a cool imagination, Daisy."

"You'd never know from looking at me, huh?"

"Well, I didn't say that. But it's cool. I like the way your brain works."

"I don't. Too weird. I creeped myself out. I never went back to that job. I haven't even been downtown since, I don't think. It sort of ruined it for me."

Glen finally found a parking spot in an alley two blocks from Pink's. He straightened the car and killed the engine.

"We can walk from here. It's not far."

"Is this parking spot legal?"

"I don't know. We won't be gone too long."

"Okay. It's your ticket."

"See, you guys aren't the only ones who don't care about doing illegal things."

"You're a rebel, Glen."

"That's what she said."

"Are you kidding me? That doesn't even work there. Not even funny."

"I know. I'm forcing it."

"That's what he said."

"Ha! See, your brother's got it. Take notes, Glen. Take notes."

"I'll take notes on how to steal my mom's car, if that's what you mean."

"Very funny. Don't tell."

"I'm not going to tell. Just stop messing around with the Korean Mafia. Or Daisy's porn pirates."

"It wasn't porn!"

"Sure."

Tim

IRONICALLY, HE OFTEN experienced a sort of sensory deprivation during shows. The sonic onslaught was so powerful and taxing, it made it impossible to process all senses simultaneously. The sound levels were so high and the crowd so thick at the Troubadour one night, he felt his eyes blur during W.A.S.P.'s set. The throng turned into a swirling mass of distorted faces and melted bodies as if the scene were one giant watercolor and some godlike power was dousing them with an enormous eyedropper from above. Periods in which he could focus were gradually outnumbered by periods in which he felt blind. He could see, it wasn't that. It was just that shapes and colors lost all form. The dominant sound drowned out everything else, including his sense of sight. It was as if he couldn't process more than one sense at a time, lest he overload his brain from the incredible density each portal of experience had to offer.

Another night, he purposely attempted to flip-flop this phenomenon. Armored Saint was unleashing a tidal wave of sound, and he felt his vision begin to blur. Fighting to hang onto his sight, he steeled his eyes, forcing himself to attach his gaze on a distant focal point—the image of two girls moving to the music in slow rhythmic gyrations at the top of the stairs to the green room. He forced his perception of shape and color to remain acute, and in doing so, his ears failed him. He could no longer distinguish individual notes spilling forth from the lead guitar. He could no longer hear the rapid bass line that had been so pronounced just moments before. Each drum sounded like a distant dull thud, the guitars and singer's voice blended into a muffled cacophony of a freight train heard as if he were standing underground.

He didn't freak out. He was used to music having bizarre effects on his body. He'd heard bass so loud, he thought his heart might get damaged vibrating against his ribcage. He knew his eardrums took a beating every show. It once took three days for his hearing to return to normal. The overwhelming nature of the environment made him wonder if he was suffering permanent damage. At times, it was hard not to become overwhelmed and flee, driven by a panic-laden impulse for self-protection. He'd hear screams in his own head and realize they weren't hallucinations caused by the various harmonics that swirled around the room. They seemed to be his own body's bellowing for escape from the merciless assault on its sensory organs.

Glen

Glen and Mike sprawled out on the couch in the apartment Janine and Michelle shared in Reseda. MTV's "Headbanger's Ball" blared as best it could from the tiny speaker in the old Sony television in the corner. There was still time to catch the headliner somewhere, but they had decided to stay in. Nobody worth seeing was playing the Country Club. And no one was in the mood to drive over the hill to check out what was going on in Hollywood. It was hotter than hell in the Valley, but not much cooler anywhere else in the city. Glen foresaw four or five straight upcoming weekends with shows he'd be attending. He had decided to lay low and take a rare break from the scene.

"Haven't all his victims been east of downtown? It's like he's sticking to the San Gabriel Valley."

"No, he's not just in the San Gabriel Valley. He's in the San Fernando Valley now. Attacked someone in Burbank a couple months ago and shot a couple in Northridge last night. Didn't you see the news today? Shot a woman in the face. He's like right up the fucking street now!"

"He's one sick bastard too. Writing messages in his victims' blood on the walls and shit. Satan stuff. Devil worship."

"Plenty of that going around these days."

"Yeah but this dude is the real deal. I get a sense he means what he's saying. He's not just going for shock value."

"Like some of the posers on the Strip."

"Exactly. Hey Glen, remember that guitarist dude we met who said don't ever break your guitar in the name of Satan?"

"Yeah, he was pretty messed up."

"Said Satan told him to snap the neck of his guitar. Like Satan needs another piece-of-shit Yamaha as a sacrifice."

"What did he say afterward that was really funny?"

"He said, 'I might worship Satan, but now I'm playing air.' Friggin' hilarious. He—"

Janine suddenly ran in from the hallway, a look of terror on her face.

"Someone's in the alley! It's the Night Stalker, I know it! Oh my god, oh my god!"

"Are the windows closed?"

Janine hopped from foot to foot, hands aflutter, ignoring the question.

"Are the windows closed!?"

"No, the one in my bedroom is open. Oh my god!"

Glen rose from the couch. He was reluctant to play hero but figured someone had to take control of the situation.

"Hey, shut up. It's probably just some random person in the alley. But if it is him, the last thing you want him to hear is that you know he's the Night Stalker. He'll probably come in here and cut your tongues out."

He realized about a half second too late that was the wrong thing to say.

"Aaaaack! I'm calling the cops! Someone call the cops! Dial 9-1-1!"

"Jesus fucking Christ, Glen. Nice advice."

"Well shit, Mike. Why don't you do something then, instead of just sitting there? You're like twice my size anyway."

"Size don't matter when the other guy has a gun, dude."

Glen calmed Janine and Michelle down enough to get them off the phone and allow him to check out the scene in the alley for himself. He crept into Janine's bedroom with the others in tow. He turned off the light and slowly stepped inside.

"Great, turn off the light so he thinks you've gone to bed. Now he'll come in and kill you."

Janine gasped.

"Shut the fuck up, man. You're freaking everybody out."

"Geez . . . just joking, dude. Janine, you're the one freaking everyone out with your friggin' panic attack."

"I can't help it."

"Both of you shut up. Whoever's out there probably wants to kill all of us now just for some peace and quiet."

Glen made it to the wall opposite the door, then sidled alongside it until he reached the edge of the window. The Levolor blinds were drawn but the slats were open.

"You guys see anything out there?"

Mike and the girls all shook their heads.

Glen slowly pulled the cord on the blinds, raising them several inches.

"Don't open it!"

"Shhhhh. Shut up!"

In a quick motion, Glen slipped his hand through the aperture he created and slid the window shut. He lowered the blinds and started back for the door.

"That's it? Like a closed window is going to stop him?"

"You got a better idea?"

"Look out and see if he's there."

"I'm not looking out there. You look."

"Geez, such a pussy."

Mike crept across the dark room, dropping to his knees and crawling the last half of the distance to the window.

"You open the blinds, I'll look."

Glen stood with his back to the wall again, blind cord in hand, waiting for Mike to give the signal.

"Go!"

Glen pulled on the cord. Mike popped up and pressed his face to the glass. Michelle stared vacantly. Janine muffled a scream.

"Nothing."

"What?"

"There's nothing out there. Nobody. What did you see?"

"I saw someone. Or someone's shadow. I swear, there was someone in the alley. I swear I saw a hand. I thought he was reaching for the open window."

"Maybe he got scared off."

Mike was less sympathetic.

"Yeah, or maybe Janine is fucking crazy. Seeing things."

"I'm not crazy."

"Fucking Night Stalker isn't just going to get scared away."

"It could have been anybody. Maybe a burglar. Someone who didn't know if anyone was home. When he heard Janine scream, he probably split."

"Maybe he's crouched down under the window and you just couldn't see him. He might pop up any second and smash the glass. I'm calling 9-1-1 anyway. I'm not taking any chances."

"9-1-1's going to be pissed. You know how many false-alarm Night Stalker calls they probably get a night?"

"I don't care. I'm calling."

Janine and Michelle disappeared to the living room.

"Fuck, this city is gripped."

"What do you mean?"

"Captivated. Held captive. The crazy bastard could be miles across town, but people here are freaking out, acting like prisoners in their own homes."

"Nothing wrong with being careful. His victims probably weren't careful enough."

"City's gripped, dude. Gripped."

Bruce

The Denny's on Sunset was packed as usual, but they didn't have to wait long for a table.

"Hey, you ever notice that this place is always packed, but there's never a line for a table?"

"What do you mean?"

"I mean just what I said. The place is always packed, but you're always first to get a table. There's never a long line."

"That's because it's Denny's."

"What difference does that make?"

"If it were a nice restaurant, they'd have a line. People wait for a table at nice restaurants."

"Yeah? So why not wait here?"

"Because it's not very good food. It's not worth waiting for. People walk in and see a line, they're going to bail. They'll find something else, no problem. It's just Denny's."

"Yeah, but there's never a line to be seen. How do they know to bail?"

"What?"

"How do they know to bail?"

"They don't have to know to bail. They just do. You don't know how to bail. You just do it if you don't want to wait around."

"Right, but with no line, they won't have to wait around."

"You're killing me, Bruce. Do you two have to argue about this now? I just want to sit."

"We're going to sit, Princess Catherine. We just have to wait for a table.

Something Glen here thinks we shouldn't be doing. Or know how to do in the first place."

"I never said—"

"Hey, cut it out! Both of you. Jesus."

"What do you think, Paul?"

"I don't know. Denny's sucks. What's the big deal?"

"See that? Side with your brother. Go ahead."

"I wasn't even listening to you guys."

"Here we go, our table, guys. Yes!"

They were led through the crowded room to a small booth. Catherine and Glen shared one side while Bruce and Paul took the other.

"You guys getting anything?"

"Yeah, you?"

"Loan me a couple bucks, will ya?"

"You don't have money for just fries?"

"I don't want just fries. I want a Super Bird. C'mon, just tack the difference on your share of the check."

"I guess so. Paul, you having anything?"

"Super Bird."

"Alright! My man! Super Bird! Put it there, little man."

Bruce extended his hand to meet Paul's high five, but Paul just stared at him.

"I'm not high fiving you in Denny's. Maybe at a Dodger game or something, but not here."

"That's the way, Paul. He just wants to get in good with you so you'll lend him money next time."

The four of them ordered and passed the time looking through an *LA Weekly* at the upcoming schedules of the clubs they liked. When Catherine was done, she passed it to Paul so he could look at the comics.

"You shoot the show tonight, Bruce?"

"You saw me there, didn't you?"

"I don't pay attention to you. The only reason people see you is because you're so freakin' tall."

"Of course I shot the show. Ron likes my work."

"You should ask him to do his next album. Or maybe he can use some of your live shots in the liner notes."

"Maybe. Keel, man! Ron was on fire tonight. And Marc Ferrari? Insane!"

Bruce played a riff on air guitar in front of his mouthful of gritted teeth.

"Hey guys!"

Daisy called to them from a booth in the corner.

"Oh, hey Daisy."

"You guys like Keel?"

"Yeah, they were awesome."

"Woo hoo!"

Daisy was with three other guys who looked a little embarrassed when she raised her voice.

"Who's she with, Glen?"

"I don't know. I think they were at the show, though."

"She's going to take three guys home tonight?"

"I wouldn't put it past her."

"Hosebag."

"Bruce, leave her alone. I've known far worse."

"Yeah, like who, Princess? I didn't think princesses hung out with slutty girls."

"Stop calling me princess. And what? You want me to get the slutty girls' numbers for you?"

"No, thanks. Hey, speaking of numbers, though. Check out that blonde in that booth over there. You guys seeing this?"

"The one with the bandana or the other one?"

"The one with the bandana."

"Yeah, she's not bad. You going to do something?"

"Heck yeah, I'm going to do something. You got a pen?"

"No. You going to write her a note?"

Bruce had already bolted to his feet and made a beeline to the waitress station.

"Dani, I'm grabbing a pen from here! I'll give it right back, I swear!"

Nobody heard any objections, and Bruce was back in an instant. He grabbed a napkin and started writing.

"What are you going to say?"

"You'll see."

After a minute, he handed the napkin to Glen.

"'I can die happy now because I've just seen a slice of heaven.' Geez, man."

"What do you think? What do you think, Catherine? Would that work on you?"

"Hell, no. I have more self-respect than that."

"What do you mean, 'self-respect.' Respect has nothing to do with it. I'm just paying her a compliment."

"You just gonna hand that to her or give her your number or something?"

"I'm not done. Let me have it back. I'm writing my number."

"You're never there, Bruce."

"No big deal. My dad can take messages."

In another minute, the three of them were watching in anticipation as Bruce slowly sidled up to the girls' table. He placed the napkin delicately in front of the blonde with the bandana, turned slowly enough to avoid looking like he was making a quick getaway, and then casually strolled back to their table.

"What's she doing? I don't want to stare. Paul, you have a good angle. What's she doing?"

"Nothing. It looks like she read it. But her expression hasn't changed. She's just sitting there. Now her friend is reading it."

"Are they looking interested or are they laughing?"

"Hey, shut up, Catherine!"

"What? I'd be laughing. Laughing might be good. They might be giddy with embarrassment. Are they blushing, Paul?"

"I don't think so. No laughing, either. They're just talking like before."

"She probably gets napkins dropped on her all the time."

"What a bitch! She could have at least acknowledged me. Smiled or something. Or at least like shook her head no. But nothing? She's acting like nothing happened?"

"That's what I'd do. I'd be too creeped out to make any sudden moves."

"You're no help, Catherine."

"I think she's got a point."

"You're no help either, Glen."

Unexpectedly, a guy in ripped jeans at the table across the aisle leaned over and offered his take on the situation.

"Sorry, dude. I think she wiped her mouth with it."

Bruce looked at him, not surprised that others around him could overhear his failure.

"I don't care if she wiped her ass with it."

Glen nearly spit out a mouthful of water on the approaching waitress.

"Who had the Super Birds?"

"Right here, Dani. Can I get a napkin, please?"

"Yeah, can I get my pen back?"

Charlie

"Welcome to the reactor, Mike! Welcome to the reactor!"

Mike was making a beeline to the Troubadour's foyer doors to secure a spot close to the stage when he was intercepted by Charlie who practically leapt into his arms from the bar.

"Whoa, Charlie. Good to see you, too. You been drinking?"

"Come into the bar, Mike. I've got to tell you something."

"Nah, I'm heading in, man. I want to grab a spot up front."

"No, really Mike. It's important. It'll take like one minute. Just come in the bar first."

The way Charlie insisted, Mike half expected someone to be waiting beyond the bar entrance with a baseball bat, ready to beat him over the head and flee with his cash. If it were his birthday, he would have assumed Charlie had been hurriedly elected to lure him to his surprise party.

"Just tell me here, Charlie. What difference does it make?"

"No, Mike. No. Just follow me. Pleeeeease?"

Mike was used to seeing Charlie in various stages of declining sobriety. This was close to a record, however. It wasn't even 9:00, and he already looked and acted completely wasted.

"Alright, man. If it's so important to you."

"Thanks, buddy. Hey, I want you to meet . . . um . . ."

Charlie led them to the first table past the doorway. Two nondescript metalheads were seated there with 7&7s. Long hair. Leather. One wore blue jeans. They could have been in a band, but so could 90 percent of the club. They looked a little annoyed that Charlie had returned.

"This is um . . . hey, what are you guys' names again?"

"Frankie and Jamie."

"Oh yeah. Mike, this is Frankie and Jamie. We just met when I got this crazy idea. And then I saw you out the window, so I had to jump you, man. I had to bring you in here to meet them and tell you."

Mike shook hands with the guys at the table and said hello in a way that he hoped conveyed that he had nothing to do with Charlie's behavior. They smiled at him in a way that he took to mean they'd prefer he and Charlie leave them alone.

"This is Mike, guys. He's cool."

Charlie turned to face Mike as if the next words he spoke were a secret of the privileged.

"I was in the bar here. And I heard Jamie say—"

"I'm Frankie."

"What?"

"I'm Frankie. Whatever, dude. Just tell your story."

"Ah, right. It was Frankie. I heard Frankie say . . . Frankie, what the fuck did you say?"

"Nothing to you, man. Nothing to you."

Mike smiled as if to apologize.

"Right, but I heard it . . . Oh yeah! Frankie said, 'That band was like a nuclear bomb went off' or something like that. Didn't you, Frankie?"

"Something like that."

"Yeah, and it gave me this idea. You know this club?"

"Yes?"

"You know this club?"

"Of course I know this club, Charlie. I've only been coming here for like eight years."

"Right. Ok, you know this club. This club . . . get this, Mike. This club . . . it's the nuclear reactor!"

"Yeah?"

"Yeah, man! It's the nuclear reactor! And the bands . . . the bands are the nuclear reaction inside the reactor. The bands create the power! Get it?"

"Yeah, I get it Charlie."

"No you don't. Because the best thing of all . . . the best thing . . . what are we?"

"Huh?"

"What are we, Mike? What are we?"

"Uh . . . fans?"

"Yeah, fans. What are we? The fans . . . what are the fans?"

"I don't know, man."

"We're the uranium! We're the fucking uranium, man!"

"Okay."

"Yeah, see . . . they put us in the reactor. We go in the reactor, the music hits us, and BOOM!"

Several heads turned, saw Charlie, and immediately turned back.

"Not so loud, man."

"Sorry . . . Boom. We generate the power. I mean, we help the bands generate the power. The reactor needs the uranium to get that reaction! And we're the fucking uranium, man!"

"I get it, Charlie."

"No, but what you don't get yet . . . you don't get yet . . . is that, after the show?"

"Yeah?"

"After the show? The power doesn't stop going when you shut down the reactor. The uranium keeps on generating power. It's radioactive! And it just keeps on making heat and power, and it doesn't stop."

"Okay."

"So, they have to open the doors!"

"What?"

"They have to open the doors, man! Of the reactor. They have to cool the place off or there'll be a meltdown! And all that heat . . . all that power . . . it's got to be released! So, they open the doors, man. They have to open those doors to let the pressure and steam out. It escapes into the streets! It goes spilling out into the street. Right on Santa Monica Boulevard. And all the way down Melrose, man!"

"Yeah, I guess that's what we do, man."

"Fuck yeah, that's what we do! We're the uranium, man! The reactor can't run without the uranium!"

"No, I guess it can't. Where did you learn all this, Charlie?"

"Oh, I've been watching a lot of PBS. There was this show on about Three Mile Island. Scary shit. But very educational."

"Nice, Charlie. Nice. You keep learning. C'mon, why don't you say goodbye to your friends here and come inside the showroom with me. I think there's a spot with your name on it right up next to the stage."

"Alright, Mike."

The two at the table allowed themselves to look grateful for a second.

Charlie left them without a parting word. He followed Mike back into the foyer and through the double doors into the showroom.

Those drinking at the bar could faintly hear his excited voice before the doors swung shut.

"We are the uranium! We are the uranium, man!"

Summer

PAUL WASN'T MUCH for mingling away from his brother's side, but he decided he'd give the Rainbow parking lot a once over. He ducked around a small crowd that had placed itself smack in the middle of the driveway's mouth, walking circuitously enough to make himself look weak for not just barging right through their little klatch. After regaining a position in the center of the lot, a few bodies unexpectedly shifted in front of him and he found himself face to face with a tall woman with a cascade of lush brown ringlets framing a perfect smile.

Summer.

He was immediately caught off guard but forced himself to greet her.

"Hey, I know you! I talked to you after the Pandemonium show at the Roxy a few months ago!" This was the best he could do. He meant to say he was happy to see her—had been thinking about her more than he'd care to admit, actually. But what came out sounded like a feigned delay of recognition and feigned wonder at the probability of running into her again at another show, on another weekend like so many weekends before.

"Yeah, that's right. Tell me your name."

Crap. It would have meant so much if she'd have remembered his name. But he didn't exactly throw it around much. Most just called him Glen's little brother.

"Paul."

"Hi, Paul. Good to see you again."

Obligatory. It's always good to see people again. Even when it has absolutely no impact on the quality of your night whatsoever.

"Yeah . . . good to see you."

He had nothing more, at least not while making eye contact with that smile.

"So, are you taking my advice?"

"Sorry?"

"My advice. Are you getting out and seeing new things?"

"You remember that?"

"Of course I do. You just never told me your name. But I remember everything."

"Oh, that's cool. I don't know. I guess I'm trying to get out a little. My friend and I discovered this little club. It's called the Lhasa Club. Have you heard of it?"

"Sounds exotic. No, I haven't."

"Yeah, most people probably haven't. It's pretty small. It's down Santa Monica a ways. In a seedier part of Hollywood."

"Seedier than the Strip? That's saying something."

"Yeah, it's pretty dark. They have strange bands there. Pretty experimental stuff. Nothing like this."

"Well, it's good to experiment."

He wondered if this was an invitation to ask her out. He suddenly wondered what she'd think of the Lhasa Club. He immediately decided it was too weird, too risky a place to bring anybody who wasn't already madly in love with him. He wanted to ask her out somewhere, though. Despite the fact she was obviously considerably older than he and would probably laugh at the idea. But there wasn't anywhere he could think of that would impress her. He felt useless standing there in silence trying to think of a place.

"Well, I should let you get back to your conversation."

"That's alright. This is a conversation, too. I like talking to you."

"You do?"

"Sure."

He felt he needed something to engage her. He needed something to keep her there. He needed a connection, and he couldn't believe Summer was there and seemingly receptive. He leaned a little closer than he felt was appropriate. It was frustrating how awkward this woman made him feel, but he was past the point of no return.

"Can I ask you something?"

Her eyes widened slightly but her smile didn't waver.

"Anything."

"Do you ever get tired of it? I mean—"

"I know what you mean. No, not really."

"I mean, this whole scene. You know what it feels like to me sometimes?"

"What?"

"No offense or anything. Because you seem different. But it seems like so many people here are just living sort of dead-end lives."

"How so?"

"Well, they seem to have ordinary lives during the week that they aren't too happy with. Nobody is really doing much out there. And then the weekend comes and they get dressed up and go out to the clubs. It's like the highlight of their week. Like they're only living for Friday and Saturday night."

"You could look at it that way."

"Isn't it a little sad? I mean, that's why I ask. Don't you ever get tired of it? That routine?"

"I see what you mean. I get it, I really do. And I guess you can say I live a little for the weekend too. It's a lot more exciting out here than what's going on the rest of the week, for sure. But . . ."

"But, what?"

"But, I don't have any regrets."

"None?"

"None. There's nothing wrong with doing what makes you happy. And this makes me happy. I don't have to do it. I choose it. I feel a part of it, and I enjoy it. I've got some really close friends here. And I love the music. That's why we're all here, right?"

"I guess so."

"So, I'm having a good time. And what's wrong with that? If I had to go back in time and do it all over again, I'd be right here."

"Good for you."

"Yeah, damn right, good for me. And good for you. Life's too short."

"Yeah. Okay. Thanks for answering that for me."

"No problem."

He didn't know where to go next. He just tried not to make it look obvious that he was content to simply keep staring at her smile.

"Paul?"

"Yeah?"

"No regrets."

He had only begun to nod in agreement before she was gone.

Daisy

Denny's was crowded, but a table was waiting for them.

Glen and Paul piled in on one side of a booth. Daisy and Janine slid into the other.

"Where's Catherine, Glen? I never see her around."

"I'm not sure what she's up to tonight. She doesn't come out as often as she used to."

"What's going on with her? She find a boyfriend or something?"

"I don't think so. I mean, I don't know. She doesn't tell me much."

"You should tell her to come hang out with us. I like her. She's sweet."

"Sure, I'll let her know you asked about her."

Janine suddenly perked up.

"Hey, Paul. What do you think? Ozzy solo or Ozzy with Black Sabbath? Are you old enough to know Black Sabbath?"

"Of course I know Black Sabbath. But I'll take Ozzy solo any day."

"Really?"

"Yeah."

"Why?"

"Randy Rhoads. He was awesome. Totally made Ozzy's solo career. I don't think Ozzy would be who he is today without Randy. He'd just be Ozzy from Black Sabbath."

"But Tony Iommi, dude."

"Yeah. Tony Iommi is overrated."

"Oh my god. Most people I know are huge Black Sabbath fans. They'd fucking kill you if they were here right now. Iommi is like fucking God. What do you think, Daisy?"

"What do I think, what?"

"Ozzy solo or Ozzy with Black Sabbath?"

"I don't care."

"How can you not care?"

"Because I don't."

"What do you think, Glen?"

"Ozzy solo."

"See?"

"Geez, what the hell is wrong with you people? Black Sabbath is like . . . c'mon . . . Sabbath!"

"Yeah, whatever."

Bruce suddenly appeared, looming larger than life over the table.

"Look who I found! You guys like the show? Geoff Tate . . . Insane!"

"Yeah, great show. You wanna sit down?"

"Sure. Never thought you'd ask. You girls going to squish together and let me in or what?"

"Eww, no! There's no room. And you look like you need a shower."

"Hey, I've been about five feet away from Queensrÿche, covered in sweaty bodies all night."

Bruce grabbed an empty chair nearby and clumsily plopped it alongside their table. He fell into it, half blocking the aisle.

"Oh sure. You don't ask the guys to squish together and sit with them."

"Guys don't have pussies, ladies."

"Fuck off, Bruce."

"Well, maybe Paul here does."

"Hey!"

"Leave him alone, Bruce."

"Just kidding, little man."

"Ask Bruce."

"Ask me what, little man?"

"Ask him, Janine."

"Okay, Bruce. Who do you like better, Ozzy solo or Ozzy with Black Sabbath?"

"Oh, give me a break. Don't even ask me that."

"Why not?"

Glen and Paul tried to stifle their laughter.

"Are you fucking kidding me? Hello? Randy Rhoads? Ozzy solo. Ozzy is the luckiest son of a bitch on the planet. His career would have gone nowhere if he didn't meet Randy."

"See?"

"Well, he's biased. He's a Randy freak. I heard you take girls to the cemetery where he's buried and have sex on his grave."

"You heard what?"

"A rumor that's floating around. That you do that with girls."

Glen interrupted.

"That couldn't possibly be true."

"Why not?"

"Because if Bruce were getting laid, we'd all be hearing about it from him."

"Very funny. The question you should be asking is Ozzy Black Sabbath or Ronnie James Dio Black Sabbath. That's a question."

"Oh c'mon, Bruce. Ozzy Sabbath. No doubt."

"I don't know. Ronnie is pretty insane. I'm leaning toward Dio."

"Wait, Dio with Black Sabbath or Dio solo?"

"Shut up. This is getting out of control."

The waitress came over to take their orders. Everyone was set on what they wanted by that point. She asked Bruce last.

"I'll just have a side of fries. Unless you guys want to donate to the Feed Bruce Foundation."

"No, that's alright Bruce."

"Side of fries, then, Dani."

The waitress had begun to walk away before Bruce realized he had forgotten something."

"Hey, Dani?"

"Yeah?"

"Ozzy solo or Ozzy with Black Sabbath?"

"Huh? Oh, Ozzy solo. I'm not a big fan of Black Sabbath."

"Aha! I rest my case!"

Janine simply shook her head and looked at Dani as if she had betrayed her. Dani left without saying another word.

"You really think Dani listens to Ozzy? That's kind of hot."

"Shut up, Bruce."

"What? You'd do her if you were a guy. Or maybe a girl."

"Hey, speaking of getting laid, tell Janine what you did in the mall the other day."

"What?"

"Oh, c'mon Bruce. With Daisy? Probably to annoy Daisy?"

"Oh, yeah. You tell her, Daisy."

"He walked around the Glendale Galleria with a giant panda down his pants."

"A what?"

"Not a real one. A stuffed one. A stuffed panda. One of those huge ones, like you see people win at carnivals. He stuck the head down his pants like it was giving him head and walked around the whole mall with it."

"Where'd you get it?"

"That's what you ask? 'Where did you get it?' Who cares where he got it. He's perverted. It's gross."

"I just did it to embarrass Daisy. She was bright red. Everyone was staring."

"Why do you guys fight so much? It's because you secretly love each other, I bet."

"Yeah, right."

"I'm sure. Don't gross me out, Janine."

"Well, who do you love, Daisy?"

"I don't love anyone, you know that."

"No, she loves everyone. That's her problem."

"Fuck you, Bruce."

"Geez, guys, can you believe this?"

Glen and Paul sat silently. Janine insisted.

"C'mon Daisy, there's got to be someone special in your life."

"Like Jesus."

"Shut up, Bruce!"

"Alright, alright."

"No, Janine. There's no one. Why is that a problem?"

"I never said it was a problem."

"I mean, it's the whole scene. If I love anything, it's that I love the whole scene."

"But I mean a person."

"It is like a person. One, big collective person."

Bruce snickered into his palm.

"What?"

"I'm keeping my mouth shut. Don't tell me to shut up and then ask me 'what?'"

"Why are you laughing?"

"Well, if you think the scene is like one big person, it's like you have to have sex with everyone in the scene to equal having sex with the person. And you seem to be making progress, Daisy."

"Okay, forget I asked. Shut up again, Bruce."

"Told ya."

"I mean, why are you so wrapped up in my sex life? What business is it of yours who I'm having sex with? And what business is it of yours who I love?"

Janine bristled.

"Sorry, I was just asking. But, you are a little obsessed, Bruce."

"Obsessed with what?"

"Daisy. You always criticize her but then it's like you are really interested in who she's with and what she's doing."

"I am not."

"Yes, you are."

"Well, maybe I'm just looking out for my little hosebag."

"God! Shut the fuck up, Bruce!"

People at nearby tables stopped talking and turned their heads.

"Hey, Daisy, you're going to get us thrown out of here again. We're lucky the manager even let us in tonight."

"Sorry, Glen. Just tell your friend to shut up."

"Glen . . ."

"Seriously, Bruce. Leave her alone. Just shut up."

"Okay, okay."

The waitress arrived with a tray full of plates. They made room for her to deliver each one. Bruce liked her smile. She never seemed frustrated by him.

"So, Dani . . . Ozzy solo, huh?"

"Heck yeah. Randy Rhoads. Are you kidding me?"

She smiled again as she left.

"Okay, you want to know who I'm in love with, Janine?"

"Not really, Bruce."

"Dani, man. Insane!"

Tim

He usually hung out in the bar until they asked him to leave. And lately, they pretended not to notice. They may not have pretended—you'd have to lower your gaze quite a bit to find him in a crowd of boots and stiletto heels. It's not like he'd drink if they were to serve him. He just liked the crowd there. There was something more warm and friendly about the dimly lit bar compared to the sidewalk and glaring streetlights outside.

The youngest on the scene, he felt well-known, and took comfort in the fact that most everyone was very welcoming and friendly to him. Only a few drunk assholes would make the occasional predictable jokes about being out past bedtime or shine spotlights on his innocence and virginity. Once, he was accused of being too young to have pubic hair. But for the most part, even though he never engaged in conversations, he got accepting handshakes from the guys and sweet smiles from the girls. He didn't mind too much that they were the same smiles reserved for puppies and kittens and meant nothing more in the way of physical attraction.

"Hey, little man. Didn't I see you at Judas Priest?"

He didn't have much of a memory for faces but was pretty sure he'd never seen this guy before. And he missed the Judas Priest show at the Long Beach Arena everyone was raving about.

"No. Sorry. Not me. I didn't go to that show."

"Oh, okay, man. Not to worry. There was a young guy backstage that you remind me of."

His first thought was to be impressed this guy was not only there but also backstage at one of the most talked about concerts of the year. People assumed Tim went backstage to any show he wanted because of his father's connections, but that was not the case. He rarely even got tickets. His father almost never cashed in favors for Tim's benefit. His second thought was that this guy was just looking for an opportunity to broadcast through the bar that he was backstage at Judas Priest in hopes that some hot chicks might hear him. What a tool. But he seemed nice enough. He talked to Tim like he was a real person, not some stupid little kid hanging out where he didn't belong. He didn't even seem fazed that someone Tim's age was socializing in the bar.

Tim figured he'd try being more social for a change.

"It was a great show, I hear."

"Yeah, it was. Pretty cool."

Tim mistook what he would soon realize as modesty for a sudden lack of interest in conversing with such a child. Still, there was something very easygoing, friendly, and nonjudgmental about the man. Tim had already decided he liked him. He thought a logical question would be to ask how he got backstage but feared it might come across as a test to see if the guy was lying to him about it. He decided against it but felt the need to try to continue the conversation.

"Um . . . are you in a band?"

It was a safe question. Any dude with long hair and fairly nice clothes was in a band. Most of the guys in the bar on any given night were in bands. Some of the girls too.

His new friend allowed a slight smile to creep across his face but never revealed if the question was a blow to his ego as Tim later feared it was. He nodded only slightly and pointed at something on the other side of the bar over Tim's head. Tim turned, and there on the wall, amid several others, was a band poster. It was a studio shot of Great White. And posing front and center in the picture, trying not to look like he was posing, was the man Tim was talking to.

It took a fraction of a second to recall that Great White had opened for Judas Priest at the Long Beach Arena.

Embarrassment for both of them overwhelmed him, but Tim tried to keep a composed demeanor.

"Oh . . . .wow . . . yeah, that's impressive. I'm sorry I didn't—"

"That's okay." He held out his hand. "I'm Jack."

He introduced himself as if Tim still didn't know who he was. There was not a drop of arrogance added to the exchange despite the greater rift between them one might perceive from such a revelation. Jack didn't seem the least bit bothered by not being recognized. Maybe he could excuse it by Tim's age and apparent lack of experience, but Tim sensed that he was speaking to a man who had a firm grasp on the reality that he was not quite a headliner. And even if he were a headliner, he'd still be generous enough to speak to a wide-eyed young fan as if he were just another guy in the bar.

After they shook hands, Tim made a conscientious effort to maintain the conversation with the same level of interest and energy. He didn't want to come across as either a groupie or a stammering idiot who isn't used to being in the presence of someone who's actually experienced a bit of success in the business. People also assumed that since his father had connections in the music industry, Tim was frequently in the presence of famous musicians. But this was also untrue. Aside from letting him walk down the hill to the clubs, Tim's father sheltered him from the business and especially his clients.

Tim found it hard to think of what to say next. There were suddenly so many questions that he couldn't ask, questions too personal or too much from the perspective of an outsider looking in. He secretly wanted to hear about everything that went on backstage at Judas Priest. Everything. But he censored every question as coming from the mouth of an innocent amateur. He wanted Jack to believe that this was just another night for him in the bar at the Troubadour.

Jack got pulled away suddenly, into a social circle too tight for Tim to crack by tagging along.

"Hey, it was nice meeting you." Jack extended his hand again.

"Yeah, thanks. Nice meeting you, too. Take it easy."

He wanted to say he hoped to see him again sometime, but even that made him sound like a groupie in awe of the rock star. He was gone before another word could escape Tim's mouth.

Mike

He walked the streets alone. He did that once in a while. He liked the solitude, especially after being crammed shoulder to shoulder with a roomful of sweaty people for the past three hours. The Whisky emptied a bit earlier than expected, and instead of making the trek up the hill to stand outside the Rainbow, he headed east.

He didn't provide an explanation. It was not necessary. Friends who knew him well enough knew this was just something he did from time to time. As if he had to. No one ever worried about him. Mike could take care of himself.

For several blocks, Sunset was rife with the usual amount of Saturday night traffic. Where the Strip started to twist and turn among giant billboards and entertainment industry office buildings, he remained walking straight on Holloway, passing quiet apartments, well-manicured hedges, and jacaranda trees. Only a few cars passed by in this half-mile stretch. The quiet helped his mind wander.

He thought of his mother and how quickly her health had deteriorated. She required an oxygen tank around the clock now. He wondered how much longer she'd be alive. He wondered if his sister would want to stay in the house after she was gone or sell it. He wondered if they'd maybe rent out part of it or continue to take in others for free like their mother had, giving guys in the scene a place to stay and something to eat once in a while lest they starve on the streets. This led his mind to a sense of relief of having his own apartment. But he laughed to himself that the place obviously didn't mean much, with him preferring to walk great distances to find a little solitude rather than slink home and have all he wanted. He felt guilty about the place, too. His mom busted her ass to take care of him all his life. And now that she needed to be taken care of, he was gone. To take his mind off this, he thought of his job, but only briefly. It was rather mundane. But he thought of the sacrifices he made to keep it, telling the guys in Poison they'd have to find another roadie. Then his mother returned to his thoughts, thinking about how she had helped those guys so much. He remembered wondering if she loved some wannabe rock stars who liked to wear her clothes more than she loved her own son. Guilt returned. Had the decision to leave Poison damaged their friendship? Despite everything his mother had given them? He hadn't seen any evidence of this. He felt they were still friends. Then he wondered if he even had any genuine friends. He pondered the strength of friendships forged on these streets. He assumed them to be stronger than others founded in more traditional circumstances—but he wondered. The scene had its artifice. Why shouldn't the friendships crafted there have it too?

He passed Barney's, voices spilling from its capacity crowd. He quickened his pace past the lot until he had crossed Santa Monica. He continued east with no idea how far he'd go. Santa Monica was quieter than Sunset but not by much. Steady streams of cars slowly filed down each lane. He thought again of guilt. He wasn't religious, but he wondered if he needed salvation. Forgiveness. Absolution. He played with this last word in his mouth, silently repeating it to himself. He remembered having first heard it in high school. Absolution. Absolution is the solution. Absolution is restitution. Absolution is an institution. Absolution from prostitution. He toyed with the rhymes and smiled to himself.

He thought again of his friends. Many of the fans he hung out with every weekend were friends. He had no doubt they'd always be there for him. He thought of the other bands he knew. He wondered if any of them considered him a friend. He was a friend as long as he came to the clubs and bought tickets and brought others to do the same. He was a friend if

he helped pass out flyers. He was a friend if he hauled gear. But he wondered if anyone got signed, would he still be a friend then?

He came across a 7-Eleven in a strip mall just before Fairfax. He decided to drop in and buy a Coke. He stopped short of the door when he
heard a bellowing voice coming from the space next-door. He shifted his
direction to get closer while stepping back to look up at the sign. It was an
income tax preparation company office. Large vertical blinds were drawn
in the windows to prevent him from seeing much inside. Through the
cracks between slats, he could make out a large crowd of people. It was
dark inside, but colorful lights were flashing. The voice boomed through a
microphone, and Mike quickly realized it was speaking Spanish. It sounded
like a vivacious church sermon of some kind. He laughed to himself at the
thought of a Catholic church taking up residence after hours in a tax office. He searched for a connection there but found only conflicts of interest. Judging from the frequent ovations from the congregation however,
the voice seemed to speak of a truth that was very important to them. He
could only make out a few words here and there.

Nuestras almas . . .

A raucous response punctuated every sentence.

Espiritu . . .

His mind flashed to standing outside the Rainbow and Roxy, and
hearing no sound carrying outside from within.

Nos bendiga . . .

Passersby would never know the intensity or the depth of the ocean of
sound inside the clubs.

Nuestro sacramento . . .

He wondered if larger venues also sounded so subdued from the street.
He'd never been by one during a show without having gone inside.

Sangre de cristo . . .

Church.

Nuestro salvador . . .

He had his own church. They all did. And they sought salvation every weekend.

De la vida en calles . . .

But he didn't know what it meant to be blessed.

Los calles de los angeles . . .

The crowd roared approval as he stood frozen in front of the window.

He suddenly strained to extricate himself from the sermon, as if he were moments from bursting through the door and imploring their acceptance. He walked nine more blocks before realizing he had forgotten the Coke.

From the Whisky, he had traveled two miles. The sign before him on the corner of Vista and Santa Monica read Oki Dog. People filled the tables outside under a canopy of potted trees. The line for food inside went nearly out the door. Another that originated outside at a window went around the side of the building. At one table, a tattooed man in his forties held court among a throng of rapt teenagers holding skateboards.

He wondered what it was like to be a disciple. He wondered if he already was one. Maybe he could save himself. Or maybe he didn't need saving. He was curious what the man could have been saying to such an attentive audience. But the feeling he didn't belong crept over him once again, and he forced himself to move on.

He turned around and walked back to Sunset.

Paul

Suppliants
Banging your heads against an altar every night
Is there salvation
Through six strings and the thousand decibel screams?

I stand in the dark, baptized by the light
Kliegs and spots
And the cityscape's billion stars

I don't believe in prayer
Every hymn of praise
Leaves silently from gaping mouths
Instantly devoured by the sound waves
Awash over all

But the chanting masses
Have faith
Believe their offerings are bestowed upon some great receiver
Instead of deaf ears

Salvation is a tricky thing

To be saved
One has to believe he has been led astray
To be found

Is to admit you have been lost

To be pure
Is to embrace the derelict grit
And to not only accept it

But to hold it dear

1986

Charlie

THE SIDEWALKS WERE still damp from the day's rain. That didn't stop
Charlie from sitting on the curb, legs splayed across the gutter, daring the
cars on Sunset to clip his feet. He stared at the asphalt, darkened by mois-
ture, and watched to see how many tires would hit the little puddle in front
of him before it was dissipated into oblivion.

The headliner at the Roxy had only been on stage for twenty minutes,
but Mike emerged from the sweatbox of sound to check out the scene outside. He'd seen Armored Saint so many times recently, he decided to grab
some fresh air. Charlie was alone among the traffic. Both the Rainbow and
Roxy hummed with capacity crowds, but no one else was on the sidewalk
at the moment. He sat down on the curb beside Charlie before realizing
how wet it was.

"Hey, Charlie Tuna! What's up?"

"Don't call me that, man."

"Charlie Tuna?"

"Yeah. I don't even like Starkist. Chicken of the Sea, man."

"Not Charlie the tuna. Charlie Tuna. The DJ. The guy on the radio."

"Charlie Tuna is like some sort of orca and shit."

"Orca?"

"Yeah. Killer whale, man."

"No, the DJ, not the . . . wait . . . you think Charlie Tuna is an orca?"

"Yeah, he looks like one. All big and black and white."

"He's a tuna. His name is Tuna. He sells tuna. Why would an orca sell
tuna?"

"I don't know. They're all fish."

"A tuna . . . . What? Dude, an orca is not a fish."

"It lives in the ocean. It swims. It's a fucking fish, man."

"An orca is a whale, and whales are mammals."

"No way, man."

"So are dolphins."

"What?"

"Mammals. Dolphins are also mammals."

"I know dolphins are mammals. They breathe air."

"But you just said if it swims in the ocean it's a fish."

"No I didn't. I said whales and orcas swim in the ocean."

"But so do dolphins and they are mammals. So why can't a whale?"

"Because whales suck, man. Never mind. Just don't call me a whale. And don't call me an orca. Or a tuna."

"I'm not calling you a tuna. I'm calling you a DJ. Haven't you heard of him?"

"A DJ named after an orca?"

"No, a DJ named after a tuna."

Charlie leapt to his feet suddenly. There was a couple leaving the Rainbow just then, and he ran over to them. Charlie had no fear of strangers.

"Hey, man. Sorry, lady and man. Let me ask you a question."

The couple stopped walking and stared at him.

"Is Charlie Tuna an orca or a tuna?"

"Charlie Tuna the DJ?"

"NO!!! Not the fucking DJ!!! The orca. Or the tuna. You know . . . Starkist?"

"No, I don't."

"You don't eat tuna?"

"No."

"Aw, fuck you, man."

Charlie left the couple dumbstruck and returned to the curb. Mike shook his head and tried to hide his smile.

"Couldn't help you, huh?"

"No. Who the fuck hasn't heard of Starkist?"

"They knew Charlie Tuna, though."

"Stop fucking with my head, Mike."

"Sorry, Charlie."

Mike

IN THE END, all their mother wanted was to see her boys play one last time.

She had put a roof over their heads after they got kicked out of the apartment on Sweetzer. It was only a tiny guest house in the backyard of her rambler in the Valley, about as far removed from the Hollywood scene as you can get while staying within the city limits. But beggars can't be choosers, especially beggars with a lot of gear.

She had put food in their mouths when they'd be living on one or two Carl's Jr. or Naugles meals a day otherwise. She was stretched thin with Mike and Flor to raise—and Flor still living at home at that—but she didn't mind. She knew what their music meant to her kids.

She had even let them raid her closet when they were looking for scarves or boas to wear onstage. As if she'd ever own a boa. She never questioned their wardrobe choices or their use of hairspray, makeup, and lipstick. She refused to assume the role of nagging mother in some areas. She let them be whatever they wanted to be, as long as they didn't bring drugs into her house.

Like so many others, she cheered from afar after they made it. Like others, she never asked for any credit. Never bragged about having known them or having cared for them like they were her own sons. They didn't do a good job keeping in touch, but she didn't mind. She knew they were busy. That lifestyle makes it hard not to move on and become preoccupied by bigger and better things.

She worried that Mike might be bitter, having served as a roadie, only to quit six months before their big break because the hours of his paying job kept getting in the way of his ability to make it to load-ins on time. But he rarely showed it. He'd talk about how he almost got to go on the road with them. How he'd have been hanging out with established bands like Ratt and Quiet Riot. But he did so with reverence in his voice, never regret. He seemed to accept the choices he made and the chances he'd lost. Everyone in the family couldn't help but gasp in muted envy when a video clip of them playing in a sold-out stadium emerged. But after a while, genuine happiness for the once-starving artists tempered any woeful feelings about what might have been.

That night had been magical. A private concert for a select few in the very backyard in which they'd taken refuge when it felt like no one was listening. Their mother beamed all night, walking on air if she could only stand. Even the neighbors didn't mind. Great cover band, they must have thought.

There's still a photo from that night on Flor's dresser. Sitting in her wheelchair, an electric guitar across her lap, Rikki's hands seen sneaking through her armpits to prop it up from behind, fingers from both of her hands tap dancing across the fretboard like she were Eddie Van Halen with an oxygen tank, flanked by Brett and C.C., each holding his own guitar in the same pose—both hands hammering out a solo on the fretboard, heads cocked, faces scowling the put-on visage of self-proclaimed rock gods. Their mother wears the same hammy scowl—that same expression that tells you, this business . . . this business is difficult. So difficult, it's easy, if you've got the right attitude and the right swagger.

As easy as dying.

Delaney

"WOULD YOU LIKE something to drink?"

"Sure, that would be great."

Danny wound his way through the crowd to the keg in the corner. He filled two plastic cups while looking around the room for anyone else he might know. Only Glen and his brother were recognizable. He made his way back and handed a cup to Delaney.

"Thanks."

"It's Coors Light, I think."

"Okay."

"I mean, I'd expect even less at a party like this. Nobody in Hollywood has any money. So, Coors Light, you know . . ."

"I said it's okay. It's not a big deal. I'd drink whatever they had."

"Alright. I just . . ."

"Danny, relax. You don't have to be so uptight. I'm having a good time."

"Good. I'll try. Hey, Glen and his brother Paul are here. We should go say hi."

Delaney simply nodded and led the way across the room.

"Hey, Glen. Danny wanted to say hi."

"Hey, Delaney. I've introduced you to my brother Paul before, right?"

"Only every time I see you guys. Hey, Paul."

"Hey. This is our friend Justin."

Delaney didn't realize the guy standing behind Paul was part of their group. He had his back to them, staring at a group of guys sharing a beer bong. He said hello quickly and turned his attention back to them.

"Hiya, Glen, how ya doin'?"

"I'm good, Danny. You guys having a good time?"

"Yeah. I guess I should be thanking you for introducing us."

Delaney rolled her eyes but smiled.

"That's alright, man. No thanks necessary. No complaints, either."

"Har, har. Very funny."

"You know I like joking with you, Delaney."

"Yeah, huh? Hey, what did you think of the show, Paul?"

"It was cool. They sounded great. Probably better than the other times I've seen them."

"Yeah, The Brats. They kick ass. Do you still hang out with Paul Hansen, Glen?"

"Well, I talk to him when I see him. I talked to him a little tonight. But I wouldn't say we hang out."

"Your brother knows a lot of famous dudes. Or dudes that are going to be famous."

"I know a few. No big deal."

They chatted for several minutes while people filed in and out of the living room of the small apartment. Danny finally got the courage to ask Glen if he could speak to him in private. He wanted to report how the night was going and to ask advice about getting at least a good-night kiss out of it. Delaney felt it was obvious what his intentions were, but thought it was cute. She was left with Paul and Justin, and Justin still hadn't turned back around.

"You guys having fun?"

"Yeah."

"Doesn't your friend talk? What's his deal?"

"He does. He's just distracted. Sightseeing. He doesn't get out much."

"Ha. I get it. I might do a little sightseeing myself. Hard not to."

"Yeah, I guess."

"I'm going to find a bathroom. You guys need anything?"

"From the bathroom?"

"Har, har, very funny. You're like your brother, you know that?"

"No."

"Well you are. No, not from the bathroom. From anywhere."

"No, we're good."

"Alright. Stay out of trouble, you two."

"We will."

Delaney made her way across the living room, turning heads as she went.

Catherine

"HEY, I HAVEN'T seen you in a while."

"Yeah, I know, Paul. I haven't been coming out that much. Kinda took a break from the scene. You too, from what I've heard."

"Well, not much of a break. I still see a couple shows a month. Maybe every other weekend or so."

"Glen told me sometimes you stay home, or go out somewhere else with your friends. He made it sound more often. I bet he misses you when you're not around."

"Heh, yeah, right."

"No, really. I bet he does."

"He doesn't act like it."

"He acts like big brothers are supposed to act. That doesn't mean it's not true. Hey, here he comes. Pretend we aren't talking about him!"

She said this last part purposely so Glen could hear.

"Talking what about me?"

"Nothing, Glen. Just chatting with Paul. Your little brother is cool. What happened to you?"

"What do you mean? I'm cool too."

"Not nearly."

"I'm cool. Aren't I Paul?"

"I'm obviously cooler. According to Catherine, at least."

"Yeah, and I know cool when I see it."

"I bet you do. Hey, I was just coming over to borrow you for a second."

"For what?"

"I've been talking to Danny about Delaney. He's on a date with her tonight and nervous as hell. I'm giving him advice, but he doesn't trust what I'm saying. I told him I'd get you to provide him the female perspective. Would you mind?"

"Sure. I mean, no, I don't mind. Where is he?"

"Over by the keg, see?"

"Wow, he does look nervous. Delaney's not even around and he's nervous."

"Yep. I figure he'd believe advice coming from you. But don't let him know we talked about it. He'll think I spoon-fed you what to say."

A young woman interrupted suddenly, nearly stumbling between them in order to get close to Glen. She slurred her words conspicuously.

"Hey, you know who you look like?"

Glen was taken aback, but not totally shocked. He was used to drunk people in his face.

"No, who?"

"Brad Gillis from Night Ranger. Doesn't he look like Brad Gillis from Night Ranger?"

She appealed for verification from anyone nearby who was listening.

"I've heard that before, yes."

"Wait! Are you Brad Gillis from Night Ranger?"

"No, I'm not."

"Are you sure?"

Paul and Catherine laughed loudly.

"Yeah, I think I know who I am."

"No, I mean, are you sure you're not lying to me? Because you don't want me to bother you or ask for your autograph?"

"I'm sure I'm not lying. Sorry to disappoint you."

"So, you're not Brad Gillis from Night Ranger?"

Catherine intervened.

"He's the other Brad Gillis."

"Huh?"

"Stop it, Catherine. You're confusing her. No, I'm not Brad Gillis from Night Ranger or any other Brad Gillis for that matter."

"Oh, okay . . . Wait! You look like Sammy Hagar, then! Are you Sam— no, you're not Sammy Hagar, huh?"

"No, I'm not Sammy Hagar either. My name is Glen."

"Are you in a band, though? You look like you are in a band."

"I'm not in a band. I just enjoy the music."

"Oh, that sucks. You need to join a band, Brad."

"Glen."

"Huh?"

"My name is Glen."

"Oh yeah, huh? Not Brad. I'm sorry. I called him Brad, didn't I?"

Again, she appealed to anyone who would listen.

"Sorry to disappoint you, uh, what's your name?"

"Tracy."

"Sorry to disappoint you, Tracy."

"That's okay. Just join a band, Brad."

Again, Catherine and Paul had a hard time stifling their laughter.

"I'll try."

She made her way off to another group in the room.

"See that, Catherine? And you said I wasn't cool."

"Ha, yeah. If being cool means you look like cool people. You are in, man."

"Paul doesn't get mistaken for rock stars, do you, Paul?"

"No."

"Are you kidding me, Paul? Jimmy Page?"

"Oh yeah, I've gotten that before."

"Leave him alone, Catherine. You're going to give him a big ego."

"Hey, you should follow Tracy over there and tell her you're Jimmy Page. She'd probably believe you."

"Jimmy Page was my age in like 1960."

"She'll still believe you. She's wasted. Glen, you should have told her you were Brad Gillis. It would have made her freakin' week. Or year."

"Sorry, not into deception. Besides, I don't want her as a groupie."

"Your loss."

"Let's go talk to Danny before Delaney gets back and he screws everything up."

"Alright. Sit tight, Paul. We'll be back."

Paul turned around to find Justin who had ventured off a few paces closer to the beer bong. He sidled up next to him.

"See that drunk girl over there? She thinks my brother is Brad Gillis."

"Cool."

Delaney

SHE WASN'T GONE long. Men she encountered were never unwilling to expedite the process. She attributed their success to equal parts youthful enthusiasm, the excitement of the taboo, so easily stoked by the danger of getting caught, and her own alluring charms, not to mention technique. She put the most weight, erroneously enough, on the last of these, often underestimating how powerfully efficacious the first two can be for men in their youth.

She didn't mind the brevity. Satisfaction was highest at the initial point of contact, and being penetrated meant being victorious. It didn't matter how much longer it took to get things to a conclusion. The quicker the better, actually.

She never came. The concept itself, like her ability to achieve her own pleasurable ends, was far removed from her psyche. She couldn't, or so she thought, and so she didn't. From the initial contact, she was in control, men growing weaker in the knees by the second until nearly withering at their most vulnerable moment, and this was all the pleasure she desired. She owned them, and it was when they were at their strongest, before losing themselves inside her, that this realization was most fulfilling.

When she returned, she felt the need to explain the stain on her dress. She claimed she was in the bathroom and got splashed by water when the faucet came on stronger than expected. The fact she was in the bathroom was the only truth to the statement. Paul and Justin believed her, never questioning why she felt the need to explain herself so determinedly. Paul thought maybe she feared they would accuse her of peeing herself, but the stain was far too low on the dress for that to be realistic.

They probably wouldn't have even noticed it had she not brought it to their attention. They bought the water excuse, not imagining for a second a stain that size could be attributed to another source in a bathroom. They had no idea that more evidence of her encounter continued to drip down her thighs.

Delaney was grateful she didn't blush easily. She made a mental note to avoid that guy in the future. Far too large a load, she thought, smiling to herself and wondering how many people might catch on and realize what she'd been up to the last five minutes.

Glen

The crowd at the Palladium had been whipped into a frenzy before the headliner even took the stage. Anticipation surged through the group packed on the floor. Glen and Paul held their own among them a few bodies deep from the front. Every so often a surge would come over them. Bodies constricted and released in strong undulations, pushing ever closer to the stage. Several times, Paul felt his feet leave the floor. He'd get picked up, not by hands or arms but by the squeezing together of bodies on either side of him. He'd float like this for seconds until the pressure subsided and he was put back down. A few moments would pass and the pressure would return. After a few cycles of this, he noticed that a crack in the floor appeared a farther distance away. He wondered how many feet he could drift this way until the density of bodies between him and the stage grew too thick.

Glen had been slowly separated from him. It could have been because he weighed about fifty pounds more than Paul. He was able to root himself more firmly to the floor, resisting each surge as it came. It was as if Paul were being swept away in a riptide. It felt not unlike watching somebody drown in front of his eyes. He was about to call out to him to see if he was alright when the lights cut out and an explosion of sound overwhelmed his senses.

The first power chords through the Marshall stacks seemed to push the crowd back on its heels. For a fleeting moment, Glen felt blown back by the sound. Paul felt bodies rigidly stand at attention for a split second. Then drums and bass kicked in, laying down a driving rhythm. Finally, the singer took the stage, belting out the first words of the song.

Then the place erupted.

Paul and everyone around him hurtled forward. The front row hit the edge of the stage, compressed into a mass, and ricocheted back. Shoulders and elbows jostled about his ears. His feet lifted with the uprising of a crest. He made the mistake of trying to take a step moments before they returned to the floor. And he was down. His shin banged against the hard wood. A foot kicked him in the neck. Someone stepped on his body, scraping a hard boot sole against his ribs as he stepped off. Paul tried to put his hands to his head to protect himself, but his arms became entwined in the ankles that surrounded him. Someone's heel landed millimeters from his face.

He felt two arms encircle his stomach and hoist him up off the floor. He was lifted just high enough to straighten his legs and get his feet under himself. He regained his balance quickly, knowing that he was going to get only one clear shot at recovering a standing posture before being down among the stomping feet again. He was successful, standing again quite still, until the next wave of pressure crushed the bodies against him and slowly dragged him a short distance from this newfound foothold. He never saw who it was that picked him up.

Somehow Glen reached him. He gracefully sidestepped bodies as they surged against him and was able to slip in front of the few layers that separated them. Not that it mattered. It's not like he could prevent each crushing wave that pounded them. It's not like he could shield his brother from the onslaught of music and human energy that synergized in front of their eyes. He couldn't hear his own voice, so he knew it was pointless to try to speak. But he grabbed Paul by the shoulder and looked at him as if to ask if he was okay. Paul nodded, but looked like someone struggling just to keep his head above water.

A little over an hour later, with two songs and an encore to go, Paul had had enough. He turned to Glen and began to tell him he was going to try to step back a bit to try to find a calmer area. But he realized it was futile after the first words fell silently out of his mouth. Instead, he just motioned with his head and turned his back to the stage. Moving away from the stage proved easier than heading toward it. Each undulation of the crowd seemed to propel him toward the raised section at the back of the floor where people watched much more casually, leaning on the low walls that separated them from the hardwood. Once he felt released from the most volatile mass, he turned to the side, figuring it would also be calm along the walls of the hall. He found a spot he could squeeze into underneath a balcony.

He stayed to see the final songs, but bolted out a side door as soon as the house lights came on. He hoped Glen would be wise enough to just go to the car and meet him there. He staggered to the parking lot, feeling like he hadn't set foot on solid ground in days. When Glen arrived, he was sprawled across the back of the Firebird, drenched in sweat.

"Dude, you look like you almost drowned. Washed up on shore."

"That was crazy. I thought I was going to get crushed. Like you hear about those shows where too many people are pushing toward the stage. And you get stampeded."

"Yeah, I was a little worried about you for a second there."

"You didn't get caught up in it? You're barely sweating!"

"Oh, I'm sweating all right."

"Not as much as me. I'm soaking wet. It's not all mine, either."

"Eww. Hesher sweat. Let's go."

He unlocked the Firebird and opened the door for Paul.

"Here, take a load off."

Paul flopped down in the passenger seat, nearly stumbling over the threshold. He was happy to see Sunset wasn't as congested as he had expected. They'd get through to a canyon road or all the way to the freeway soon enough.

"Good show, though. Did you like it?"

"Yeah, it was alright. Just crazy. I've never been in a crowd that crazy before."

"Yeah, I've been in a few crazier ones, but that one was up there."

They drove without speaking too much. Paul reclined the seat but not so far as to make it impossible to see the city streaming by outside his window. He watched it in silence, the steady ringing in his ears drowning out all sounds.

Daisy

"PAUL! SHE SAID she'd go!"

"What?"

Glen walked from the bedroom into the kitchen where Paul sat eating.

"Daisy. She said she'd go with you. To the prom. Remember?"

"I thought she said she wasn't interested."

"She changed her mind. She said she'd go. You should take her."

"Why did she change her mind? What did you tell her?"

"I just told her how it would mean a lot to you. That all the girls at your school are stuck-up bitches and you aren't interested in them. And how she'd look better than all of them. She never went to her prom. She dropped out of high school before she had the chance. I think she's curious what it would be like."

"Daisy doesn't strike me as the type who would care about a prom, or the girls at my school, or any school."

"Well, I also told her that you were hung like a horse."

"What!? And that worked!? That's what changed her mind? Jesus . . ."

"Hey, whatever works. You should take her."

"So, she's expecting to have sex? I mean, just like that, you tell her I'm hung like a horse, and now she wants to go with me?"

"Yeah. I said it, and she said okay."

"Just like that? 'Okay'?"

"Yeah. She said okay. What's the big deal?"

"What a hosebag."

"Hey, she's your prom date now. Don't call her that."

"She's not my prom date. I just can't believe . . . I mean . . . she knows me. She's never shown any interest in me like that. It kinda sucks because she shows interest in just about everybody else. You and I are just friends to her, I guess. But she thinks I have a big dick, and now suddenly she's interested? Isn't that messed up?"

"Not really. I mean, that's Daisy. What did you expect?"

"I can't believe you're getting me laid and I'm disappointed. What if she's disappointed? I mean, I'm okay, but I'm not exactly John Holmes. You're kind of setting me up for failure here."

"I don't think she's going to care. She might not even be interested in that. She might have just decided to go to help you out."

"Yeah, help me out because she thinks I'm hung like a horse. Geez, no pressure or anything."

"Don't worry about it. You don't have to do anything. Just take her. It will be great."

"I don't know . . ."

"Think about it. All those snobs thinking how special they are. And then you walk in with Daisy, all dressed up. She'll blow them all away. They're going to be thinking, 'Damn, Paul!' They'll be totally impressed, and it will shut them up because they'll be too shallow to say anything. All the guys will just stand there jealous with their mouths hanging open. It'll be great. They'll be talking about it the rest of the year. How Paul's the stud of the century."

"I don't know. It'll be awkward."

"It's Daisy, man. C'mon, she's harmless. She's just helping you out. And picture it. She'll get made up so she's totally hot. She'll blow the room away. And yeah, you might get laid out of it as well."

"I don't even know if I want to stick my dick in that. That's scary."

"Just double bag it, man."

"Jesus. I can't believe she said she'd go . . ."

Bruce

GLEN DECIDED HE'D host the next after-party during the last after-party. He wasn't sure they'd even go for it, with so many people coming from Hollywood, but everyone he told at the Country Club said it sounded great. Still, he figured only about half of those who said they'd be coming would actually show up. But all of them did. He blinked and all of a sudden, 150 people were in his backyard.

His mother made frequent trips to the back door to see what was going on. After a few talks with Glen about the condition of the lawn, she assumed she'd done all she could and gave up spying. But this would be the first and last after-party he hosted there.

Paul spent most of his time on the outside of the crowd, marveling at its size. He chatted with Catherine a bit and said hi to Grant, but that was the extent of his socializing. About an hour in, he wondered how long it would last or if people would disperse quickly when they'd decided the time had come.

"Psst . . . Paul . . . Paul . . ."

He thought he heard something, but didn't specifically hear his name through the crowd noise.

"Psst . . . Paul . . . Paul!"

That time he heard it. He turned to see Bruce crouched in the shadows behind the chain-link gate on the path at the side of the house. Paul walked over and kept to the darkness.

"What do you want?"

"Is your mom up?"

"Yeah. Do you think she could sleep through all this noise?"

"Is she outside or inside?"

"Inside. Why?"

"I don't want her to see me. I'm not allowed around here anymore."

"Yeah, I know."

"Do me a favor, huh?"

"What?"

"Go inside and make me a sandwich. Bring it out here for me."

"No way!"

"C'mon! Why not?"

"Because I'm not making you a sandwich."

"Why not?"

"What do you want me to do? Just go in the kitchen and make you a sandwich?"

"Yeah? Why is that such a big deal?"

"Because my mom will see me and ask who the sandwich is for. And she'll probably know it's for you."

"Just say it's for you. That you got hungry."

"No way."

"Why?"

"Because I don't just 'get hungry.' She'll know I'm lying. I never just make myself a sandwich."

"Well, just say it's for someone else then."

"No, because she'll know 'someone else' is you."

"How?"

"Because nobody else is desperate enough to ask me to go inside and make them a fucking sandwich! Who the hell's going to ask me that? 'Excuse me? Nice party you have here. Would you mind fixing me a sandwich?' Are you crazy? Of course she'll know it's for you!"

"C'mon dude! She won't know."

"Yes, she will."

"C'mon man! I'm starving."

"Aren't we all, man? Aren't we all?"

"Aw, thanks for nothing, man. Thanks for nothing."

Bruce slunk back down the path the way he had come.

"Hey, Bruce!"

"What?"

"Stay out of the light going down the front driveway. My mom likes to stand in the kitchen and look out the window."

Delaney

"I DON'T KNOW what it is, Glen. I just don't get it."

"I don't know what to tell you."

"She likes me. I know she does. At least, she says she does. But I have no reason not to believe her."

"Yeah."

"And she's attracted to me. I mean, again, that's what she says. I doubt a girl like her would lie about something like that."

"Right."

"So why not?"

"I don't know."

"Why not me?"

"I said, I don't know, Danny."

"She'll fuck practically anyone that walks. Anyone in a band, at least. But I've asked her about that. She says she's had boyfriends who weren't in bands. I explicitly asked her if she wasn't interested in me because I wasn't in a band, and she said no. She said that had nothing to do with it."

"What did she say it had to do with, then?"

"She didn't. She wouldn't. Or couldn't. She just sat there saying, 'I don't know.'"

"I don't know either, man."

"It's like I'm killing myself for her. I'm so nice to her. I do favors for her all the time. I treat her with respect. I take her places. I listen to her. I do everything you're supposed to do."

"Maybe that's the problem."

"What?"

"Maybe you're too nice. She's probably one of these girls who's not used to being treated well. Maybe she doesn't like it."

"That doesn't make sense."

"Sure it does. She really likes you, so she won't fuck you. She'll only fuck the guys who treat her like shit. Maybe that's all she thinks she deserves. Or maybe, if she fucks you, she's afraid you'll leave her, just like all the guys she has these one-night stands with."

"So, I have to start treating her like shit to get her to sleep with me?"

"Sounds pretty messed up, but you might have found your answer."

"Sounds really messed up. Then what? We have sex and I dump her?"

"I don't know. She'll probably be too scared to stick around after that. It makes sense, man. If she has sex with you, she'll lose you. So that's why she won't have sex with you."

Suddenly, Danny's younger brother Brandon came crashing through the front door, slamming it behind him without a care who might be asleep after midnight on a Saturday. He called from the kitchen without bothering to walk down the hall.

"Danny?"

"Yeah? What's the matter with you? Don't be so loud."

"Sorry, excited."

"Why? How was your date?"

"Awesome. She gave me a blowjob while I was driving home on the freeway."

Glen and Danny looked at each other in shock.

"Isn't he a virgin?"

"Yeah."

Brandon burst into the room.

"I swear. A blowjob right on the freeway!"

He stormed out again, heading to the bathroom.

"Congratulations, buddy."

"Thanks! I came on the off-ramp."

He slammed the bathroom door behind him without another comment.

"Just kill me now, Glen. My little brother is going to be getting more pussy than me."

Summer

GLEN AND PAUL reached the corner at Doheny with a green light but slowed their pace to check for cars making right turns in front of them. Sure enough, an old VW bug with its blinker on came flying down Santa Monica toward the intersection with no apparent attempt to slow down. It took the turn in front of them a little faster than it should have for the sake of propriety.

The passenger-side window swung into full view. It was open. Summer's face was immediately recognizable, angled toward them, mouth agape but curled into a huge smile. She looked like she had just run into an old friend she hadn't seen for years. Her face was bright and dazzling, luminous in what was otherwise a dark interior. Her huge mane of curly hair flew behind her head, suspended in the warm night wind like a halo. Her arm shot forth, fully extended out of the window, her hand in a gesture that appeared more an attempt to grasp than to wave at them. Her words were a blur going by, but they could tell it was an invitation up the hill, to follow them up Doheny to the Strip and the Rainbow.

The entire exchange was over in a flash, but the image of it lingered over the intersection like the streak of a bottle rocket. Like tracer fire. As if having been photographed in the dark, Paul could see spots every time he blinked.

Forgetting for a second how long the major blocks were on the way up to Sunset, Paul briefly entertained the idea of following the car on foot. He didn't know how to ask for Glen's permission to go to the Rainbow. It was usually he who restlessly waited to be taken home. It was he who had grown tired of that social scene, where every conversation seemed shallow and anemic.

"Hey, do you . . . want to follow them? That seemed like an invite."

"Naw. She was just being friendly. Just saying hi."

"I bet they are going to the Rainbow. We could go hang out for a while."

"Heh, you are usually the one wanting to get going home. Sorry, not this time. Gotta be up early in the morning."

"Did you see the way she looked at me?"

"Just now? She was just saying hi. I think you are imagining things. Wasn't that a dude driving the car?"

"I didn't notice. All I saw was that smile. Really, you didn't see anything in it?"

"I don't know what you mean. I saw her smile. That's about it."

"She seemed so happy to see us. Or me. Or you. Do you think it means anything?"

"I think it means you've got a boner for her."

"Shut up. Seriously, I've had some pretty cool conversations with her. I always thought she saw me as too young for her, though. But that wave, that invitation . . . it looked like it meant something."

"Well, I guess it means Summer's here."

Tim

He walked all the way down the hill on Doheny but hung a left into the alley before he hit Santa Monica. It was a habit of his to check the dumpsters at the end of each month. A milk crate was lying alongside the first one in perfect position to give him the necessary height to look all the way inside. He eagerly headed for it and stepped up before he realized there was someone standing a few feet away, behind an upright refrigerator box.

"Hey little man, how you doing?"

Tim immediately heard the trickling splash on the pavement and realized what was happening. He stepped down off the box and retreated several paces.

"Oh, uh . . . sorry."

"That's alright, man. Just taking a leak."

"Uh, okay. I'll come back later."

Tim retreated farther.

"Hey, it's alright. I'm not like the first guy to take a whiz in an alley, you know? No big deal. I didn't mean to scare you off."

"Uh, I know. I'll just—"

"C'mon. It's like you're going to run off and call the cops or something. Guys pee in alleys all the time, man."

"Oh, I'm not calling the cops. Don't worry."

"Oh, I'm not too worried. Sorta joking. Hang on, though."

He zipped up and stepped out from his hiding place to face Tim.

"I thought you looked familiar. You're Tim, aren't you?"

"Yeah."

"Hey, I'm Walt."

"Hi."

Tim thought he recognized the face, but he hadn't known the man's name. That was usually the case in his social interactions in the scene. He was grateful Walt didn't offer his hand to shake.

"So, what are you doing in the alley, Tim? Gotta pee too?"

He laughed heartily enough at his own question to make Tim realize he probably wasn't too sober.

"No, just looking around."

"Ah, dumpster diving! What are you looking for? Booze?"

"Uh, no. Posters. They throw them away every month and put up new ones."

"Ah, cool! I never knew that. Don't worry, I won't horn in on your territory. Be my guest."

Walt stepped aside to let Tim pass.

"No, that's alright. I'll come back later. Maybe when it's daylight."

"Ah, want to let it dry out a bit? I see. Smart kid. Sorry to uh, rain on your parade."

Walt thought that was hysterical too.

"That's alright."

"Hey?"

"Yeah?"

"Doesn't your old man work in the music industry?"

"Yeah."

Again, the familiarity with his personal life didn't surprise him.

"Well, can't he get you all the posters you want for free?"

Tim was glad this question came up.

"Actually, the clubs use promotional material that's not available any-where else. Stuff the bands make that's not like what you can buy at stores or that record companies have. I mean, they might have a few copies, but not any for distribution."

"Sounds like you know a lot about this."

"Yeah. Well, sorta. I just like collecting the flyers and the other promo gear."

"Cool, well, good luck. I'm going back inside to get another beer. You coming?"

"Yeah, sure."

The two left the alley and hung a left on Doheny.

"I got to warn you, though, man . . ."

"What?"

"The Troub hired some new security. They're total goons."

"What do you mean?"

"Big angry dudes. Short hair. That was their first mistake. I mean, c'mon, hire some security who understand us."

"Oh."

"Yeah, and from what I've seen already, they're just way too uptight. Pushy. Bossing everyone around. They don't get it. Harshing everybody's gig. Out to persecute us. Just like The Man."

"Okay, thanks."

Tim kept such a low profile, he didn't expect the change to affect him.

The line to get in the Troubadour showroom was already long. Tim decided to check out the bar before going back and buying a ticket. He'd never heard of the opening act anyway. He figured there was no rush. When they approached the entrance to the bar, there was a large, muscular, short-haired man in a tight yellow T-shirt checking IDs.

"See what I mean? Alright little man, you're on your own. I'm going to go my own way. Good luck to you."

"See ya."

Walt ducked between bodies in line, showed a stamp on the back of his hand to the bouncer, and quickly headed inside.

Tim wasn't sure what to do but found himself slowly following the few people in front of him as they produced wallets and driver's licenses and made their way in. After the bodies cleared, he was face to face with a surly looking bouncer just inside the foyer.

"The lineup for the show is outside along the wall, kid."

"I know. I'm just checking inside."

"For what?"

"I don't know. Just checking?"

"Listen, punk. You gotta be twenty-one to enter here. Go get in line if you want to get inside."

Charlie poked his head out of the bar, ears perked as if he were a hunting dog.

"Hey, man. This is little Tim. He hangs out with us all the time."

"Don't 'hey, man' me. He don't come in if he's under twenty-one. And if this kid even had an ID, I'd know it was fake. He looks freakin' twelve."

"No, he's like fourteen. C'mon, let him in. They don't serve him alcohol. He just hangs out."

"Why don't you mind your own business?"

The bouncer turned to fully face Charlie who still only peered partially out the doorway into the foyer.

"This is my business. This is all our business. Don't you know who this kid is? I mean, who his father is?"

"I don't care who his father is."

"Well you should, man. His father is a great man. His father is what makes stars out here, man."

Tim wanted to quickly turn and leave before he was responsible for Charlie getting tossed out.

"That's okay, Charlie. I'm leaving."

"No, no, little man. You stay. This guy's got to leave. "

Charlie addressed the bouncer again.

"You know what, man? Little man has been coming to this bar since before you were born, dude."

"You're drunk and you're going to find yourself out on the street in a second."

"This guy has been here a long time. His father lets him. His father is huge. Really. You better listen."

"Don't tell me what I better do, sweetheart. I'm not letting him in, and if you know what's good for you, you'll get back in there and mind your fucking business. Or get the hell out. Either way."

"I'm not moving until you let little man in."

"Oh no?"

The bouncer grabbed Charlie by the arm and jerked him fully into the foyer. He then twisted his shoulders to face him out the door and gave him a single, solid shove. Charlie nearly sprawled face first on the pavement before being grabbed by a couple guys who had gotten in line behind Tim.

Charlie was red-faced in anger, spitting and slurring his words.

"Hey, fuck you! You know who we are, man!?"

The bouncer took a step forward but restrained himself from laying another hand on Charlie.

"I don't care who you are. I don't care who this kid is or who his father is. All I care about is the rules. And the rules say he don't come in. And the rules say you are outta here for arguing with me!"

"You should care who we are, asshole! You should care! We are the angels, man! We are fucking angels!"

Mike appeared from the bar and got between Charlie and the bouncer, who now slowly clenched and unclenched his fists at his side. Charlie didn't seem to notice Mike and kept yelling.

"We are the angels! We watch over these streets. This city, man. This is the city of angels, you know that!? And we are the angels. We are innocent and gentle. And what happens? We get pissed on! We have no rights. We're just young and stupid. But we take care of each other. We don't need you to—"

"Let's go, Charlie, before you get hurt."

Mike gently grabbed Charlie by the arm and began walking.

"Mike! Hey, it's Mike! He's an angel, too! But you, sir. You are not an angel!"

The crowd that had gathered laughed and cheered.

Tim had made his way back up the sidewalk toward Doheny amid the chaos. Mike walked Charlie over to the bus bench and sat him down, not sure if he should try to get him back in the club after he cooled down or chalk it up to a wasted night. He noticed Tim walking away.

"Hey, Tim! Go back, man. Get in line. Go to the show."

"No, it's alright."

"No, it's not alright. You shouldn't have to leave. You didn't do any-thing wrong. Did that guy tell you to leave?"

"No, I'm just leaving. I'm sorry I got you kicked out, Charlie."

Charlie seemed too much in a daze to find Tim with his eyes. He spoke instead in his general direction.

"It's okay. You are an angel, my man. I always stand up for my fellow angels."

"C'mon, Tim. Just get in line. We're going to try going back too. Let's just go watch some music."

Glen and Paul turned the corner. Mike immediately noticed them and continued.

"Here's Glen and Paul. Look! C'mon, Tim. Go with them. Go have a good time. Don't go home, man. That sucks."

Tim quickly acknowledged Glen and Paul with a nod.

"No, that's alright, Mike. I'm just going to head out. Some other time. I'll catch you next time, alright?"

Glen and Paul looked confused as Tim began walking past them, turning right up Doheny.

"Hey, you need a ride?!"

"No, thanks, Glen. I'll walk."

Tim disappeared around the corner.

Glen and Paul silently stood staring at Mike and Charlie, huddled to-gether on the bus bench as if Charlie still needed comforting.

Mike muttered to himself.

"Fuck."

"What's going on, guys?"

"Oh, nothing, Glen. Just a misunderstanding."

Charlie perked up to see who Mike was talking to. He smiled.

"Ah, Glen and Paul . . . More angels."

Glen

THE LINE OUTSIDE the Troubadour nearly reached the corner. Glen and Paul waited while Mike walked Charlie back to the front to see about getting back into the bar. Mike had briefly filled them in on the new security staff and what they had missed.

With the line growing in length, the bouncer who threw Charlie out had moved from working the door to doing crowd control on the sidewalk. He kept telling people to keep the line against the wall, but groupings of people in conversation kept allowing it to drift out in the middle of the sidewalk. By the time he got one end of it against the wall, the other end had already drifted away from it. He'd get those people to reform a cleaner line, only to have it fall apart again at the other end.

Ted, "The Button Man" as everyone called him, strolled casually up the sidewalk holding a slab of cardboard with many of his wares pinned onto it. He managed to stay out of the bouncer's way, and he greeted Glen and Paul as he passed. He'd gotten to know Glen from seeing him before and after so many shows.

Mike quickly made his way back down the sidewalk, nodded a quick hello to Ted, and kept moving until he found Glen and Paul in line.

"Hey, just wanted to let you guys know I got Charlie back inside. New bouncer at the door. Didn't have a clue about what had happened, so we just walked right back in."

"Cool."

"Ooh, shouldn't have said that too loud. Dickhead is working out here now. That's him, the guy who hassled Tim and Charlie."

"Oh, okay."

"I don't think he heard me. Dickhead."

"I don't think he's paying attention. Too busy pushing people around."

"Look, I'm going to go back inside. You should come. Hang out awhile and get your tickets later. Oh, shit. Maybe they won't let you now. Especially Paul. Stupid new rules."

"No, it's alright, Mike. We're going to check out the opener. A friend of Grant is playing with them. I told him I'd check it out."

"Okay, buddy. I'll see you back in there."

"Hey, it just occurred to me . . . are there two lines? Is this the line to get tickets or the line that goes right into the club?"

"Just one line I think. Anyone who isn't going in the bar is filing in behind the bouncer."

"But don't we get our tickets first at the box office?"

"I don't think they're using the box office tonight. Doing everything right inside the door."

"Are you sure? I've never seen that before."

"Well, maybe because of the new security or something. More stupid new rules."

"I doubt it. Let me just go see if the box office is open."

"If you want. I don't think I've seen anybody using it."

Glen started to make his way up the side of the line just as the bouncer was making his way back along it. They met about twenty feet from Mike and Paul.

"Hey, get back in line."

"I am, I'm just seeing—"

"You're not seeing nothing. Nothing to see. Now get back in line."

"What? I'm just walking up to—"

"Get back in line!"

The bouncer stood with his feet apart, blocking Glen's way.

"I'm just—"

"Yeah, yeah, you're just nothing. Get the hell back in line!"

As he began to make his retreat, Glen turned his face to the street. He didn't have time to turn the rest of his body before a fist crashed down upon him. It smacked off his left cheek with a dull thud that silenced the crowd that had turned to witness the commotion. Before he felt the pain, Glen was on his backside on the sidewalk. In a purely reflexive action, he stiffened his upper back and neck to keep the back of his head from smashing on the cement. The bouncer immediately moved closer to stand over him, shaking a finger in his face.

"You want another one!? You want another one!?"

Glen was in too much shock to answer. He cowered slightly and slowly pushed himself backward as he came to his senses.

It took a second for Mike and Paul to process what had just happened. Paul shouted in disgust at the bouncer who now straddled his brother's fallen figure, legs apart, and had the momentary notion to rush forward and kick him in the balls. Eight years of playing soccer would finally come in handy. He hesitated, realizing the bouncer probably weighed exactly twice his size and would surely lash out at him more savagely than he had at an unthreatening guy who simply wanted to ask about where to buy tickets to the show. Only Mike and Ted moved forward.

Ted helped Glen back to his feet while admonishing the bouncer.

"This is a good person here! He did nothing to you and had done nothing wrong. Don't you dare lay a hand on him!"

Mike stepped between the bouncer and Glen. He was direct with his words as well.

"It's over, man. You're done. You're also done hitting people."

He turned to someone in line and shouted at them.

"Go get Tony! Run in the bar and tell them to get Tony!"

The guy moved quickly, rushing toward the front of the line. A few minutes later, Tony arrived with another security guard. Glen had gotten back in line by now. The bouncer and Mike stood face to face on the sidewalk, but neither said a word to the other. The bouncer attempted to appear as if he had returned to his duties, keeping his eyes on the line, to make it stay close to the wall, but he never moved an inch to perform the actual task.

"What's going on here?"

"Tony, this guy just hit my friend for no reason. Punched him in the face. All the guy did was ask a question about buying a ticket to your fucking club. He didn't threaten him or anything. Ask anyone out here. They all saw it."

"That's true, Tony. I saw the whole thing. Glen didn't do a thing."

Tony looked disgusted. He turned to the bouncer.

"Is that true?"

The bouncer said something under his breath to Tony. The two of them exchanged more words that no one could hear. Tony gestured that the bouncer should follow him, and the two made their way to the entrance of the club and back inside.

Mike walked back over to join Glen in line.

"You okay?"

"Yeah. The bastard waited until I was turning around. I never even saw it coming."

"You're not bleeding at least. I don't even see a bruise or anything."

"He got me right on the cheek, so no. It's actually not that bad. Just totally surprised me. I was on my ass like that. Wham! I never saw it."

Tony came back outside. He found Mike and Glen in line.

"Hey, you okay?"

"Yeah, I think so."

"That guy is not going to work for me anymore. I put him inside. He knows he can't touch anybody like that. He won't touch you again, I promise. And he won't be back after tonight. That's it."

"How do we know he'll leave us alone?"

"He will, Mike. I told him. I promise. And if he messes with you, just come get me again. I'll throw him out myself."

"This new security you hired . . . I don't know, man."

"It's a new contract. Our contract with the old company ran out. I don't know. Probably a big mistake."

"Get the old guys back. They treated us with respect. They were cool dudes."

"Yeah, I'll see about that."

Tony suddenly spoke more quietly, just to Glen.

"You're okay, right? I mean, this will go away? He won't work for me again. You're okay with that, right?"

"Yeah, I'm okay."

"Because I don't want—I just want you to be okay. Nobody treats you kids that way. It's not right."

"Don't worry, I'm fine."

Tony shook Glen's hand and walked back inside.

"What was that about?"

"He wants to make sure you won't sue him. You probably can, you know? Probably could get a lot of money for pain and suffering and emotional distress."

"I'm not going to sue anybody. I'm alright."

"Yeah, but you could. He knows that. He's probably pretty worried at this point."

"Whatever, man. I just hope he wasn't full of shit. I hope he's really firing that guy."

"You still want to go in?"

"Yeah. I hope that guy stays away from me. I can just see him blaming me now for getting him fired."

"We won't let him touch you. Don't worry."

"Thanks. Damn . . . never saw it coming."

The line started moving again. Mike simply shook his head.

"What the hell is going on tonight? Man, fuck this city."

Paul

We seek redemption among

The nipple-pierced, self-carved, ash-painted, and coal-dyed
Meeting Hasidics for lunch on Fairfax
Equally clad in the black
Of penitent goth

Hollyhocks springing from the fumes of Vermont

Formica cafes
Atomic and Onyx
Clifton's and Rae's

Shimmery slick steel of Gehry
Crushed ceramic, sand, and grit of Rhodia
Glass of Koenig

Lotuses blooming a tapestry
To conceal the submerged evidence
Of a thousand homicides

Backyard amalgams of sage and chlorine
Pier undersides fermenting sea spray and urine

Poets who write of traffic in halting rhythms
And urban landscapes in sprawling verse

Neighboring artifacts lying dormant in peaceful galleries and in tar

Mansions and cardboard shacks
Case study to no study
Old Victorian, modern ranch, bungalow
And cinder block complexes

Travertine and ragweed
Concrete encroaching desert
Sand on the boulevards
Oaks in the crosswalks

Four-level interchanges
And footpaths past cougar dens

Revivals in gilded halls
Statuesque among flea markets and bodegas
Red carpets stained
From another era's folly

Ed Ruscha and the old lady of the freeway
Victor Clothing's bride and groom
Carousel horses running free
Epic poetry in stucco and spray paint

We are Russian and Hmong
Slavic and Farsi
Pidgin and Korean
Arabic and Bostonian
And we all speak a little Spanish every day

We are all nonnative

We are the blessed
Cast out and damned

We are The Angels

Charlie

The driveway and sidewalk outside the Rainbow were packed as usual. The crowd from the Roxy had spilled out half an hour ago, and many of the audience at the Whisky had made their way up the street to join them.

It's a landscape dominated by circles. People stand in circles to afford as much inclusion as possible among large groups. Circles cluster together in order to pack everyone into the tight space between the two buildings, yet touch only in tangent points, limiting contact between groups. People who depart company with one group to find out what is happening in another wind their way among the circles in serpentine paths, arcing along the outsides, squeezing through tangents and arcing again in another direction, like negotiating an array of interlocking gears, until they find a group willing to expand in diameter to accommodate them.

So, when someone cuts through the crowd in a straight line, it's noticeable. Almost unnerving. It implies intent, direction, purpose—motives that rarely describe those who comprise mingling crowds in driveways after midnight.

Mike made a beeline straight through the mass of humanity. He sliced off arcs of circles with segments drawn with no regard to symmetry. He bisected nothing, simply cut a direct path on the shortest route possible, jostling shoulders and hips along the way, hit the sidewalk at a diagonal and didn't break stride or direction until he had crossed Sunset and disappeared into the darkness of the alley where he had parked his car.

Glen wasn't standing in any of the circles that had been fractured, but he noticed. He watched Mike until he disappeared into the darkness, wondering what the hell was going on. He directed his attention to the buzz of a small crowd next to the entrance of the Rainbow. Their chatter swelled until the buzz morphed into a series of discernable remarks.

"Where did they find him?"

"Parking lot of some apartment on Selma. Over by Cahuenga."

"Stuffed in a fucking dumpster, man."

"Shit, what a way to go."

"OD?"

"Who knows? Probably."

"Somebody kill him?"

"I don't know. How else would he get into a dumpster?"

"Could have fallen in. That dude was always wasted."

"Can you imagine? Taking out your trash, and there's a fucking body in the dumpster?"

"Wonder how long he was in there before he was found."

"Poor dude. Just having trash and shit dumped on him until somebody actually decided to look inside."

"Maybe he started stinking."

"What?"

"Maybe."

"That dude was messed up, man. I'm not surprised. I mean, no offense to the dead, man. But that guy was like a ticking time bomb waiting to go off. Same old story. Bound to happen. Just bound to."

"Some go out in style at the Chateau Marmont. Some get stuffed in a fucking dumpster."

"Shit, remember when he got thrown out of the Whisky for stage diving?"

"Aw man, I was at that show!"

"Fucker just wouldn't stop. The bouncers kept warning him. Kept pulling him out of the crowd. But the guy just kept jumping back on stage every chance he could get. Lucky people kept catching him, too. That dude was out of control. Just throwing himself off head first and shit."

"We were just at the Troub last week and he got thrown out of the bar. Pissed off the new bouncers."

"Yeah, I was there, too."

"Man, what a way to go, though."

"I know, man. Stop doing that shit. It'll mess up your life."

"Dude needed AA. Or NA. Or Al-Anon, Narcalon, whatever the hell they call it. All of it."

"Remember when he got all up in Rikki's face about wearing lipstick and eye shadow? 'For an ugly guy, you sure make a pretty girl!' Remember?"

"He fucking hated glam, dude. Liked the music okay. Hated the look. I think the dude had issues."

"Not everyone likes the look. Takes balls to wear makeup and scarves and shit."

"I tried telling him, dude, Mötley Crüe wears makeup all the time. They just make it look more metal than pretty. He didn't care. Said he'd never raid his mama's bathroom drawers."

"Shit, his parents. Are his parents still around?"

"I don't know. I heard plenty of shit about his dad. I don't think he spoke to him. Probably got thrown out of the house years ago or something. I don't know about his mom."

"I wonder if they know."

"They must by now. Don't they do that notify-the-next-of-kin thing? Have someone come identify the body? My cousin had to do that when my uncle died. Fucking sucks."

"He didn't have any brothers or sisters?"

"Not that I know."

"I don't know. He never talked about his family around me."

"Naw. Dude was an only child. Probably scared his parents from having any more."

"Ha, you imagine him as a baby, man? Probably climbing the curtains.

Stage diving off the fucking couch. Listening to heavy metal on his Playskool turntable."

"Dude. Crazy."

"A fucking dumpster."

"Crazy."

Daisy

"Wow."

"Wow?"

She gave Paul a look as if to say don't do it. Don't fawn over me. Don't stand there like a dope. Shut your mouth and stop staring at me. What's the matter, you've never seen a girl get dressed up before? But she could tell he was sincerely impressed. More than that, he was blown away. She secretly admitted that it made her want to blush. She couldn't remember the last time she had.

"Um, sorry . . . but yeah, wow. You . . . um . . . you look great."

She was radiant. He could find no other words. Her face was gorgeous. Absolutely stunning. He had never seen her like this, and despite appearing totally caught off guard, deep down he wasn't surprised. He had recognized this natural beauty that occasionally crept out from beneath heavy swaths of eyeliner and mascara. He had noticed these gentle curves of her mouth even after they'd been overloaded with dark lipstick. But now her hard lines had been replaced by delicate strokes from an artist's palette. Her eyes twinkled, cheeks glowed, lips burst forth in a splash of crimson. He had known this face although she'd always kept it hidden.

She wore a white calf-length gown, trimmed in lace. It fitted tightly at the waist and along her torso to show off her thin and petite physique. Thin straps delicately hung from her creamy smooth shoulders, rising off the contours of her breasts where they met a neckline that dipped just enough to entice. He had seen her in much skimpier outfits, but her chest had never looked so good. She was gathered into an amazing display of décolletage, only slightly overflowing from the lace that accented every revealing edge.

"You look nice too. Very handsome."

It was only a cheap rental tux. He suddenly felt ordinary standing next to her. Perhaps recognizing the incongruity as well, she appeared to reconsider her own appearance.

"It's not too fancy, is it?"

"No, it's perfect."

"I mean, I've never been to a prom before, or really even seen one. I figured I had to dress a little differently than what I usually wear on Saturday nights."

"No, it's awesome. You look like Lita Ford."

"Really?

"Yeah. I like the lace. It's got that rocker touch to it, but it's elegant like a prom dress. It's . . . it's perfect."

"Thanks. Debbie helped me. I mean, with the makeup."

She was surprised at how flustered she'd become. She blamed it on him. If he had just been casual like most guys when she opened the door, she wouldn't have cared.

"You really think it's okay?"

"Daisy, you look beautiful."

No one had ever told her that before.

"Oh . . . here."

He handed over the corsage in its plastic case. He didn't know if he should open it for her or let her. He resisted the urge and felt relief to see her pop open the case easily enough. There was a large decorative pin included in the package. She took it and immediately affixed the corsage to the point where a shoulder strap met the bodice of her gown.

"Oh. Maybe I should have let you do that. Was I supposed to?"

"I'm not sure. It's just as well. I probably would have stabbed you with that thing. Got blood all over your white dress."

"That would be pretty cool for a club show. But not tonight, huh?"

"No, definitely not tonight. No blood."

She chuckled, thinking she heard somewhere that laughing at your date's jokes is an art form that should be practiced by conscientious girls. She grabbed her purse and made her way back to the front door, realizing for the first time she wasn't used to walking in such a thin heel. She stumbled as she pulled the door open, banging her knee in the process.

"Fuck!"

"You okay?"

"Yeah. Heh, that wasn't very ladylike, was it? I guess you can take the girl off the Strip, but you can't take the Strip off the girl . . . Oh god, forget I said that. That just sounded wrong."

She let him walk out first so she could turn on the porch light and lock the door behind them. The next step made him nervous, but he made up his mind he would open and shut the car door for her.

"Hey, you have the Firebird! Glen let you borrow it?"

"Yeah. He got a ride from Danny tonight. Most people will probably be arriving in limos. I hope you don't mind."

"No, I've always loved the Firebird. It's a cool car."

"Cool car with a noisy transmission."

He opened the passenger-side door and waited for her to step in.

"Always the gentleman, Paul."

"I guess so. Don't let that get around."

"Don't worry, I won't."

He made sure her dress was tucked neatly inside before shutting the door. She giggled a little, which made him self-conscious. He hated the feeling of putting on such an elaborate, formal show, especially for someone who only knew him as a sloppy little kid that hung around his big brother a lot.

He hadn't thought about Glen much, but as he pulled away from the curb, suddenly comforted by the distraction driving brought, he replayed in his mind their conversations about taking Daisy to the prom. Glen told him she was going to blow the room away. People that thought of him as a shy loser would wonder how the hell he'd gotten so lucky. He smiled to himself at the thought of the club scene suddenly becoming the next big trend, as suburban boys in fancy cars braved his music and his crowd in a desperate attempt to get laid, never realizing that they represented the very ideals everyone else in the room was rebelling against.

Glen was right. When they entered the ballroom, jaws dropped. A few girls giggled, but Paul knew that's what jealous girls do. A few guys stared, mouths open. Paul wanted to arrogantly tell them to stop drooling as he walked by with Daisy on his arm but restrained himself. Don't gloat, he told himself. Take it all in and enjoy it. He didn't need to tell them to eat crow; they already were.

The ballroom looked incredible. Twenty-one stories up, surrounded by floor-to-ceiling windows on two sides, they seemed to float over the valley lights below. They walked over to the edge of the room to take a better look. He pointed out the 101, stretching west across the valley floor and east to the Cahuenga Pass.

"The Hollywood sign is just over that hill there."

"Really?"

"Yeah. And the Hollywood Bowl is on the other side of the pass, there."

"Cool. I've never been there."

He thought of the overlook and the prospect of taking her there later.

"Man, I could look at this view all night."

"It's pretty."

"It's pretty, but it's peaceful. Do you know what I mean? I mean, there's all this activity going on down there. Think about it . . . all the cars, all the people, all the electricity flowing through all those lights, thousands of houses, thousands of families, all this . . . stuff, you know? It's crazy. Total chaos. But it's peaceful and beautiful if you just step away from it a little."

"I guess so."

He hadn't meant to say so much. He was secretly hoping she might see things the same way. It didn't seem she did. He remembered her story about the buildings downtown and how the peaceful quiet scared her. That was in darkness, though. This was different. Still, he decided not to push it.

"Hey Paul, how's it going?"

It was Rob, a stuck-up rich kid who had spoken to Paul one other time in his life—when he asked to borrow a pencil in math class in eighth grade. Paul was shocked that Rob of all people would approach him, but from the looks of the group of guys and their dates watching the exchange from nearby tables, it was obvious he was somehow nominated to be the one to get the lowdown on Daisy.

"Hey Rob. It's going well. Nice view, eh?"

"So . . . who's your date? She doesn't go to Truman, huh?

"No. This is Daisy. She's from Hollywood. I know her from the club scene."

"Nice to meet you, Daisy."

They shook hands and Rob slinked off without saying another word. He didn't even wait until they were out of view before he started whispering to all the curious faces in the crowd that received him.

"Sorry about that. I guess everyone is curious about who you are."

"That's okay. It makes sense. They've never seen me before."

"It would be nice if they actually talked to you, you know. I have to warn you, most of the people I go to school with aren't very nice. You're probably going to be ignored most of the night."

"They don't seem to be ignoring me."

"Well, I mean . . . yeah, they're going to stare. I was expecting that. But they probably won't want to talk to you much."

Daisy looked confused.

"I'd take that as a compliment. They've never seen such a pretty girl before."

He hoped this would comfort her, but it didn't seem to.

Paul suddenly realized two major weaknesses in his plan. First, everyone he respected and admired, who would be genuinely interested in meeting Daisy and hanging out with them, wouldn't be caught dead at their senior prom. They all thought he was crazy for going but wanted pictures of everyone else's reactions. Second, he wouldn't be caught dead at his senior prom either. He hated dances. He didn't even dance. Suddenly, the prospect of sitting at some table with Daisy, alone otherwise, watching everyone he didn't like have a good time was a really stupid idea. These people didn't mean anything to him. He realized their jealousy wasn't as important to him as he had originally imagined.

Not seeing anyone he'd feel comfortable sitting with, he led her to a table that looked unoccupied save for a few drinks left unattended there. When the song changed and several people left the dance floor, it soon filled with six others he didn't know. They were nice enough to suffer through the obligatory introductions, but nobody they sat with paid much attention to either of them after that.

They passed the time sampling the food, drinking iced tea, and watching others dance. The longer the night wore on, the more self-conscious they grew. Daisy thought it strange how she could totally cut loose and slam dance with a room full of strangers, totally flirt and get picked up by a different guy every night. But here, with a nice guy that she knew fairly well, she felt like a fish out of water. She thought dancing might help loosen them up a bit. She resolved to ask him at the start of the next song.

Suddenly "Let's Go Crazy" dissolved into "Addicted to Love" and she saw her chance.

"Hey, do you want to dance?"

"What?"

"I said do you want to dance?"

"I'm sorry. Maybe when a slow one comes on?"

"C'mon, don't worry about it. Just get out there. Nobody's watching."

"No, I actually think they'll start watching once I get out there. Nobody needs to see that."

"Fine. Don't say I didn't try."

She stared at her iced tea.

"Hey, I'm sorry. Maybe this was a bad idea. I'm not being very much fun."

"No, no, that's okay. These are your schoolmates. I understand. I don't want you to be uncomfortable. I just thought if we danced maybe it would be better."

"No, not better. Sorry. Didn't I warn you? I'm not much of a dancer."

"Maybe we can request some metal and bang our heads."

"Ha! That will definitely draw attention. But I'll do it if you do."

"No, that's okay. I doubt they even have the songs we'd like."

"You're probably right. I'd like to see some of these people at the clubs. They wouldn't even survive. I talk to people sometimes about shows I go to, and they look at me like I'm crazy. Like I'm a violent punk rocker. They don't know the difference."

"I bet."

"Hey, I'm sorry you agreed to come to this. I mean, that you have to subject yourself to this. I'm glad you came. I just don't think it's much fun for you."

"Don't worry about it and stop apologizing. I'm glad I came. I never went to my prom. Hell, I never even finished high school. It's kind of fun to see what I missed out on."

"Not a lot, I guess?"

"Well, not much. But I'm glad to be here. Don't feel bad about me. Really. I've been on far worse dates, trust me."

The word *date* stung him a bit. He'd normally be overjoyed to hear a girl refer to what they were doing as a "date," but he hoped Daisy didn't see it that way. If it were a date, he wouldn't want it to go down this way. He wouldn't want it to be a big disappointment.

An audible sigh was heard from the crowd as "Time After Time" came on, and the dance floor slowed into a collective sway. He decided not to blow this chance. He felt he owed it to her to at least dance a slow dance.

"Hey, it's a slow one. Do you want to dance?"

"Sure."

She took his hand as they walked to the floor. He felt heads turn as they passed tables and made their way to a bare patch of parquet.

Neither of them knew what they were doing but it didn't matter. At that age, nobody really knows how to slow dance. They just held each other and sidestepped their way through it. She was relieved that he never stomped on her toes. He was relieved that he survived it without making a fool of himself.

And for a moment, he felt totally content.

When their song ended, and "Walk Like an Egyptian" began, she led him off the floor and back to the table. He thanked god she didn't make him try to dance through that.

They stayed awhile longer. They watched the limbo contest. They watched the slide show, Daisy noting that Paul wasn't in a single photo. He simply shrugged as if to ask if she was surprised. She poked him in the shoulder to let him know she was kidding. They crowned the king and queen, more dancing ensued, and Paul felt it wasn't rude if they left at that point.

They made their way past crowded tables on their way to the exit. He didn't care if heads turned or not. He'd done what he came here to do. It was a gimmick. It may have worked to some extent. But it was over. He didn't care what anyone thought anymore. He felt more comfortable with Daisy on his arm now that the goal was no longer to make others jealous. Leading her across the room, he was suddenly glad he'd come, more so because that happiness had nothing to do with impressing any-one else.

"Hey Paul, you leaving already?"

Another popular kid named James blocked his path with Rob grinning at his side. There was something confrontational in their posture. For a fleeting moment, Paul thought of the utter inanity of bullies at a senior prom, not letting weaklings pass. They seemed to soften after he responded, so he figured he was imagining things.

"Yeah, we're going to head out. Have a nice time."

"You took your own car, huh?"

James turned and winked at Rob who continued to smile like an idiot in expectant joy.

"Yeah. Well, my brother's car, but—"

"Ah, I see. Couldn't afford a limo with the money you spent on the escort service."

Rob burst after failing to stifle a roar. Giggles erupted from the two nearest tables.

Paul was speechless, struggling with the conflict of firing back a retort or trying to ignore it, until Daisy interrupted his train of thought.

"At least he's getting laid tonight, you fucking losers!"

Paul was hoping Daisy hadn't heard the joke. Or at the very least, it had gone over her head. But he turned and saw Sunset Boulevard etched across her once pristine face. Every beer-soaked bar, every piss-filled alley, sweat-stained spandex, torn fishnet, scuffed Capezio, dusty boot, flammable hairdo, broken drumstick, broken guitar string, broken-down whiskey-breath microphone spit screen, neon, exhaust, asphalt, stained-glass-shattered dream. It was after midnight and Cinderella was gone. Checked out. The Daisy he knew so well stood in her place, looking totally incongruent with the elegance still draped over her.

But this shift from the demure only intensified everyone's laughter, and Paul and Daisy left it trailing behind them until they got into the elevator.

"Sorry about that, Daisy."

"Don't worry about it. Those guys are losers. I hope you don't let that shit get to you."

"No. I don't care what they think."

"Good. You shouldn't."

He suddenly chuckled to himself.

"What?"

"Do you know you pretty much admitted back there that you're a whore?"

"I did? Ha, ha! Yeah, I guess I did. Well, like they say . . . I always calls 'em like I sees 'em."

The elevator doors opened to reveal the lobby.

They drove back over the hill in waves of silence, separated by awkward attempts at conversation.

"Prom king and queen . . . what the fuck is up with that?"

"Huh?"

"I mean, who started that tradition? And why do we keep it?"

"I don't know."

"Hey everyone, I've got an idea. Why don't we take a vote and decide which guy and girl are the most popular and they can lead us? They can lead us as we blindly follow each other, trying to feel less insecure about ourselves. Who can lead us so we don't feel so insecure?"

"Heh. You're funny."

"I'm serious though, Daisy. Isn't that just a weird concept? Who the hell thought that was a good idea?"

"Just makes people who didn't win feel bad, I think."

"I mean, the social hierarchy at my school is bad enough. They don't need to vote in people to rule over us underlings."

"I don't let anyone rule over me."

"Me neither. I just don't like the idea."

"Well, if you let it get to you, it's like they are ruling over you."

He sat in silence as they crept through the traffic merging off the freeway onto Highland.

"Uh, oh. Did I offend you?"

"No. Sorry. I was just thinking."

"About what?"

"Nothing important. I'm sorry, Daisy. I dragged you into this other world of mine, and it wasn't very pleasant."

"I keep telling you, stop apologizing. I liked it. I had a nice time."

"Seriously? That was a nice time?"

"Yeah."

"Wouldn't you have rather been at whatever show is at the Troubadour or Whisky tonight?"

"Not really. There'll be other shows next week. And the week after that. How many times do you get to go to a senior prom?"

"Once is enough for me."

"Yeah, but you'll be glad you did it. Now you won't have to wonder what you would have missed."

"Ha! True. Absolutely nothing."

"Hey, I got an idea!"

Her sudden excitement shocked him out of his cynical stupor.

"What?"

"Let's go to Pink's!"

"Seriously? You want to go to Pink's? Dressed like that?"

"Uh, huh."

She was suddenly beaming.

"You're not worried about getting mustard on that dress?"

"I don't care. C'mon, the food at that prom was so chichi. I need a fucking hot dog!"

"Okay. But you just walked into the biggest 'That's what she said' joke of the decade."

"Aaaack!! Paul! Don't pimp it! Just bust it out. 'That's what she said.' C'mon!"

"Alright, alright, forget I said anything. . .That's what she said."

"There you go! Again!"

"That's what she said."

"C'mon, louder!"

"That's what she said!!"

"Here let me show you."

She rolled down the window of the Firebird as Highland crossed Hollywood Boulevard and stuck her body out up to the waist.

"THAT'S WHAT SHE SAID!!!!!"

"You're crazy, you know that? You're going to fall out of the car!"

"I don't care! THAT'S WHAT SHE SAID!!!! PAUL, YOUR DATE IS A WHORE! THAT'S WHAT SHE SAID!!!! PAUL, YOU GO TO SCHOOL WITH A BUNCH OF SNOT RAGS! THAT'S WHAT SHE SAID!!!!"

Heads turned all the way down Highland. Cinderella was insane. Flat out loco.

She plopped down on the seat with a bounce and a sigh and rolled up the window.

"Feel better?"

"Much. Thanks."

He had nothing left to say. He just shook his head and smiled.

"Paul, you're going to have to do something about that shit, you know?"

He didn't have to ask what she was referring to.

"Like what?"

"Like fucking graduate or something. What the hell are you waiting for?"

"I'm getting there. One more month."

"Jesus. Get that shit going. That's the best revenge. Get the fuck out of there and never look back. Just, 'See ya!'"

The word *revenge* made him hesitate. Did she know? Did she know this was more about him using her to make himself look good than him taking her out for a nice time?

He remained quiet as they crossed over to La Brea. He got lucky in finding a parking spot in the alley behind Pink's. He killed the engine and slipped off the seat belt, but she stopped him before he got the door open.

"Paul."

"Yeah?"

She leaned close to him.

"Don't worry. Some of those bitches totally want to fuck you now. You are a total stud in their eyes. We may not have gotten to them all, but we got to some. I'd say it was a pretty good night."

She kissed him on the cheek and bolted from the car before he had a chance to blink.

Pink's was jammed as usual. But they managed to procure two seats outside, the generous offering of an older couple who thought they looked cute in their prom attire. And they talked.

They talked even more effortlessly than they had at the prom. They talked openly about dreams and aspirations, about pending adulthood, about the music scene and those they knew who seemed to be on their way, those who deserved to be, and those who didn't.

He commented on her glibness, how she seemed much more relaxed since they left the dance.

"Well, I'm back in my element."

"Uh, huh. I see."

"Yeah. Just put me on a city sidewalk. Hollywood, West Hollywood, hell . . . Reseda. It doesn't really matter where."

Two hours later, he pulled up to her bungalow not knowing where the time had gone.

When she opened the car door and stepped out, he hustled around to be there to accompany her up the front walk.

His mind again raced with replays of conversations he had with Glen about Daisy and her agreement to come with him to the prom. He reminded himself of Daisy's comment about him getting laid tonight. He suddenly felt nervous. He'd spent the whole night with her and still couldn't tell if she was serious about all that. And he still couldn't tell if he wanted to go through with it.

She opened the front door only part way and sidled into the aperture. Halfway in, she stopped and turned to him.

"I want to thank you for a lovely night. No one has ever treated me so nicely before. You made me feel special. I don't know why, but I was nervous at first. But you made me feel very comfortable."

All his questions were answered.

"Thanks for coming, Daisy. I know it wasn't exactly your element, but you pulled it off beautifully."

"Yeah, I think we did some damage."

"No, that's not important to me. I mean, just you. You were beautiful. You can be . . . I mean, you don't have to worry if you felt out of place. You were—"

"You have to get out, Paul."

"Huh?"

"Just get out. Finish school, get out, don't look back."

"Thanks, Daisy."

"Promise?"

"Promise."

She kissed the corner of his mouth, said good night, and gently closed the door.

Paul

Many touch you on a whim
With a fleeting loveless affection
That can only befit a drunken afterthought
Or a punctuation mark on a debaucher's latest sentence

They shower you with hollow come-ons
Faceless bravado
Leave bouquets of regrets on your bedside table

It took a slew of formality
And a total absence of reckless spontaneity
An utter lack of impulsive abandon
And heartless caprice
Before I touched you
Before I held you

The hundreds of staring eyes
May as well have been blinded by our radiance
For in that moment there was only one light in the room
Abashing any measure of darkness that dared serve as aegis
To the cause of negative space

And among every force that ever shunned me
That ever left me on the outside
Abandoned and lost
I found a safe haven
A shelter in the storm
Sanctuary

You held me
As the light held us
Suspending our fears
In blissful security
Over the masses below
Over the hue and cry of a world waiting to swallow us in its depths

Cinderella
Where the hell did the time go?
I watched you transform into a princess before my very eyes
A vision of an angel in white
Captured in a single sphere of light
Floating above countless breaths of color

But now your prom dress has turned to leather
Your corsage a funeral token thrown in the grave of your youth
Your glass slippers have been
Crushed to dust on a West Hollywood sidewalk

Your image simply a memory
As the dying warmth of your embrace
Leaves not a remnant strong enough
To dance in the face of ridicule
Over an endless sea of light.

Bruce

HE FIGURED HE'D couch surfed his last wave for a while.

Mike was getting tense. And while he never let guilt into the equation—never let feeling that he was taking advantage of someone's good nature or that he was imposing too much get in the way of a decent meal in his stomach and a decent roof over his head—he knew when he was pushing his luck.

He was a master, actually. He'd ride a gravy train until things got tense. And right before he'd piss someone off past the point of no repair, he'd graciously pack up and move on, as if doing them a favor, leaving behind a bridge he might be able to venture back across someday. Everyone had a different breaking point. He could identify them all.

For Victor, it was two weeks.

For Justin, a week.

Grant, a week.

Daisy, two nights. He was too much of a burden on her social life.

Janine and Michelle, two nights. Women just seemed to value their privacy a lot more.

Tony and John, a week.

Ron, a week and a half.

Glen and Paul, he never found out. But their mother lasted four nights before nagging Glen enough to make him leave.

Mike, a week.

He was going to push it to an eighth night but decided against it. Not after noticing the vacant dirt lot behind Mike's building and how in the week he observed, nobody seemed to care what went on there. It was an empty space that had somehow not yet fallen into a state of urban neglect, save for the high weeds growing there. No trash, no signs of illicit activity, no signs of vagrancy. Just nature taking its course in a place where concrete had not yet encroached.

So, he decided to go it alone for a while. Instead of racking his brain for the next person to ask a favor of or the next friend to possibly alienate, he decided to live out of his car instead. He'd done it before. Years ago, when his father kicked him out, he spent enough weeks in a Chevy Nova to earn the cash to convince Neil he could pay rent like a good roommate for a couple months.

As Mike was getting ready for work, he told him he'd be leaving that night, to which Mike offered no argument or resistance. He gathered those of his belongings that had made it into Mike's place, stuffed what he could into his green suitcase, and carried the rest down to the street where he crammed everything into the back of his Honda Civic hatchback.

Getting into the vacant lot was easy. There was no fence, and an old driveway cut out of the sidewalk but otherwise leading nowhere made hopping the curb unnecessary. He realized from this entryway there must have been a building or a house on the lot at some point. For now, it was just an empty field.

He swung the Honda behind the building, far enough away so as not to be an obvious eyesore to the residents but close enough to avoid being seen from the street. Satisfied, he killed the engine, cut the lights, and sighed. This would be home for now. He reclined the seat as far as his possessions in the back would allow and thought about all the success stories he'd heard that began this way.

"It's just an empty field behind his building?"

"Yeah."

"Huh. I never noticed."

"Me neither, until this week."

"Did you tell Mike you're staying there?"

"No, I just told him I was leaving and wouldn't be staying another night."

"So, he doesn't know you're camping out in the field behind his place?"

"No."

"Don't you think you should tell him?"

"Why?"

"I don't know. I'd probably want to know if my friend was living out of his car in a vacant lot behind my place."

"Why? It's not like he owns the property. It's none of his business."

"Yeah, but what if someone is bothered by it? One of his neighbors, say. When they find out you're a friend of his they're probably going to be pissed at him."

"They don't have to find out. I won't say anything."

"Even more reason to call the cops. Just some strange homeless dude living out of his car behind the building."

"Nobody's going to call the cops. I bet nobody even knows the field is there, or if they do, they don't think about it much. It's easy to ignore."

"Until there's a fucking Honda parked there."

"Naw. We'll see. C'mon, my car's green. It's, like, camouflaged. And, whatever . . . I'll just move the car somewhere else if anybody says anything."

"Sorry, dude. No space in my backyard."

"Very funny."

Mike

"I'm heading up to Gil Turner's for a Coke. Anyone want to join me?"

"Sure, Mike. Hang on a second."

Glen checked with Paul to see if he wanted to come as well, then asked Daisy to save them a seat if they opened the doors before they got back.

They had been standing in front of the Roxy in the dusk of a blistering day that seemed reluctant to cool off. The three of them loped past the Rainbow and Gazarri's, up the slight grade toward Doheny and the prospect of finding comfort in front of one of Gil Turner's many refrigerated drink cases. Just the rush of air conditioning hitting them upon entering was worth the entire trip.

"Hey, it's June first tomorrow. New *Guitar Player* should be here."

Mike detoured his beeline to the soda case to peruse the magazine racks. Glen checked out the drinks while Paul scanned the candy-bar displays.

"Hey Glen! Come over here. You too, little man."

They walked over to find Mike looking confused, a magazine splayed open across his enormous left hand while his right hand rubbed his chin.

"Check this out. Quiet Riot retrospective. Old pictures, some with Randy. Then these when Carlos first joined the band. Check these out. Look familiar?"

"Hey, Bruce took that! That one, too. Cool!"

"That's what I thought. But look at the credit."

"Photos by Alan Bassich. Who is Alan Bassich?"

"Obviously, the guy who took these shots. At least these here in this set. Look, the ones with Randy are by guys named Mark Devereux, William Reid. Then all of these with Carlos . . . Alan Bassich. This one is at the Troubadour. That's where Bruce told me he shot these. He has all of these in his suitcase. He showed them to me. Told me he shot them at the Troubadour. Quiet Riot's first show after Randy and that other guy Greg left and Carlos joined up."

"Do you think they messed up the credit?"

"No, how could they? And Bruce would have told everyone if his shots were going to be published."

"Then, what are you thinking?"

"I'm thinking Bruce is a fucking liar."

"He has prints of all these, though. It's not like he cut them out of a magazine. How did he get them? How did he know where they were shot?"

"I don't know. Did he ever show you the negatives?"

"No. Not of these, at least."

"I don't think I've ever seen any of his negatives. Except for totally recent shit. I wonder how many of those old photos he stole from someone else. Or has been taking credit for shooting."

"Maybe they just got the credit wrong."

"Think about it, Glen. Bruce has those other shots. The ones of Randy? The ones early on, at Disneyland and all that? He said he didn't shoot those, but those look like prints. You can buy prints like that from collectors. I've seen them at tourist shops. You know, where you can buy old headshots of actors and shit? They probably have guys selling rock photos too somewhere. Why wouldn't they?"

"Yeah, but why would he say he didn't shoot the ones of Randy and lie about the ones of Quiet Riot?"

"To make his lies more believable! I mean, c'mon. Of course he didn't shoot the ones of Randy. What, he just happened to miraculously be at Disneyland the same day as Ozzy and his band, and they just agreed to pose for him? Of course he didn't shoot those. But shots of guys on stage

. . . he can take credit for all of them. Who's to say he wasn't there in the crowd, clicking away? We see him do it all the time."

"Yeah, but I've seen his stuff. He's good. He could have shot those other ones. He's got that kind of talent."

"Yeah, but have you ever seen him shoot any legitimate bands? I mean, bands that have really made it? He's at the clubs all the time with his camera. But he has no proof he shot the big concerts. He's told us about them, but we wouldn't know."

"He told us he shot Billy Squier from the stage."

"Exactly! How can we prove he's lying? Unless we find the same pictures in a fucking magazine with someone else's name on them! I mean . . . shit . . . Scorpions, Judas Priest, Maiden, Queensrÿche . . . maybe he didn't take any of those."

"Queensrÿche wanted to take him on the road. He said they saw those shots he took and loved them. He was supposed to send their manager more."

"He never did, huh?"

"No."

"Of course not. You know why? Because the fucking liar never took them in the first place! He didn't want to get caught in a lie. I bet the band never had any interest in him at all. He probably made the whole thing up. They'd probably know any shots they saw were taken by someone else. Like the actual photographer they hired."

"Wow."

"You bet your ass, 'wow.' I wonder how much he's been lying about other stuff, too. About anything. I don't trust a thing about that guy now. I'm going to buy this magazine and show it to him. See what the fuck he has to say for himself."

Tim

THE BUZZ WAS that David Lee Roth was inside. Tim thought it might be fun to wait around to see him stumble out the front door and count the number of hot women in his party. It was already pretty late, so he figured it wouldn't be much longer.

Tim hadn't been to any of the shows in the area tonight. He was home and had long since gone to bed before realizing he couldn't sleep. The Rainbow was just a short hike down the hill. So, he threw on some clothes and headed out.

Several circular clusters of people filled the space between the bar and grill and the Roxy next-door. Tim stayed on the periphery, speaking to no one but listening to snippets of conversations as he passed.

No one spoke to him. The people he knew the best weren't outside. No one familiar enough to approach him and initiate conversation appeared. So, he kept moving in silence. He preferred being an outside observer to a participant anyway, especially among a crowd this size.

"Dude, that set was rocking tonight."

"Better than the one at FM Station last month."

"Dude, FM Station sucks."

Tim laughed to himself and moved alongside another group.

"I did not!"

"Yes you did. You totally did."

"No!"

"Wait, wait . . . what did she do?"

"Danced on the table at Denny's."

"She did?"

"No! I didn't, I swear."

"You just don't remember."

He moved along and paused briefly near a group on the sidewalk.

"Tell him about the Night Ranger after-party."

"You mean the party that wasn't?"

"Yeah."

"We got some tip that they were staying at the Holiday Inn on Highland. So, we go over there after the show, the one at the Palladium?"

"Yeah, I was going to go to that show. Heard it kicked ass."

"It did. Anyway, we go for the after-party, right? I don't know how, but the guy has a floor number at the hotel and everything. So, we get off the elevator and the hallways are totally quiet. No party, no people, nothing. We're thinking we got the wrong place. We're about to give up when a door to one of the rooms opens and Jeff Watson comes out with a hot blonde."

"No!"

"Yep. Totally true, swear to god. He looks at us like 'What the fuck? How did you find out?' and get this. This guy's little brother was with us. He goes chasing Jeff down the hall!"

"No way!"

"Way! But it's not like Jeff is running from him. I mean, he got out of there pretty quick before that. Took off for the elevator. But his little brother starts running to catch up. Like he's chasing him down."

"Did he catch him?"

"No, we grabbed his ass. We were like, 'Calm down and shut the hell up. He's going to think we're groupies. Act dignified.'"

"Hilarious."

"So, we had the right place after all. But there was no damn party. The party was just a rumor, I guess. We got the fuck out of there. Jeff Watson looked like he was on his way to call security or something."

"Holy shit! That's insane. What a story, dude."

"I know, huh?"

Tim moved on.

A purple Stutz Bearcat occupied the spot closest to the sidewalk and therefore closest to the crowds that huddled in the entryway to the parking area. No one ever touched it or stumbled into it, however. Its fanciness seemed to breathe "Hands Off" over the crowds. The California license plate on its rear bumper sported only three letters: F I G. Its owner dressed in fancy purple coats and sashayed in and out of the Rainbow on a weekly basis. Everyone just called him "Fig." Without the getup, he would have looked like a generic fifty-something-year-old resident of West Hollywood. But there was no mistaking him or his car.

Next to the Stutz, a pink Corvette. Tim never saw anyone ever drive these cars. They simply appeared and disappeared. The Corvette belonged to well-known model Angelyne, who was able to afford large billboards of herself across town and a fancy sports car doing seemingly nothing except self-promotion. Tim stood near the cars but with enough distance so that nobody would fear he was messing with them.

"You totally want to fuck him."

"Shelley!"

"You do, admit it."

"I do not. I swear!"

Tim moved on.

"Hey man, can I bum a cigarette?"

"Here."

"Thanks."

"Irvine Meadows, man. I don't know. The sound there sucks sometimes. I'd rather go to the Greek."

"The Greek sucks. No acoustics. Sound just goes right into the mountains."

"Yeah, but Irvine Meadows. I don't know."

"Were you on the lawn?"

"I have been. But I've been in the seats too. It's not much better."

"I think it is. The seats are cool. Back on the lawn, the sound gets a little lost."

"You ever been to the Starlight?"

"Didn't that place burn down?"

"No, that's the Starwood. And they tore it down. The Starlight is an amphitheater in Burbank. Starlight Bowl."

"Oh, yeah."

"Now, that place rocks. Great sound."

"Yeah, the Starlight is alright. But Irvine Meadows . . . it's not too bad."

"Well, like I said, I'll take the Greek any day. And the Starlight. More bands ought to play there."

"Too small, man."

"Really? Isn't it like the size of the Greek?"

"No way. Much smaller. They've got like Cal Fest, but it's mostly small bands coming through there. You'll never see a big show there. Bands that graduate from the clubs can play the Starlight, but not much else comes through. Bands get too big for it after that."

"I saw Quiet Riot at Cal Fest."

"Bang your head! Metal health will dri-ive you ma-ad!"

"They played Cal Fest?"

"No, in the audience. I swear, the whole band was walking around in the crowd."

"The whole band was there? And they weren't playing?"

"Yeah. Well, maybe it was just Carlos and Rudy."

"Dude."

Tim moved on.

"Fuck that, man!"

"No, you don't get it."

"No, I get it. Just fuck that."

"Really, let me explain."

"Yeah, explain this, dude. Just fuck that."

Tim moved on.

It was a warm night as usual. Men wore short-sleeved T-shirts or shirts with the sleeves cut off. Women wore low-cut tops showing plenty of cleavage. Tim wondered how often women caught him staring. He tried to be subtle, but the scenery was always difficult to ignore. He moved closer to the entrance to the Rainbow.

"Hey, you drinking tonight, man?"

"Yeah, of course."

"Someone take his keys, man."

"Shut up. I'm not even drunk. Now, last weekend. That was another story."

"Dude, how'd you even get home?"

"I don't know. I can't remember."

Tim moved on. He stood on the sidewalk for a while.

"So, we get up to the room . . ."

"Yeah?"

"These guys have got the mirror off the wall. They've got these, like, huge mirrors over the dressers there. And they've got it pulled off the wall. It's lying on the bed, and they're doing lines of coke off it."

"No way."

"Yeah, like somebody brought all this coke but nobody thought to bring a mirror. Desperate times, man. Yanked that fucker right off the wall."

Tim moved closer to the entrance to the Roxy.

"Totally gave him head in the bathroom."

"Eww. That bathroom's gross."

"I know. Total turnoff. But where else are you going to go when you can't wait?"

Tim moved back into the parking lot. He made his way to the deepest part where people still congregated, farthest from the street.

"Two weeks, man, it's going to be killer."

"I'll be there, man."

"You thought this show was cool. In two weeks, they're going to tear it up. You can play a lot louder at the Whisky. Or at least, it seems louder. Small room."

"Rad."

"Come check it out. I'm going to be doing some stage diving. It's going to be crazy."

Tim moved on.

"KMET, man."

"No, KLOS."

"KLOS? Fuck that. KMET."

"KLOS."

"What do you guys think?"

"KMET."

"A little bit of heaven, 94.7, KMET. Tweedle Dee!"

"KMET."

"No fucking comparison, dude. KMET."

"Fine, KMET."

Tim moved on.

"Castle Donington, man. We gotta go. Monsters of Rock. They always have an incredible lineup. It's going to be Ozzy, Def Leppard, The Scorps, Motorhead . . ."

"All in one show?"

"Yeah, man."

"And they play in an actual castle?"

"No, I don't think so. They just call it Castle Donington. Donington Castle. I don't know. I think it's a big field. Maybe there's a castle nearby. Probably."

"If they played in a castle, that would be rad."

"I don't think you could fit all those people inside a castle. Not for a show, at least."

"Well, that sounds great, but there's one problem, man."

"What's that?"

"How the hell are we going to get to Scotland? Or England? Or wherever the hell it is?"

Tim sidled over closer to the entrance to the Rainbow again.

"We ran into John Candy at the Troub last week. Hanging out backstage."

"Really?"

"Yeah, man. He was wasted. Drunk off his ass. But still funny. We practically had to carry him down the stairs. He's a big dude."

"John Candy likes heavy metal?"

"Loves it."

"Huh. I never would have thought that."

"Yeah, man. That dude rocks."

Tim moved on.

"Oh man, that's funny."

"I know. Just straight up asked her: 'Can I borrow your lipstick?'"

"What did she say?"

"What could she say? She said yes and handed it over. She didn't want to tell him no."

"Too funny."

"I don't know about this glam shit anymore. It's getting out of hand. It's weird to take your girlfriend to a show where the dudes in the band are prettier than she is."

Tim decided to head home. He'd see David Lee Roth another night. He made his way back through the crowd to the sidewalk, hung a right on Sunset and another right on Wetherly. As he slowly climbed back up the hill, he could still make out bits and pieces of conversations echoing through the night from the crowd below.

Mike

"HEY GUYS, WE'RE meeting up at my place."

"Why your place, Mike?"

"Yeah, c'mon Mike. I never go to the fucking Valley."

"Just meet up at my place. Something we've got to do. I'll tell you when we get there."

"You gonna confront Bruce?"

"I already did. He says he never took credit for any Quiet Riot photos. Says he never shot them. But I know for a fact he told me he took the ones in that magazine. He told you, too. Otherwise, you wouldn't have recognized them as his. Besides, I don't need a group of guys to confront Bruce. I can handle that clown myself."

"What are we doing, then?"

"You'll see."

Half an hour later five guys congregated on the sidewalk in front of Mike's building, waiting for him to emerge from the underground parking structure. They laughed and shared Bruce stories, trying to outdo each other by the extent to which Bruce had taken advantage of each of them. Glen was sharing the story about how his mother banned Bruce from the house, but how during the Stainless Steel after-party Glen volunteered to host in his backyard, Bruce snuck up the driveway to the side gate.

"He calls Paul over. Paul, I should let you tell it."

"No, you're doing fine."

"He calls Paul over. He says, 'Psst. Hey Paul.' He's hiding from my mom, right? He says, 'Paul, go inside and make me a sandwich!'"

"No."

"Yes."

"The selfish fuck."

"The selfish mooch fuck is what he is."

"Did you, Paul?"

"What? Make him a sandwich?"

"Yeah."

"Hell no. My mom sees me making a sandwich at midnight, she's going to know exactly who it's for. She probably would have stormed the party. 'Where is he? I know he's here somewhere! Where is he?'"

The slamming security gate cut off their laughter. Mike didn't head straight toward them, but instead angled himself down the sidewalk, motioning for them to follow. They didn't know exactly what Mike had in mind, but they knew he'd had it. They all had. He led them around the corner, then up the driveway that led to the vacant lot behind the building.

Mike stopped walking and lowered his voice, casting an illicit atmosphere over the gathering.

"I'm done, everyone. Official. Fucking done. After tonight, that dude's no longer my friend. He's a mooch and a fraud. A fucking liar. Anyone who wants to make excuses for him or defend him can just leave right now."

Nobody flinched.

"I figure we send him a message that it's over. He's through as far as we're concerned. He never was anything. But whatever he thinks he is, he's through. Over. Done. I'm just tired of the bullshit, man. And I don't even know what's the truth anymore."

Nobody said a word. Five nods broke the stillness.

"He's been sleeping in his fucking car over there. See it? Dumbass probably didn't think I'd notice."

"So, what are you going to do?"

"*We*, Paul. What are *we* going to do . . . I say we flip it."

Five sets of eyes scanned the group for signs of dissension. Five sets of eyes found only grins of anticipation.

"Seriously. Just flip the fucker over. He won't be able to flip it back himself. It'll rot there. Like a helpless turtle. Asshole will be up shit's creek where he belongs. Major wake-up call."

"What if he's in it?"

"He's not in it. I dropped him off at the show tonight and he immediately asked Ted if he could crash at his place tonight. He's been couch surfing the past couple days. It's too hot to sleep in the car, and the pussy's too scared to sleep with the windows rolled down. Idiot doesn't even know I've kept tabs on him this whole time since I tossed his ass out."

"Dude, your neighbors will be pissed. Upside-down Honda growing weeds and shit out of it in their backyard."

"John, this is LA. You think I know my fucking neighbors?"

They followed Mike over to the green hatchback. The space between the front seats and the back window was crammed full of clothes, boxes of random belongings, *LA Weekly* and *BAM* magazines, and a small green suitcase that once served as a portfolio—a testament to a talent that had now lost all credibility.

Mike quickly assessed the elevation and walked around to the driver's side which rested on slightly higher ground. He put his massive hands on the edge where the roof met the tops of the doors. He pushed and the whole car rocked. He pushed again and it rocked farther.

"C'mon guys, help me rock it. We get it in rhythm and then we can shove it right over."

Everyone except Paul joined Mike on the driver's side.

"Paul, you coming?"

"No, I'm just going to watch if that's alright."

"Suit yourself. But we might need those muscles, man."

"Yeah, right. I'll be here if you do."

"No problem, little man. Just stay the hell out of the way so we don't crush your ass."

They all pushed together. The car nearly lifted off two wheels. They released and pushed, released and pushed, building momentum. The car rocked more and more recklessly, rattling and squeaking more obscenely with each shove. Mike slowly chanted to maintain an even rhythm.

"Push . . . push . . . push . . ."

When the car was clearly getting air under the driver's side wheels, Mike counted down for a big final surge.

"And, three . . . two . . . one!"

They shoved their hardest. The driver's side lifted farther than ever. The car seemed to hang there, perfectly balanced on two wheels, for what seemed like several seconds. Until, smash.

It landed with tremendous force on the passenger side, then rolled right over on its roof in one fluid motion. The door frames buckled severely, all six windows on the sides of the car popped and shattered, sending safety glass flying in all directions. Clothes, magazines, and other random papers spilled out of the sides as if the crumpling of the roof created too much pressure inside the vehicle and it could no longer contain those things that had packed it full. Everything Bruce owned leaked like toothpaste out of a freshly opened tube.

No one cheered. No one expressed awe or amazement. The shattering of glass and scrunching of metal spoke for them. It was loud enough to wake the building. Nothing legal could possibly sound like that, so they jogged, then sprinted out of the field and back to their cars. Paul was the last to turn the corner, giving one last look at the uninhabitable mass still seeming to creak and groan in the darkness.

Mike jumped in the back of Glen's car.

"What do you think, Glen? Can I crash at your place? I don't think tonight's a good night to meet the neighbors."

Paul

The first time I saw you, you sat on the edge of the stage
Shooting photos right up the lead singer's nose
And I asked myself
What gives him the right?
How can I get a gig like this?
Not having to fight for position
In a stinking, sweaty mosh pit
I'd have a front-row seat every night

And there you were
At every show
Towering above us all
You'd hold your lens
Like a great cannon
Or third eye
And you captured that magic we sought
Night after night
Under those hot lights

So when I woke up one morning to find you sleeping on our floor
It had that look what the cat dragged in innocence to it all
Nights get long
Mornings creep up, sly
Sometimes it's safer to crash where you are
Than to crash in the traffic and the DUIs

And you showed me a suitcase
A veritable treasure chest
Of photos and proofs
Magazine clippings and business cards
Your portfolio, albeit crammed in a space
That seemed to betray the glory of your career

Living out of your Honda
Like the classic starving artist
Parked in a big field behind Mike's place
Stuffed to the gills
With every scrap of your work, your passion
Your life in a compact space

And the stories you'd tell
About everyone you knew
Those who were taking you on the road
Or those who just wanted to
But had no road yet to travel
There were more than a few

So, when they said you were lying,
I had a hard time believing you could
Until I realized what good money could buy
At any tourist shop on Hollywood

And some of your most incredible shots
Appeared in magazines
With a byline that wasn't yours
How could you think these would never be seen
By us, those desperate to be a part of your scene

We marched through the field that night
Soldiers of another kind
But on the warpath all the same
I admit it was surprising to see such a thing
Just how easily the car was lifted
Everything shifted
Its contents were sifted
But that's what anger can bring

Good thing you weren't in it
We didn't want to hurt anyone
Just stop the lies and deceit
Just put an end to what had been done

And hundreds of photos, papers, old clothes
Spilled like blood from its guts out the windows
As the car rolled
And the roof was crushed
Under the weight of so much emptiness.

We left everything strewn about
Proofs, prints, and negatives
Were left positively abandoned
Like the wounded left to die
Amid the wreckage wrought from our wrath

You see, in our little world
We are desperate for a role model
Someone who doesn't forget our names when he makes it big
Or checks out in a plane crash
Or ODs on his glory

We are like children on the sidewalk staring down the long lines of
    cars
Quietly mumbling "Don't leave us behind"

You lied for your own selfish needs
You probably didn't mean any harm
But it screwed us all the same
These kids who played right into your game
These orphans who wished they too had a name for themselves
These lost angels in search of inspiration
In a Sunset desert with no sign of salvation

In a field
Where success and failure are so close together
They are easily confused as the same

Summer

"Hi, Paul."

He nearly choked on his spit. Among the throng of bodies spilling out of the Roxy onto the sidewalk, still leaning into one another, leveraging position for what there was to see outside on a new stage as it were, Summer had found him.

"Hey, Summer! You were in there?"

"Yeah. Surprised?"

She looked radiant as always. Her ringlets intact and shimmering. That smile filling him with warmth and a sense of purpose.

"Not really. It's just that I always see you out here, but never inside."

"I don't really mingle inside. Too hard to have conversations with the music and everyone shouting into everyone else's ears. That's what outside is for."

"I don't mingle either. I'm not good at it. I just come for the music. Glen is off talking to some people, as always. I don't do that much."

"I know. I see you watching the shows down close. I'm usually off to the side. I like watching the crowd as much as I like watching the bands."

"I've done that too. When it gets too crazy up front."

"You haven't been around much, Paul. I mean, I haven't seen you, aside from that time on the street, from the car?"

"Yeah, I remember. No, you're right. I haven't been coming so much lately."

"Anything going on?"

"I'm graduating high school next week."

He felt like such a child, being proud enough to share that.

"Hey! That's great." She playfully socked his shoulder. He realized aside from a handshake, this was the only time she'd ever touched him. "Doing anything special?"

"Not really. Just graduating is enough."

"I bet."

He stood silently, unable to maintain eye contact with that smile. He struggled for something to say but nothing seemed profound enough. He yearned to impress her, to engage her in a way he knew most in that scene probably couldn't. He fantasized of the amazing, intellectual conversations they could have, someplace peaceful, overlooking the chaos that surrounded them. But he froze when she was around. Nothing worth talking about ever came to mind.

"Are you still exploring?"

"Huh?"

"Other clubs? Other music? Remember? We talked about it before."

"Oh, yeah. Um, well, a little bit, sure. Nothing really worth sharing."

"I never got to the Lhasa Club. I should put it on my list."

He should have invited her right then, but he knew it would put her in the awkward position of saying no, of blowing the difference between his romantic attraction and her simple friendliness out into the open. He'd rather live with the illusion that she might have said yes.

"You remembered, though. That's pretty cool."

"I told you, I remember everything."

"I don't, obviously."

She giggled. It felt good to make her laugh.

"You're going to need that memory in college, you know."

"How do you know I'm going to college?"

"I can tell. You are, aren't you?"

"Yeah. Santa Barbara. So, I won't be too far away."

"You will, though. That's good. That's growing."

"Did you?"

"What? Go to college?"

"Yeah."

"No. Didn't finish high school, either. Well, got my GED, but that doesn't really count in my book."

"Huh."

He didn't want to insult her but was afraid his facial expression already had.

"That surprises you?"

"Yeah, I heard the GED exam was hard."

She giggled again, and he was proud of himself for bailing them out of an awkward moment with humor.

"No, seriously, you are very intelligent. I figured you at least graduated high school, probably went to college."

"It takes more than intelligence to graduate anything, you know?"

"Yeah, I guess so. But . . ."

"But, what?"

"Well, it's none of my business."

"No, go ahead."

"But, why? Or, why not, rather? Why'd you quit school?"

"That's a long story. I just wasn't in the right space for it at the time. If I were myself back then as I am now, I would have finished no problem. I was going through a lot in those days. It happens. A lot of talented people don't achieve much because of other obstacles. Thanks, though. For saying that you see me as someone with that potential."

"Oh, yeah. I see . . . I . . ."

"Yes?"

Her smile was killing him. He could barely remember his own name in her presence. He wanted to tell her he saw endless potential in her. He wanted to tell her she inspired him. He could only stammer and censor himself. He hated how his words sounded so profound and touching in his head, only to seem silly and awkwardly idealistic out loud.

"Hey, there you are Paul. Hi Summer, how've you been?"

"Hi, Glen. Just chatting with your awesome brother here. I'm good. How about you?"

"Good, you know, same as usual. You ready to go, Paul?"

Glen's interruption was an unwelcome rescue from a precipice to which he wanted to cling for a lot longer. He wanted to let himself go. To fall. He wanted to see the plunge his words could cause. He wanted to speak up for a change. To face the consequences they'd bring.

"Yeah, I guess so."

Only acquiescence.

"Hey . . . Paul."

Summer gently grasped his forearm at the elbow. She leaned close to him as if to share a secret. Her lips practically kissed his ear and her voice dropped to a whisper.

"These people? This scene? It saved my life. It saves it constantly. Because if I didn't have this years ago, I'd be dead right now."

Her closeness shocked him more than her words. He didn't know what to say.

"We all find our salvation in different places, in different ways. The city is a beast, but there is always shelter to be found. Always sweetness. No regrets, Paul. Remember? No regrets."

"Yeah."

She straightened until she towered over him as usual, still smiling, still looking him directly in the eye, emerging from the exchange like someone with nothing to hide. Having revealed very little, actually. Her bravery only attracted him even more.

She nodded once and threw her arms around him in a tight embrace.

"Goodbye, Paul."

Glen

Daisy nearly tripped running to the Firebird, not regaining her balance until she was up against the passenger side door. She opened it and collapsed in the deep bucket seat, all in one motion, laughing all the way. Glen pulled away from the curb in front of her house before the door had even fully closed.

"Whew, sorry I'm late. Debbie, man. She fucking talks and talks sometimes."

"No big deal."

Daisy noticed the new addition hanging from Glen's rearview mirror.

"Hey, nice tassel. I thought you finished high school a long time ago."

"I did. That's Paul's."

"Oh yeah, he graduated! Shit, is it June already?"

"Yeah, for the past twenty days or so."

"Time flies, man. So, why do you have Paul's tassel?"

"He doesn't have a car of his own, so we hung it up in mine."

"Oh yeah, huh? Well, that's cool, big brother."

"Yeah, I guess so."

Daisy took the tassel in her left hand and combed its strands with her right.

"It's pretty."

"Same one I got, just a different number on it."

"Where's yours?"

"I don't know. I had it up for a couple months but took it down after I got sick of looking at it. It's probably in a box somewhere."

Daisy separated the strands into two equal sections, then took a few strands from each to make a third approximately the same size as the other two.

"So, where are we going, Glen?"

"I don't know. Anybody you planned on seeing tonight?"

"No, not really. Nobody really good is playing."

"Yeah, my thoughts exactly. Rainbow?"

"Sure, I guess."

Daisy began braiding the three strands of the tassel. She pulled the strands tight after every round to make the rows of braids compact.

"What did you do today?"

"Not much. Hung out with Debbie, mostly."

"Not a lot to do when you're stuck hanging out with Debbie, huh?"

"Yeah, you can say that again."

Daisy wove as many rows into the braid as possible, then let it go and watched the strands slowly unwind. When it had restored itself, she grabbed them, combed them out with her right hand, and began the process again. Glen took his eyes off the road frequently to look at her hands as they worked.

"So, where are we going, Glen?"

"You just asked me that. I thought we agreed on the Rainbow?"

"Oh yeah, I guess so. I don't know."

"You don't want to go?"

"No, we can go. Let's go see who's there."

"Have you eaten?"

"Yeah, I ate a little with Debbie."

"Well, I might get a pizza. You can have some if you want."

"Thanks."

Daisy completed a second braid on the tassel. She admired it for a few seconds before letting go and watching it unwind. She let it finish before grabbing it and combing it out again. Then she started braiding once more. Glen looked at her more squarely.

"What?"

"Nothing."

Sensing he was getting annoyed, she let go of the tassel. The few rows she'd just finished braiding slowly unwound. She turned to watch the parked cars and buildings go whizzing by.

Mike

HE WAS ABLE to find a spot in Yamashiro's lot before having to use the valet. He breathed a sigh of relief. He'd come up here several times and never once set foot in the restaurant. He didn't even know if this was legal, or against their policy. He decided it was easier to ask for forgiveness than permission, find a spot himself, and see if anyone stopped him. So far, no one ever had.

He made his way to one of the narrow footpaths carved into the hillside beneath the line of sight of those entering the restaurant and those parking their cars. He walked out until the trees in the garden no longer obscured his view and stopped at the point where he felt most surrounded by the city lights.

Long, beaded streaks of color lay parallel tracks down the steady grade to the south, sagged through the middle of the basin, and climbed the Baldwin Hills on the other side. Another set of tracks cut these lines into grids at perpendicular angles, stretching from the haze beyond downtown all the way to the beaches.

Each quadrant was filled with hundreds of twinkling droplets of color. The heat waves coming off the landscape made the entire scene shimmer like an effervescent pool. Together with the steadily droning hum that rose from the basin floor, the city appeared to vibrate to a constant pulsating rhythm.

Mike breathed another sigh.

"Pretty cool, isn't it?"

He didn't realize he wasn't alone. He had stopped a mere fifteen feet from another person without even noticing anyone there. The young man stepped out of the shadows and moved closer to him.

"Justin?"

"Yeah, how's it going, Mike? I thought that was you."

"Hey, man. Imagine running into you up here."

The two shook hands.

"I know. Small world, huh?"

"I haven't seen you in a long time, man. You still coming to shows?"

"Yeah. But, not much. I haven't been coming regularly."

"Well, you ought to come hang out."

"Thanks, yeah, I should."

"You still going out with that redhead? Um . . . Angie?"

"Annie. No, we aren't really seeing each other anymore."

"She like, puked all over your car, didn't she?"

"Yeah. Thanks to you, remember?"

"Oh yeah, sorry. Yeah, Glen told me. I guess that was my fault. Honestly, I thought she could handle it."

"Obviously not. I had to handle it. It was nasty, man."

"Heh, heh. Yeah, sorry. Really though, you should come out. You seeing anyone else these days?"

"No. Otherwise, I probably would have brought her up here with me."

"Yeah, that would have been smooth. Well then, fuck it. Come out alone. Then you can hit on all the hot chicks."

"Sounds good. So, you come up here just for the view, or did you eat?"

"Oh, fuck no. I can't afford that place. I've never even gone inside. I just like their view."

"Me neither. I'm always worried they're going to hassle me. Make me buy something before I can park up here. But I guess they don't care."

Mike felt relieved he wasn't the only one with this fear.

"I know, huh? I've never been hassled. I think they know it comes with the territory. Plenty of people come up here and don't go inside. People are making out up here all the time, and the dudes are too cheap to spring for dinner in there. They have to know if they're going to have a view like this, they're going to attract a bunch of people."

"You come here often?"

"Yeah, I come up here once in a while. When I want to take in the whole city."

"Me too. There are a lot of viewpoints I like. This is one of the better ones."

"Yeah, it's pretty nice, huh?"

"Helps me think. You can think about a lot with a view like this."

"I know what you mean."

"Like, every light has a purpose."

"Yeah, I guess so."

"Yeah. Streetlights, porchlights, office lights, traffic lights, store signs."

"Yep."

"It's the darkness that gets me."

Mike looked at him side-eyed.

"How's that?"

"The spaces between. That's where the truth is."

"Damn, man. You're getting deep."

"Heh, yeah, sorry. I do that sometimes."

"So, you're out here in Hollywood just being philosophical or were you at a club tonight?"

"Nah. I just went out for a drive and wound up here. I do that sometimes, too. Just drive around."

"Not me. I hate driving in this fucking city."

"Yeah, I guess I'm used to it."

Mike got quiet. Justin could sense he wasn't in the greatest mood.

"So, Mike, how have you been? What's going on with you these days?"

"I been alright."

"Yeah? You don't sound convinced."

"Actually, it's been a pretty shitty year."

"Really?"

"Yeah. My mom died in February."

"Oh, I'm sorry."

"Yeah. It's tough. And my friend died last month. You hear about Charlie?"

"No, sorry. I haven't been around. He died?"

"Yeah. They found him in a dumpster, man. Fucking sucks."

"Wow."

"Yeah. Charlie could be annoying sometimes. But he was harmless, you know? He didn't mean any harm. He didn't deserve to go that way. It's just sad. So many assholes in this world and they've got to take someone innocent like Charlie."

"Someone kill him?"

"We don't even know. Drugs, probably. OD'd. But I never found out how he wound up in the dumpster. And I'm not close enough to anyone to ask. I don't even know who they called to, you know, come get him. Claim the body."

"That's too bad. You have had a hard year."

"It's not even half done. Well, almost."

"I know."

They both stared at the lights before them until this time, Mike felt the silence grow awkward.

"A lot going on down there."

"Yeah."

"A lot of shit going on down there, too."

"Yep. People are down there doing all sorts of crazy things."

"Yeah, man. Like dying."

"Yeah. Spooky when you think about it."

"Looking out at all those lights. If you could see far enough, and through walls and all, you could be witnessing murder. Or someone OD'ing."

"Yeah."

"How many drug deals are going down right now?"

"Uh, huh."

"How many muggings? How many people fucking?"

Justin laughed.

"Heh, pervert."

"No, I'm serious. You are bearing witness to a lot of activity, man. Why not fucking? Especially this time of night. It's like prime time down there right now."

Justin decided to play along.

"How many people are pissing in alleys?"

"WE SEE YOU. STOP DOING THAT. SIR, PUT THAT DICK AWAY."

"Funny."

"It is funny. How something can look so pretty from afar, but you get close and it's not so attractive."

"Heh, yeah. I've thought about that. I guess that's why I like looking at it from afar so much."

"I mean, don't get me wrong. I like this city. I have a good time down there. I've had a lot of good times down there. But I've seen a lot of crap, too."

"Yeah, makes sense."

"And you can get cheesy about it, or philosophical like you, and talk about all the good things people are doing down there right now. All the progress being made. Or all the truth, right? But it doesn't take away the façade."

"The what?"

"The façade. Like, you'd expect good things to be happening in such a pretty scene, right? But you wouldn't expect the bad. So that's the façade. It looks so nice on the surface, but underneath? A lot of shit. There's your truth, man."

"I guess that's LA."

"Damn right that's LA. A lot of people struggling out there. A lot of people failing. And a lot of people scratching and crawling over everyone else's back to make it. A lot of liars and cheats. A lot of people afraid of failure. Doing what they can to avoid it. Or pretending not to."

"Yeah."

"Sometimes, I think about leaving."

"Really, Mike?"

"Yeah, but it's not like I have anywhere else to go."

"I was going to ask, where would you go?"

"I haven't figured that out yet. And it's not like it would be any different anyplace else. Any big city, you're going to run into problems."

"Yeah, I guess."

"And any place small enough not to have these problems? That's just not my style. Everyone knowing your business all the time. Everyone talking shit about everyone else. My uncle lives in a small town. It sounds awful. You have to get used to knowing every move you make is being watched."

"That's why I like LA."

"Uh, huh."

"You can do pretty much whatever the hell you want. Nobody cares. Like this restaurant. I've never been told to get out of here. Or like, go inside and order something if I want to enjoy the view."

"Yep."

"Hollywood, man. You see all kinds of shit down there. It's like people doing whatever they want in the streets, on the sidewalks. And everyone is just like, 'Oh, well. That's Hollywood. Hollyweird.' You can just do whatever and nobody cares . . . or notices."

"Kinda nice, but it sounds kinda lonely too when you think about it."

"How's that?"

"In a huge city, it's like you're surrounded and alone at the same time. It's like, there are always a lot of people around, but at the same time, nobody cares. So, if nobody cares, or nobody notices, you tend to feel pretty alienated. Pretty lonely."

"It's true."

"But I tend to go off by myself a lot anyway. Makes it easy to get over being ignored if you aren't around people to ignore you."

"Yeah, I know what that's like. I drive around by myself all the time. I mean shit, I'm up here now, aren't I?"

"Ha, yeah. Speaking of alienation, I think it's funny how the tourists clear out after it gets dark. You ever notice? In the daylight, everyone is all taking pictures, crowding around the footprints at the Chinese Theater. Looking at all the stars on the Walk of Fame. Or cruising the Strip, looking for movie stars. And then the sun goes down and they all get scared away. Only the freaks remain. All the homeless and the psychos. And us. Us heshers standing on the sidewalks in front of the clubs."

"Yep, you're just a bunch of freaks."

"I'm serious. And what's this 'you' shit? You've been there. You're one of us."

"Yeah, I guess. Just not full time."

"But you get it. You're into the music, right? Or the girls? Something brings you out here. But we're a strange crowd, man. A lot of freaks. A lot of crazy people. A lot of drunks. We scare the fucking tourists away. 'Uh, six o'clock, honey. Time to go back to the hotel. It's getting freaky out here.'"

"Ha, ha. Yeah, I guess we're a pretty motley crew. Hence the name."

"Exactly."

"You know what, though, Mike?"

"What?"

"It's pretty cool when you think about it."

"Yeah. I'm not sure what you mean, but it's a scene. We have that. And it's pretty cool when you can look at it from up here. And all you see is beauty."

Justin simply stared out at the lights until Mike broke his reverie.

"I'm out, man. I'm going to pitch myself off this cliff and join the masses."

"Huh?"

"Just kidding, man. But I am going to get back in my car and drive back down there."

"Okay."

"So, if you hear any screeching tires, slamming brakes, screaming pe-destrians . . . that's me."

"I'll try to stay out of your way."

"Yeah, you better."

Mike extended his hand.

"Nice talking to you, man. Hey, come on out to the shows more often. Tell Glen and Paul to take you. You guys can carpool. Oh wait, I forgot. You like to drive."

Justin accepted the handshake.

"I'll try. Nice talking to you, too."

"Don't stay out too late. And don't get caught. You'll ruin it for everybody."

"Don't worry, I won't. Just going to hang out a little more, looking."

"What are you looking for? Besides this truth shit."

"I don't know. Maybe some perfectly round cul-de-sacs in the foothills."

"Some what?"

"Nothing. Just got the notion to beautify a few more cul-de-sacs. That's a story for another day."

"Making the most of a dead end?"

"Yeah, something like that."

"Alright, man. I'll hold you to it. You'll tell me in the parking lot of the Rainbow one day."

"Deal."

"Take care, man."

Mike left the way he came, got in his car, and sheepishly passed the valet stand on his way out of the parking lot.

When he got to the bottom of the drive and made a right on Franklin, he turned and looked back up the hill, trying to see the footpaths beneath the restaurant. Trying to tell if it were possible to see Justin still up there, gazing out into oblivion.

Glen

THE SUN BEAT down on Santa Monica Beach at the peak of a late-June day. Towels spread to fill much of the space between the lifeguard towers and the last few feet of dry sand. Boogie boarders and bodysurfers crowded the water. Children darted about, shrieking as they dodged the wash of especially large breakers. Vin Scully called the Dodgers-Astros game from more than one transistor radio.

Waves crested and broke frequently, their leading edges arriving parallel to the coastline, only to fan out into diagonals as they splayed themselves upon the sand. Water returned to the sea a foot or more from whence it came, revealing a southern current.

Glen and Paul played around in the breakers, bodysurfed as far in as possible a few times, then hung out in the foreshore awhile to let the ocean pound them with its incessant rhythm. Without a word then, Glen stood and made his way out as far as he could stand, diving underneath the largest waves until emerging treading water on the other side of them. Paul followed.

The two floated and moved with the tide, rising and falling with each crest that passed. They were both struck by the strange sense of calm the scene afforded. The surf no longer pounded in their ears. The shrieks of laughter of those playing in the waves were suddenly almost too distant to hear. Swells passed by silently, with only a faint trickle issuing from the largest as they began to feel bottom. A subtle gurgle escaped as the peak of each crest bubbled white over its deep green mass—such delicate and fragile sounds to contrast the impending roar soon to follow. All noise on the coast and the city beyond was reduced to a faint, steadily buzzing hum.

The newfound peace made it easy to talk.

"Paul, we should do something different this summer. Make the most of our days."

"Sounds good."

"Maybe head out to Catalina for a few days. Maybe hit some of the other Channel Islands, do some hiking. San Miguel is supposed to be cool."

"Yeah, sounds good."

Glen's voice betrayed the effort of keeping his head above water.

"We could get up to Big Bear or Lake Arrowhead. Maybe do Mount Baldy. It would be different without the snow."

"Yeah, or the Punchbowl before it gets too hot."

"Yeah. And get down to TJ. We haven't been there together. Explore San Diego. We haven't been there since we were kids running around Sea World."

"Yeah."

"When do those birds come back to San Juan Capistrano?"

"I think they already did. Isn't that in the spring?"

"I don't know. But stuff like that. We should make the most of what time we have before you go off to college."

"I'll be back every summer, you know. And a lot of weekends. I'm not going far."

"I know, but you won't be around as much either."

"Yeah, I guess not."

"I just want to get all we can out of it."

"Sounds good."

"You know what I mean?"

"Yeah, I get it."

Glen paused briefly to catch his breath.

"I just don't want it to be a waste . . ."

The swells gently lifted them, let them fall, only to lift them again, nearly weightless over every crest. They stared onshore.

From this far out they could take in the length of Santa Monica, from the GTE Building at Wilshire, to the clock tower, to the pier, to the twin apartment buildings perched just outside the border of Venice. Both silently marveled at the perspective. Both contemplated the incredible amount of power necessary to sustain the mass of humanity that sprawled inland from the coastline and the amount of energy it produced in turn.

Yet everything was dwarfed by an ocean that swallowed sound, that reduced every madness, every passion, and every dream to something as fragile as a bubble borne on the peak of a wave. Suspended for a fleeting instant by nothing more than the notion of potential.

Alive. Vibrant.

Then gone.

Silently extinguished on the threshold of a world that knows nothing of promises.

Acknowledgments

I wish to thank two writers I met during the early stages of transforming these stories into text. Without their advice and encouragement, I might still be wondering if it were possible for me to complete a novel. Brian "SuperB" Oliva, thanks for the inspiration and making it look easy. Patrick Flores Scott, thanks for allowing me to geek out at the fact that I'm a lot like you, and that means I can be an author too.

Heather Miller, thank you for being a great editor and having a way with words in harmony with mine.

This novel goes out to the people in and around the Hollywood music scene of the mid-1980s, without whom these memories would never have taken shape: The Huihui family – David, Loke, and Lani; Hilary Wehrle; Gail Moyer-Kallos; David Baker; Rags; and Kat, wherever you are. And the talented musicians who unwittingly have allowed me to drop their names: David Resch, Eric Resch, the late, great Chris Resch, Glen Holland of Pandemonium; Marc Ferrari of Keel; Grant Goracy of Stainless Steel; Steve Adler of Guns & Roses; Bret Michaels, Rikki Rockett, Bobby Dahl of Poison; and Jack Russell, Mark Kendall of Great White.

Thank you to the Troubadour, The Roxy, The Whisky-a-Go-Go, The Rainbow, and The Country Club over the hill for allowing the space, night after night.

And thanks to the City of Los Angeles for raising a little hell from time to time. This is my love letter to my hometown, its haunts and environs.

Oh, and here's to Dani, the best waitress Denny's ever had…